Mary Dawson

MAKE ME LIE

RICH DEMONS OF DARKWOOD 1

C.R. JANE
MAY DAWSON

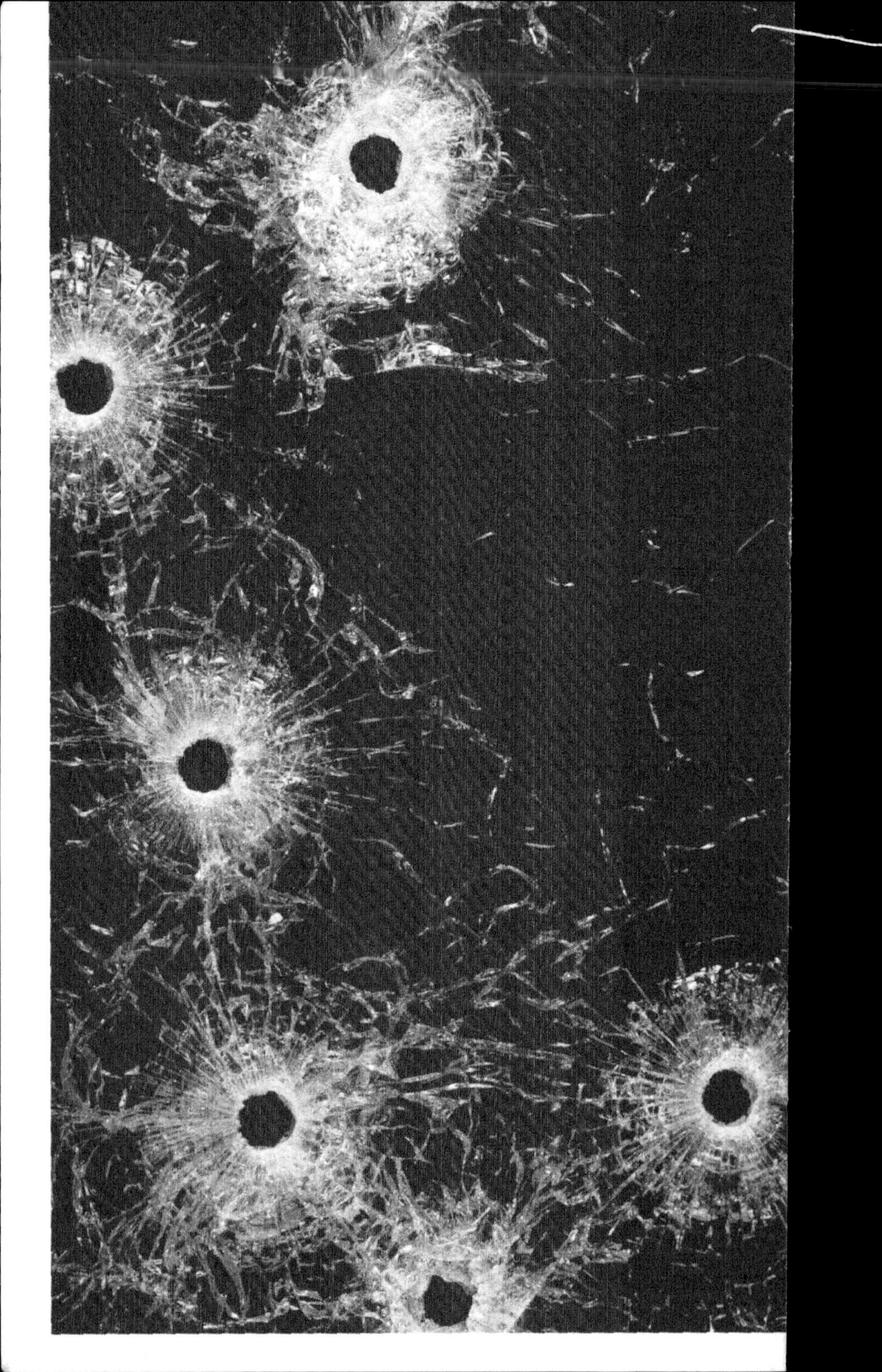

Make Me Lie

RICH DEMONS OF DARKWOOD BOOK 1

C.R. JANE

MAY DAWSON

Photograph: Wander Aguiar

Cover by Eve Graphic Design

For permissions contact:

crjaneauthor@gmail.com

maydawsonauthor@gmail.com

Proof: Jasmine Jordan

Don’t call him “sir” until he earns it.

JOIN OUR READERS' GROUP

Stay up to date with C.R. Jane by joining her Facebook readers' group, C.R.'s Fated Realm. Ask questions, get first looks at new books/series, and have fun with other book lovers!

Join C.R. Jane's Group

Join May Dawson's Wild Angels to chat directly with May and other readers about her books, enter giveaways, and generally just have fun!

Join May's Group

star-crossed

Kacey Musgraves

boys will be boys

emlyn

bad guy

Billie Eilish

Hold On

Chord Overstreet

All I Need

Within Temptation

Falling

Harry Styles

Lunatic

UPSAHL

Enter Sandman

Metallica

Fighter

Twin Wolves

Waiting Game

BANKS

I am not a woman, I'm a god

Halsey

Good For You

Selena Gomez, A$AP Rocky

West Coast

Lana Del Rey

Never Let Me Go

Florence + The Machine

Just Like Fire

P!nk

Get the SPOTIFY playlist HERE

RICH DEMONS OF DARKWOOD SERIES

FROM C.R. JANE AND MAY DAWSON

Make Me Lie
Make Me Beg

This is a college bully reverse harem series which means the main character will end up with multiple love interests. It may have triggers for some as this is a dark romance with scenes of intense bullying, murder and mayhem, and sexual scenes.

MAKE ME LIE

The world knows me as the Demon's Daughter.

He's a famous serial killer. And I may have been his accomplice.

But no one knows for sure except for me.

The dangerous, cruel men of the Sphinx secret society intend to uncover my secrets...and break me.

Stellan, my childhood crush who lost his sister to the Demon.

Cain, the boy with the face of an angel to who manipulation comes as easy as breathing;

Remington, the playboy soccer star full of secrets.

Pax, the dark psycho who hides behind his fists.

I hoped for a second chance at Darkwood University, only to have my dream ripped away the first time I kissed one of the handsome bastards.

They know who I am.

And they're determined to make me pay.

They should have thought twice about who they were playing with.

Because I am the demon's daughter. And just because they have the power, the connections, the faces and bodies of gods... do they really think they'll win?

I wanted a new life, not a war.

But if they insist, we'll see who ends up playing.

PROLOGUE

Gabriela (CROSS OUT) Delilah (CROSS OUT) Aurora

The world ended for me, then started again in technicolor, on a Tuesday afternoon in fourth grade.

I gripped the doorknob of the back door to steady myself as I unlaced and pulled off my Converse. My adoptive mother hated when I wore my shoes into the house, but these high tops took so long to get on and off, and that made it hard when I was so desperate to get through the house to my room before my "brother" Lucas caught me.

The door abruptly jerked open, and I tumbled into the kitchen, landing on the pristine white tile.

Lucas leered down at me. "What are you doing out there? Come inside, Gabriela. We've got our chores to do."

"I'll do them when Mom gets home," I said. It was safer to wait until she was home so I didn't have to be around Lucas, even though sometimes she'd get mad at me for wait-ing. If I made it to my room and locked the door, I could do my homework and read my books in peace. Even Lucas wasn't going to risk banging up the door to get to me when

Mom's house was her most precious thing—more precious than either of us. Definitely more precious than me.

I edged sideways trying to get away from Lucas, but he pinned me to the wall. "Mom is going to be so mad at you. She told us both that if we didn't do our chores, she was gonna be mad, and you know what that means."

My stomach churned. "I'll get them done."

I tried to get away from him, but he grabbed my pony tail and reeled me against his body. Lucas was seventeen, and he stank of body odor as he pulled me close. I tried to wriggle free.

"Mom said I could spank you if you didn't listen to me."

"No, she didn't." I kicked against one of the cabinet doors, trying to get loose.

"She did, and you're gonna get it from her too if you don't listen." He tried to wrench me with him, and I struggled to get free.

The two of us slipped. I kicked out, trying to get away from him. I managed to land on my feet while he landed hard on his knee and let out a grunt of pain. I ran desperately for my room with no plan but to get the hell away from Lucas while he was so furious at me.

The two of us raced through the hall. He was right behind me as I reached my room. I swung the door shut, but he threw his shoulder into it, and it banged open, knocking me back.

I fell back and slammed my head into the drywall so hard that I couldn't breathe for a second. The world spun darkly around me.

"Oh shit," Lucas said, and now even he sounded scared.

I got to my feet and saw the crack running down the drywall. There was no way Mom wouldn't see that.

"You are so screwed," Lucas said, starting to grin. "Do you

want me to tell her that it was an accident? That you tripped? Or that you had a temper tantrum and did it on purpose?"

None of those were the truth.

"Lucas," I said, stunned.

He shrugged. "Up to you, Gabriela."

He always said my name like it was a joke, but everything about my existence seemed like a joke to him.

"What do you want?" I asked.

"Nothing. Let's just get our chores done so she's not mad about that too." He slung his arm around my neck and squeezed, the sour odor of his body washing over me. The affection was confusing. "We've got to have each other's backs, little sister."

I hurried to do my chores, putting away the dishes from the dishwasher that had run while we were at school, vacuuming again, making sure the house was spotless. Lucas had less to do since he pretty much took the trash out and did chores around the outside of the house, but he came over and helped me finish cleaning the kitchen which was nice and unexpected.

When we were done, he pulled out a bag of chips and said, "Come on. It'll be worth vacuuming again before Mom gets home."

She hated for us to have snacks outside of meals, but he rustled the bag with my favorite kind of chips, and my mouth watered. "Where did you get those?"

"I picked them up from 7-11 on my way home. Lunch at the high school sucks. I've been starving all day."

"They're not from Mom's secret stash?"

He grinned. "Nope. But she really needs to get over being so weird about *us* having junk food when she's keeping Hostess cupcakes in her underwear drawer. Come on."

It was unusually nice of Lucas. The two of us ended up sitting on the couch, watching a television show and sharing chips from the bag. When the bag was empty, I ran and buried it under some trash in the kitchen to make sure Mom wouldn't find it. I sat back down to watch the rest of the show.

Lucas rested his arm around my shoulders, and I leaned into him. It felt awkward but even though he smelled bad, it was kind of nice to be close to someone, even if it was Lucas. Maybe things would be different from now on. Sometimes it seemed like he'd hated me since I moved in four years ago, when I'd been taken away from my first mom. Back then I'd cried all the time, but I'd grown up since.

Then Lucas slid his other hand down my leg. It felt like he was just petting me absently, but I froze, pretending not to notice. It wasn't absent at all. His attention was just as razor-focused on me, on waiting for my reaction.

"Lucas..." I tried to squirm away, and he grabbed my thigh, his fingers sinking painfully into my skin.

"Come on, Gabriela. Remember what I said about how we've got to watch each other's backs?"

"Lucas, please..." I didn't even know what I was begging for, but something about the way he was touching me felt so wrong.

I didn't want him to tell Mom that I'd had a temper tantrum and broken the wall. I didn't know how to fix the wall or hide it from her, even though I'd been racking my brain trying to find a way out ever since it happened. I was going to be in so much trouble, and my stomach ached every time I thought about it. Maybe if she believed it really was an accident though, she wouldn't be mad. Sometimes she could be really nice... just like Lucas.

He pushed up the bottom of my t-shirt and slid his hand

into my leggings. Just rested it there, against my bare skin just under the waistband of my panties. I closed my eyes because hot tears were building, threatening to spill over. I'd been lying to myself when I thought I was grown up and didn't cry anymore. I felt small and helpless.

"Shh, Gabriela, it's all right," Lucas said, but I knew it wasn't all right. It wasn't going to be all right. He was just touching me lightly for now, but somehow, I knew it was just going to keep getting worse and worse.

There was the rumble of the garage door, and the two of us jumped apart. I pulled the hem of my t-shirt down, pulling it taut against my body. Lucas knelt next to the couch, trying to sweep up crumbs from the chips that I hadn't noticed when I got up before; they must have been hidden under his leg.

"Shit," he grumbled. "You better hope she doesn't notice any more crumbs."

I turned and ran to my room, afraid of being caught in the living room while he fumbled with the remote.

A few minutes later, as I was turning the pages of my Nancy Drew book and trying to pay attention, I heard a familiar shrill scream. "Gabriela!"

"Coming!" I shouted back, throwing my book down without even remembering to put a bookmark in. I raced down the hall to the kitchen, where my mom was livid with rage, holding the empty chip bag.

"Did you try to hide this from me?" Her voice was the kind of white-hot that meant I was in deathly trouble.

"It's Lucas's," I whispered.

"Right, because they are *his* favorite chips that he always gets for his birthday," she said, tossing them into the trash again. "Where'd you get the money? Or did you steal them?"

"I didn't," I said. "I came right home after school."

"I told her she shouldn't have them," Lucas said from the doorway, and Mom's irritated gaze snapped to him. Before she could bite his head off, he added, "And you should see what she did to her room when I tried to take them from her."

"No, no, no," I begged as Mom towed me by the arm down the hall to my room. Her face went white with rage when she saw the crack in the wall.

She slapped me across the face so hard my vision went red. "Really, Gabriela, is there *anything* you didn't do today? Lying, stealing, destroying our house?"

"I didn't," I whimpered, but I knew she wasn't going to stop as she dragged me across the carpet to my closet door.

She rummaged through the closet, knocking one of my dresses to the ground as she pulled out a wire hanger.

I caught a glimpse of Lucas in the door, grinning, before I couldn't pay attention to anything but the pain.

That night, I lay in bed, trying to sleep despite the terrible pain. My Nancy Drew book was still lying with its spine open on the floor where it had fallen, and its pages were probably getting creased. I finally managed to get out of bed and pick it up, trying to read by the street light that came in through the window because I didn't dare get caught with my light on. Every once in a while, a car would come down the street and my page would get brighter for a moment with their headlights; I'd read frantically, skimming the page as fast as I could. I put the book under the pillow next to me, raising it just enough to hold the page up so I could drop it and hide the book at a moment's notice.

It was only because I was still awake that I heard the door creak open. I went still, letting the pillow fall, pretending to be asleep.

Lucas came to the side of my bed. He peeled back the

blanket and the sheets, and I froze, pretending I was still asleep.

How many times had he come into my room like this?

He didn't touch me again, just touched the front of his pants, then pulled his manhood out. I kept my eyes closed, wanting to scream as he jerked his hand up and down along his pale thing.

Then suddenly, he made a short, desperate sound.

I opened my eyes to see him frozen, one hand still gripping himself, his eyes and mouth wide with horror.

A bright red smile had been cut across his throat, and the man with the knife was standing right behind him. The man touched the knife to his lips, warning me not to make a sound.

Gently, he eased Lucas's dying body onto the bed beside me.

I scrambled back and off the bed, staring at the stranger.

"It's all right," the man whispered. "I'm sorry it took me so long to find you. But nobody's ever going to get the chance to hurt you again."

He reached out his hand to me. I wasn't sure what to do, but his eyes were kind.

"Who are you?" I whispered.

"They call me The Demon," he whispered back. "But you can call me Dad, if you want."

"Where are we going?"

A grin spread across his face. "That's my girl. Wherever you want, darling, that's where we're going. But first, we have to make one more stop..."

I took his hand. He frowned at the sight of the bruises on my body and said, "Why don't you pack a bag while I go have a talk with that woman who pretended to be your mom?"

"Okay," I answered in a trembling, but hope filled voice.

I was putting my books into my suitcase when I heard the faintest start of a scream, so quiet that I didn't think it reached outside the house. I froze for a second, then went on, getting my favorite t-shirts.

He came back in for me, and took my suitcase out to the car while I got dressed in real clothes instead of my pajamas. Then he picked me up, as if I were a little doll, and carried me out into the hallway.

"Don't look," he whispered to me. "Close your eyes."

But I didn't want to keep my eyes closed anymore, and I shook my head, wondering if he would hurt me like everyone else had if I didn't obey him.

But he just smiled.

He carried me into the hallway, where my mother lay half-in and half-out of her bedroom, the carpet stained dark with blood in the dim light.

"You were always only pretending to be sweet and helpless, Gabriela," he whispered in my ear.

"I was?"

"You forgot who you really were, sweet child, because you had to forget. That was the only way for us to keep you safe. But you've always been something more than anyone could realize. You've always been fierce."

I tried to understand what he was saying. Had I always known deep down that I was his daughter, that someday he would come back and claim me? That I was never really helpless, no matter how I felt?

I could leave behind Gabriela, the scared little girl who was locked in closets and beaten with anything handy. She was nothing but a ghost in the house that I was leaving behind, along with the bodies. She wasn't ever real.

The real me could never be hurt, broken...destroyed.

Especially not when I was with my daddy, and my daddy was the devil himself. I smiled up at him, and a slow smile spread across his face, as if he understood what I was thinking. He looked so handsome and strong when he smiled. He pressed a kiss to my forehead.

"My darling, precious, blade of a daughter," he murmured. "The only way anyone will ever see you as a victim again is if you want them to. And at any time, you can pull the blindfold from their eyes and show them you're always the one with the knife."

1

AURORA

I rehearsed my cover story as I drove to college.

I'd had a cover story all my life, ever since The Demon rescued me. But this time was different. My heart sped as I turned the corner and the stone buildings and green hills of Darkwood College rose in front of me.

I had to come to a stop as I joined a long line of cars waiting to turn into the campus circle in front of the dorms. As I waited, I pulled my sunglasses off and checked my face in the rearview mirror.

I'd been getting worried the swelling and bruising from surgery wouldn't go down in time. But it finally had; there was just the faintest puffiness that I couldn't quite cover with makeup. I mentally amended my cover story: I'd been partying hard the night before, enjoying one last night with my dear friends.

I'd spun my cover story out of a fantasy I'd had when I was a kid, imagining I had half-a-dozen close-as-hell girlfriends who were my absolute ride-or-die besties. Now I was bringing my imaginary friends back, pretending that I'd left them in my hometown, where we'd played lacrosse together.

I even had photos starring me and a couple of deep fakes, sitting on the front porch of a house I'd never been to, or standing pink-cheeked with our arms around each other's shoulders and red Solo cups in hand.

The face staring back at me in the mirror was pretty: high cheekbones, delicate nose, large, hooded eyes that were a startling shade of violet. I'd picked my new face out carefully. But I couldn't quite bring myself to put contact lenses over my irises, even though I knew I really should. They were the one connection I had with my birth mother, and I owed her some kind of debt.

It wasn't like me to be so emotional. "You're going to get yourself hurt being stupid," I mouthed at myself, watching my bright pink lips move, before I slipped my sunglasses back on to hide the swelling.

I didn't know then how right I was.

Half an hour later, the line of cars had finally crept forward until I was parked in front of the dorm. I checked in, then popped the trunk of my car and slung my duffel bag over my shoulder. I didn't own much, but I'd definitely have to make more trips.

The sun was shining and the campus was beautiful. The students streaming around me while unpacking their cars with their parents all seemed so happy. It made me feel like an outsider, because I was alone. I wouldn't have wanted to bring my father. Just imagining him in this scene was like imagining the beautiful setting slowly being infested by a dark poisonous blot.

"Let me help you." The voice was deep and sexy, and I spun to find myself facing a tall, good-looking guy with broad shoulders and a powerful body.

He flashed me a boyish smile. "It's a service our frat offers everyone. Whether or not they're a pretty girl."

He'd towed over a bright yellow rolling caddy. Behind him, another guy was pushing a caddy into the dorm while a girl and her parents walked behind him.

"I might not be a pretty girl, but I'll take the help," I said.

He grinned at me like he knew I knew better, then began to unload the boxes in the trunk into the cart. I stood back and watched him. There was no reason he'd open the tire well and see the weapons hidden inside, but I couldn't help feeling wary.

"What's your room number?" he asked.

I normally wouldn't volunteer any additional information about myself to strangers. In my experience, being casual with your personal information was a great way to end up locked in a wooden box.

Be normal, Delilah...Aurora. Shit.

"Four-twelve," I said, giving him a smile.

When we reached my new room, it already seemed full. A girl with long blonde hair, her parents, and a surprising number of small children seemed to fill the room.

"Oh! Get out of the way, Patrick," the blonde girl said, tugging one of the people out of the way of the frat boy and his caddy. She smiled at me, her eyes crinkling at the corners. "You must be Aurora!"

"You must be Jenna!"

"It's so nice to meet you!" She hugged me.

I'd exchanged a few emails with my new roommate. We weren't really on hugging terms but I was good at adapting to what other people wanted from me. So I hugged her back and smiled. She seemed genuinely warm and sweet just within a few seconds of meeting her, although that could always be an act.

She quickly introduced me to her parents, and to her

three younger siblings who had all come along to help her settle into her new dorm.

"Let me get the circus out of here while you unpack," she said, trying to shoo her family out. "Do you have family?"

Here. She meant here.

But I would've said no anyway. I shook my head.

"Okay! Then once I get them to give me some space, we'll go to dinner tonight. Six?" She called over her shoulder as she gently shoved her father out the door.

"Six is good," I answered.

The room felt quiet after they left. I sat down on the mattress, feeling exhausted after only a few moments of being Aurora. My whole life had been a cover story; why was this so tiring now?

Maybe I just wanted to be myself.

Then I thought about what kind of results would come up if I googled *Delilah Kane,* and I knew, no, that wasn't what I wanted.

I just wished I could genuinely *be* someone else.

By six o'clock, I'd unpacked my belongings into my room. I was glad that Jenna wasn't here to see me pull the tags from some of my clothing and hastily discard them, covering them up with crumpled paper at the bottom of the trash bin. I'd had to buy everything new, enough to make it look like I had a real past. I'd scuffed up my shoes in a hotel room, washed some of my new clothes and run them through several dryer cycles on hot, but I hadn't had the chance to do that to all of them.

By six fifteen, I thought Jenna wasn't coming back after

all, and I was relieved. This would be so much easier if my roommate wasn't nice.

Then the door swung open and she rushed in. "Oh good, you're still here! I'm sorry I'm late!"

"No problem," I said, feeling a sudden sense of dread about heading down to the dining room. "I knew you wouldn't abandon me."

She laughed. "No, freshmen have to stick together. Especially around here!"

I wanted to know why, but she was already kicking the rubber wedge that held the door open, holding it for me to go with her.

As we headed down to the dining hall, she prattled on, "I wouldn't miss dinner tonight anyway. The frat that helped our dorm move in will be eating with us tonight, and I want eye candy as much as I want some chicken tendies."

I had to smile. "How do you know everything that's going on around here? I'm pretty sure that *eye candy* wasn't in the schedule *I* got from the school."

"Oh, I'm a legacy," she said lightly. "My parents met here and fell in love here! My mom didn't just get her Mrs. degree though, she also did pre-med here."

"She's a doctor?"

She nodded. "And my dad's a mechanical engineer. Don't even get him started talking about gardening—he's engineered all these automatic watering systems and grow lights. If you walk past our basement windows in the spring and see the glow, you'd think he was growing something besides tomato plants."

"What are you going to major in?"

"Pre-med. Not because of my mom," she added quickly. "I want to be a completely different kind of doctor. She's a dermatologist. I am not devoting my life to other people's acne!"

Jenna was easy to talk to, especially since she did most of the talking anyway. The two of us separated in the busy, noisy cafeteria, and by the time I'd begun to load up my tray, I felt a little lost and alone.

But then Jenna waved at me manically from across the cafeteria. She clearly didn't care if anyone side-eyed her nonstop enthusiasm. It was refreshing.

And dangerous.

No, just refreshing, I reminded myself. Just because I knew how dark the world could be, I couldn't stop trying to believe in the happier, brighter version that co-existed right alongside it.

I walked over to Jenna and let her chatter wash over me as I took in the students around us. People were already forming into groups...or trying to. We were such pack animals.

There was a change in the air, a sudden tension, a bit of a hush. I looked up, curious about what had driven the change.

Four of the most good-looking guys I'd ever seen had just walked into the room. But what was fascinating to me wasn't the perfectly styled hair above handsome faces or the broad shoulders and athletic bodies.

It was the way they commanded a room, the way everyone had stopped for a second when they saw them. My heart suddenly beat a warning. They seemed to be in a good mood, getting food, making small talk.

But they bled a sense of power and certainty that I knew. These guys were predators.

"See what I mean about eye candy?" Jenna said, because that girl was oblivious to danger.

"Who are they?" I asked.

"Cain, Remington, Pax, and Stellan." She pointed at each of them in turn, and I sighed under my breath. She was going to draw their attention to us. "Four stars of the school."

"Really? We're not in high school anymore."

"Cain is an amazing quarterback," she gushed.

Maybe we were still in high school. Maybe high school never really ends.

What a depressing thought.

"Pax and Remington kill it on the soccer field together," she said. "And Stellan is the captain of the hockey team."

"Jocks," I said. "Oh, fantastic. I love jocks."

I glanced over my shoulder at them again. They were surrounded by girls.

"Everyone loves them," Jenna added.

"Probably not as much as they love themselves."

Jenna laughed, but I meant it.

I couldn't help keeping a wary eye on them as I continued to get my food.

I hadn't met many men like them in my life, but all the ones I had known?

They were trouble.

2

STELLAN

It was good to be king. I smirked as Leslie Baker, a cheerleader with remarkable flexibility, winked at me and flipped her hair as she walked by. I'd fucked her in the cheerleading locker room last week, but she was good enough for a second round. That back bend was a thing to behold.

I looked over and smirked at Paxton who had a girl tucked under each arm as we strolled through the cafeteria. He had a thing for threesomes, so I imagined he was setting something up. He'd been a monster in his fight this week-end. And we still hadn't gotten to celebrate properly. He'd knocked that guy out in ten seconds. That was a new record for him. Usually he liked to play with his prey first, but the fucker had made a comment about his mom and Pax had lost control.

A sharp slap to my ass made me jump and I rolled my eyes as Remy ran by, way too much energy, as usual. He let out a loud *whoop* as he rolled in and half the cafeteria answered back. Suckers.

I gazed around the room, not looking for anything in

particular, just making sure everything was as it should be. We were surrounded by simpering sheep, and sometimes it's all I could do to keep my absolute disdain for these idiots off my face. If I asked any of these lemmings to lick my butt-hole, they'd probably do it.

Absolute idiots.

And then I saw her, a face I hadn't seen before. School was just starting, but the freshman had been here for orientation and all the athletes had to get to campus early to start practicing...so the boys and I are very familiar with the freshmen *talent* available to us this year.

And the girl that I was seeing now was not in the mix.

Wide, fucking gorgeous, *familiar* eyes stared around the room.

But it couldn't be her. Everything else about this chick...was all wrong. Not wrong as in aesthetically unpleasing...just not as it should be.

Those eyes though.

There weren't a lot of people with violet fucking eyes. Elizabeth Taylor. And Delilah Kane.

There was something strange about that girl. Something almost...familiar.

I watched her nervously follow her friend around the cafeteria. I gave an automatic wink to a group of girls avidly watching me from a table nearby, but it didn't have the oomph I usually put behind those kind of things. I was too distracted watching *her*.

Why the fuck did she seem so familiar?

The girls all giggled behind me, but it didn't make me smile like it usually would. I felt like a lion stalking its prey as I followed the girl to the far side of the cafeteria where she was staring at the menu for the grill line like it held the secrets to the universe.

Her friend, who I'd seen around before, really needed to tell her to order the cheese sticks. They were the only good thing at the grill. I got in line, ignoring the look of terror from the mousy kid in glasses who was standing in front of me, and watched as she began to nervously tap two fingers against the metal railing that held the lunch trays. It looked like she was tapping out a song or something. Hmm. That seemed fucking familiar too.

She ordered her food and then walked over to the soda machine, mixing up the orange and cream sodas like a little kid. I didn't even know the school carried cream soda. The girls we hung out with were usually all about diet coke. My thoughts pittered away as I watched her take a huge gulp of her mixture, her eyes fluttering closed as if she was really enjoying herself.

I'd only known one girl who mixed her sodas like that, but...

That girl had also always been nervously tapping songs on everything, unable to control herself.

No. No fucking way. This girl looked nothing like Delilah. People grew up, but their features didn't fundamentally change. I mean, you could still tell Kim Kardashian was still Kim Kardashian as a girl, even with all the plastic surgery.

I moved out of my spot in line, as if there was a rope connecting me to this girl. I had to get closer. Some guys from the football team tried to fist bump me as I walked by, but I ignored them. I was faintly aware they were probably going to shit their pants thinking that our crew was mad at them or something, but I couldn't care less.

I stalked over until I was right behind her. I was standing way too close, creepily close if I was being honest, but societal norms had never been my thing. Not when they stood in the way of things that I wanted.

Not that I wanted that girl.

I was rambling.

I inhaled, the soft scent of coconut brushing against my nose. My cock instantly hardened. I was definitely crossing into the territory of really fucking creepy right now.

"Hey," I breathed.

The girl screeched, and I watched soda spit out of her mouth like a geyser as she jumped and looked at me.

"I'm so sorry," she said in a low, dirty voice that should be illegal for a girl that looks like her.

I searched her face without answering, trying to understand why I was so bugged right now. The blonde hair was all wrong. So were the cheekbones. The lips were a little too pouty.

I gave the girl a casual smile and then moved away, getting in a random food line and ignoring the girls in front of me who were trying to catch my eye.

The girl gave me a side glance before she ran back to the safety of her friend's side. I watched as she tapped out a rhythm on her pants, and then she pulled on her hair three times in a nervous tic.

And with that little move, there was no denying it. Somehow, Delilah Kane was standing in this cafeteria. A ghost from my past. A devil disguised in a beautiful package.

And the only person who could tell me exactly what happened to my sister all those years ago.

Aurora

Stellan. Years have passed but I'd never forget his face.

Sometimes, when things felt so terrible that I didn't know if I could stand it for one fucking minute, I'd think about him. About how normal I'd felt around him. How safe.

My heart was threatening to beat out of my chest as I surreptitiously tried to throw him side glances without him noticing. Luckily for me, the rest of the room was looking at him and his three friends, so hopefully he wouldn't notice another pair of eyes.

I was panicking. I felt like I was going to pass out actually. Because for a second there, it almost seemed like he recognized me.

But that would be impossible, right? I mean, I didn't even recognize me anymore. And he'd known me years ago, before I'd even matured.

He didn't seem like he knew me. He was laughing with that redhead next to him at the sandwich line, and his eyes hadn't once glanced my way.

"Are you okay?" Jenna asked, looking over at me, concerned, as she grabbed her chicken sandwich from the annoyed guy manning the grill station. She smirked when she saw where I kept looking.

"Stellan caught your eye already? You know, I hear he likes hot blondes, so you probably have a good chance," she teased.

I rolled my eyes and laughed nervously. "I almost spit my drink on him a moment ago. I was just checking to make sure he wasn't mad. Wouldn't want to piss off campus royalty the first day."

She gave me a look that told me she wasn't fooled, but like the nice bitch she was, she didn't say anything. I grabbed my food and followed her across the cafeteria, my appetite suddenly completely gone.

Jenna waved at a group of girls sitting at a table near the

back, and I tried to look happy to see them as she went and sat down. They all had open, friendly grins on their faces as I sat next to Jenna, but being around this many people still made me itchy.

And I couldn't see *Stellan* anymore, which should have been a good thing since, apparently, I wasn't very good at stalking under the radar. But I needed to make sure I was nothing but a clumsy stranger to him.

How the fuck had I ended up at school with Stellan Bishop in the first place?

3

AURORA

"Rise and shine," Jenna squealed. She had way too much energy for so early in the fucking morning, and I contemplated throwing my lamp at her for a moment to shut her up. But then the goddess set down a steaming cup of coffee in a bright pink, sparkly mug on my nightstand and I decided that violence was not the answer.

Anyone who understood the importance of coffee first thing in the morning needed to be protected at all costs.

I hopped in a quick shower, then ran my fingertips through my hair to double check my roots. Even though my dye job was fresh, I couldn't let it grow out at all. I couldn't let any of Delilah slip through.

Aurora. Aurora. I was Aurora now.

Stellan's gorgeous, haunting eyes rose up in my memory and my breathing quickened before I caught myself. He didn't know. I was going to be fine.

And if I wasn't?

I would run. I wouldn't hurt him.

I'd done that once before after all. I'd run to protect him from The Demon.

Someone banged on my door, almost giving me a heart attack before I realized it had to be Jenna.

"Hey!" she called. "Hurry up. You've got an eight o'clock class too, right? We'll walk together."

This girl was aggressively friendly. That was probably just what my introverted ass needed, but it was still a little overwhelming.

"I'll be there in a second."

"You don't need to waste time putting on makeup, you're already rudely pretty," she added.

I rolled my eyes and ran my fingers through my hair one last time before stepping back into our shared room. "You're very pretty too, you know."

"I know," she said lightly.

I grabbed my coffee—breakfast of champions—and the two of us headed through the dorm together.

"Do you want to get lunch together?" she asked. "When are you off?"

"I'm going to hide in the library," I answered honestly. "I love libraries. I want to take a little time to explore."

"You skipped breakfast."

"I promise, I'll eat something," I held up my fingers in a Scout's Honor sign even though I'd definitely never been any kind of Scout.

"You'd better, or I won't bring you coffee first thing in the morning. You'll have to go to the cafeteria yourself."

I'd once gone six days without eating as part of The Demon's 'training'. Skipping breakfast *and* lunch didn't faze me much.

"I'll be good, Mom," I said, and she laughed before she peeled away toward the Chem building.

I wasn't interested in Pre-Med like she was. I'd spent

plenty of time with cadavers. Instead, I headed for Price Hall, where the literature classes and offices were housed.

I could've sworn I felt someone starting at me as I went up the steps. I pretended to pause to check my phone, even though there was no one to text me; students streamed around me, heading for class, as I furtively surveyed the area for my stalker.

But I didn't see anyone.

And as a stalker myself, I was usually good at spotting one.

You're getting paranoid, Delilah, I thought, then corrected myself. *Aurora.*

But you know what they say. Just because you're paranoid doesn't mean you're wrong.

My classes that morning were all light and easy. The professors introduced themselves and handed out syllabuses. A warm, summer breeze drifted through the windows, blowing away some of the fresh-paint-and-cleaning-solvent scent of the classrooms.

I headed to the library at lunch time. My next class wasn't until two; I'd have time before then to duck into one of the cafeterias and grab a bite to eat while it was quiet.

Walking into the library was the closest I'd ever come to a religious experience. My footsteps resounded across the marble floor; an enormous domed roof covered the expansive lobby, which led to three different wings, and twin elaborate staircases led to the second-floor walkways. As I glanced around, I felt a smile come over my face.

The Demon and I had moved half a dozen times in the years between when he rescued me and when he destroyed me. He'd denied me a lot of things over the years with the goal of molding me into someone just as cold and cruel and dangerous as he was. Food. Medical care. Comfort. Friends, most of all.

But he'd never denied me a library.

Libraries had been my salvation. And this one was especially grand.

I wandered the stacks, enjoying the chance to get lost in the books, pulling a few out along the way. It would be easy to get lost in the long rows of books in this massive library, and that was exactly what I wanted—to forget myself in books for a while.

I made my way past the many community rooms with glass doors to a study carrel in the very back, hidden between a couple of shelves. I could watch my back from here. It was perfect. I leaned back in the chair, surrounded by the scent of paper and ink, and flipped through the pages.

I left the books there but took my backpack when I had to run to the bathroom.

When I came back, the books were still stacked neatly how I'd left them.

But a little folded white piece of paper was set on top of the pile, and it fluttered just faintly. As if there was air circulating. Or as if someone had just dropped it.

I lowered my backpack noiselessly to the ground and turned, my arms loose and ready for a fight.

But there was no one there.

After a few moments, I picked up the note and backed against the wall, making sure no one could sneak up on me as I unfolded it.

I know who you are.

My stomach dropped. Who could it be? Stellan? It had to be Stellan.

The peace of the library was broken for me now. I picked up my backpack and abandoned the books on the table. *Sorry, librarians.*

I was heading down the spiraling stairs toward the marble lobby when I glimpsed broad shoulders at the bottom of the stairs.

Stellan.

Waiting for me. Blocking me.

I glanced sidelong at the circulation desk beyond him, where two librarians were at work. I couldn't count on them to help me. If there was one thing I'd learned from The Demon, it was how unreliable humans are. Some days they'll help, some days they'll ignore you. But Stellan wouldn't want a public scene.

"Hey," he said, flashing a handsome, boyish smile up at me. That smile was a weapon; he'd been firing it freely around the cafeteria the night before.

"Hi," I replied cautiously, trying to go around him.

"Are you in Brit Lit 1?" He didn't block my way; he fell into step easily with me as I headed toward the doors. "I thought I saw you. I came in late, and I was wondering if I could get your notes."

I had a class with Stellan? Had he changed classes to be with me?

"I would love to, but there really was nothing to take notes on. Professor Flynn just passed out the syllabus. I'm sure he gave you a copy on your way out?"

"He did. And he told me to get notes." He flashed me a grin. "I saw you on the stairs and thought it was my lucky day."

Funny, because I saw *him* on the stairs and thought that I was fucked.

"Notes," I said. "Sure."

Maybe it was easiest to play his game, if there was one. Or maybe I was lucky and it was all coincidence. I wasn't the kind of person to gamble on luck though.

I stopped as we reached the doors and fumbled in my backpack for my notebook. I couldn't help freaking out a little, having him here so close to me. Both because of what he meant to me now... and what he used to mean to me.

"Hey," he said.

I glanced up at him, and found him frowning. He jerked his thumb at the circulation desk. "I accidentally stole a copy of *The Agony and the Ecstasy* and took it home for the summer. I came in today to give it back and pay my ridiculous fine—seventy dollars, can you believe it?"

"That's ridiculous," I agreed automatically. "You should've just bought it."

"The librarians let me off with a warning because they're lovely," he said, flashing that adorable grin over my head in their direction. Great. Even librarians swooned for this cocky asshole. He directed that gorgeous gaze back to me. "I just wanted to tell you because you seem freaked out. I didn't follow you in here from class or anything. I just recognized you and thought you could help me."

"I'm happy to," I said, then realized I was playing this all wrong. He could tell I was freaked out by how he'd just appeared. He'd probably left the note on my books, but he didn't know for sure who I was. That was why he was testing me. If he knew for sure who I was, he wouldn't bother.

I needed to lean into the role he expected me to play. Dumb bimbo who hung on his every word.

"You just surprised me, that's all," I said, giving him a slow smile, looking up at him through my lashes. "I didn't even realize we had a class together."

"Maybe we can sit together Friday."

I willed myself to blush. "Sure, that would be great," I said softly, as if I were playing it off like nothing, but was secretly thrilled.

I pulled out my notebook and flipped to the page where I'd jotted my notes. "Let's see. Three short papers, three to five pages, and one longer twelve-to-fifteen page paper. No tests, though. That's nice."

I reeled through what the professor had said. I could feel Stellan standing too close to me, radiating warmth and confidence. His gaze on my face was too intense.

The blush was beginning to come naturally, but that was okay. Let him think I was disarmed. Hopefully he thought the pulse beating too fast in my throat was because I had a crush on him.

He rested his hand lightly on my arm. "Thanks," he said, cutting into my monologue about the class. "I have to get to my Calc class. But maybe I'll see you for dinner tonight? Do you eat in the freshman cafeteria?"

"Yes," I said, because there was no point in lying.

"We make the freshmen soccer players swipe us into dinner after practice," he said with a teasing grin. "Maybe I'll see you around."

"Maybe."

"What's your name?" he asked, taking a step back, his shoulders against the door. As he pushed it open, the sun illuminated his hair with light.

Funny, because I knew Stellan Bishop was no angel.

"Aurora," I said.

"Pretty name," he responded, but I could've sworn the faintest disappointment flashed across his face. "For a pretty girl."

There was a time when Stellan's teasing and compliments left me weak.

Now, even though I smiled back at him, they left me terrified.

4

AURORA

"The trick, little angel, is that you don't want them to bleed out too quickly."

The Demon's knife cut into my arm, just below the first layer of skin, and I tried to hold in my whimper. He hated when I cried.

"See how the blood is just pebbling, right there?" he said in that breathless, excited voice that haunted my every moment. "But it hurts, doesn't it? It's really a beautiful thing."

I tried to suppress my shiver; he'd trained me to do it, but it was still fucking hard.

We both watched as a tiny rivulet of blood trailed down my arm.

"Now you try it," he said after a long moment where I was honestly afraid he was going to lick the blood off my arm. I'd seen him do it before.

He moved the knife back to the counter where he had his "tools" all set up. My heart rate slowed as his attention moved back to the main event, i.e., the man currently strapped to a medical table in the middle of the room. His gaze was flicking back and forth between The Demon and me, and there was a terrified, bleating noise coming from his throat as he continued to struggle against his bonds. I knew the struggle wouldn't last long though. The Demon would eventually inject him, and then he wouldn't be able to move at all. He'd evidently spent three years concocting some kind of venom that trapped the victim inside their body. They were conscious, completely aware of everything that was happening, and able to feel every cut against their skin, but they were unable to move.

The Demon was especially proud of that creation.

"I've been watching this guy for weeks," The Demon said gleefully as he inserted a needle into a large bottle filled with the venom. He carefully measured out just the right amount and then expertly squirted a bit of the liquid out from the top so that there would be no air bubbles. "He's had a crush on one of the girls who worked in my office. He would wait around the coffee bar in the lobby because he knew she went there every day for lunch. It was the cutest thing."

I waited for The Demon to tell me what the man's sin was, like usual, but this time, he never said...

The Demon leaned over the sniveling man. My breakfast threatened to come up just thinking about what was about to occur. If I'd known that he had this guy down here, I never would have eaten in the first place. He'd just killed someone two weeks ago, he was going way off pattern here. I'd thought that I'd been safe. I'd thought that I'd have at least a few more months...

The man slowly went still as he was injected with the venom. His eyes moved around crazily though, the only sign of the panic and utter terror he was experiencing inside.

The Demon fiddled with some buttons on the wall, and I tried not to follow the man off the edge of sanity as Sweet Caroline started to blast through the speakers. It was his go-to song when things were going to get really messy, and I'd seen enough while listening to it that it was a guaranteed panic attack if I heard the song at any point outside of the basement. Somehow, the song seemed to belong down here, in the land of nightmares. Hearing it played anywhere else was more than I could take.

My father laughed as he picked up a mechanized chainsaw, the buzzing song interspersed with the lyrics. Suddenly he turned towards me and...

"Aurora!"

My eyes opened and I sat up, my breath coming out in gasps as I struggled to shake off the nightmare determined to hold me in its grips.

Jenna was standing over me, a concerned and wary look on her face as she stared. What I presumed was my morning coffee was clutched tightly in her hands.

I wiped my face, trying to get ahold of myself before she inevitably started asking questions. Beyond the fear of somehow being recognized, I'd been most afraid about sharing a room with someone. Nightmares were something that haunted me frequently. They'd been happening less and less since The Demon had been locked away. But yesterday's note must have triggered them.

"Sorry, just a bad dream," I said hoarsely, wincing at the sound of my voice. I must have been screaming judging by how much it freaking hurt to speak. I let out a deep breath and tried to smile and not look like a psychopath while I was doing it. Sometimes I wondered if the lessons The Demon had taught me were so ingrained that it wasn't possible to escape them, no matter how many times I changed my face.

"Quite the imagination. Remind me not to suggest any scary movies. Looks like you don't need any help in that department," she tried to joke. But I could see it in her eyes, she was thinking differently about me. Just a few days in and I was already rocking this whole *be normal* thing.

Not.

"Yeah, I'm not the biggest fan of horror movies," I agreed, grabbing the coffee from her hands and stepping towards the bathroom.

After showering, I hurried to get ready. Jenna was noticeably already gone from the room, not bothering to wait for me like she had the previous mornings.

I was both relieved and upset about walking to class alone. On the one hand, it gave me a break from having to be so fucking cheerful every minute, but on the other, it felt lonely. Jenna had already given up on me. I'd already spent most of my life feeling that way, and it was an unwelcome emotion.

At least I would be surrounded by people in class, I guess.

"I've been looking for you everywhere!" Jenna shouted as she practically pounced on me as I was walking to grab lunch. I twirled around, shocked that she was acting so...normal. Evidently she'd recovered from this morning faster than I thought she would.

"You are never going to believe what just happened to me," Jenna squealed as she grabbed my hand and started to drag me away from the cafeteria.

"Um, where are we going?" I asked, practically having to jog to keep up with her.

"We have to get ready," she panted.

I was lost.

"What exactly do we have to get ready for?" I asked,

throwing a longing look behind me at the food that was rapidly going out of reach.

"There's a party at the football house tonight, and the Sphinx is co-hosting it." You would think she'd won the lottery by the level of enthusiasm in her voice.

The Sphinx sounded familiar, but I couldn't remember where I'd seen something about it.

"Why aren't you freaking out about this?" Jenna demanded, coming to such a sudden halt that I almost ran into her.

I thought about faking it for a moment, but then decided against it. I was just not that good of an actress.

"What exactly is the Sphinx, and why is this a big deal?" I asked hesitantly.

She pointed behind frat row where I could kind of see some sort of enormous concrete structure hidden in the trees. "That's The Sphinx. It's the most exclusive secret society in the whole country, Aurora. Basically, every president, every famous athlete, every famous actor...they all were members there."

I squinted at the building, feeling the inane urge to go and check it out further. Secret societies weren't really my jam—thanks to The Demon of course—but now that she was talking about it, I remembered reading about the secret societies here when I was doing research on schools.

"Do you know anyone who's a member of it?" I asked as Jenna began to pull me towards our dorm once again. "Or is it really a secret?"

"Well, it's pretty easy to guess who's a member there. I mean, just take a look at the uber popular kids and you can guess. But they do pretend to keep it secret, at least until graduation. On graduation day, the graduating members carry a special cane with a sphinx on top of it up on stage with them, so everyone knows how special they are." She muttered 'special' reverently, and I had to hold in a snort.

"Oh! And they have the biggest water bill in the state, and no one knows why," she explained excitedly.

We got to the outside of the dorm building and Jenna swiped her card to get us through the door. She was a woman on a mission as she raced down the hall almost desperately.

"How exactly does a secret society host a party with the football frat?" I asked as we burst through our room door and she made a beeline for her closet.

"They donate money," she said, like I was the biggest idiot on the planet. "But more than anything, it means *they* will be there." She stared into space dreamily.

It said a lot that I'd only been at this school for a little bit and I already knew who the *they* were that she was talking about. And knowing who *they* were had me debating if I could fake a quick stomach flu to get out of the party.

"Are you sure they'll let us in?" I asked hopefully. I mean, we were freshman, and there had to be some exclusivity to a party like that, right? I couldn't imagine the frat hosting the entire college at the party.

"That's just it, though. It was the craziest thing that's ever happened in my life. I was standing in the hallway, talking to one of the girls in my psych class, and Stellan stopped and said hi to us. And then he specifically asked if we were planning on coming tonight and told me to bring a friend!" She began to throw dresses out of the closet furiously. "I still can't get over it."

"Are you sure you want to bring me?" I asked, still bothered by how she reacted this morning.

"Of course! We're roomies, it's only a matter of time until we're besties too."

Now I was definitely thinking of getting the stomach flu. It couldn't be a coincidence that he was asking my roommate if she was coming to the party tonight. While a small, small part of me was a little bit hopeful that he just thought I was hot or something like that, The Demon didn't raise idiots. He was trying to get close to me, and I didn't understand why.

"I'm not feeling that good," I told her, trying to sound at least a little bit pathetic. But like I said, I wasn't a good actress.

Jenna froze and then turned around to stare at me, a determined gleam in her eyes. "You are going to get your cute butt into a hot dress, and you are going to this party. I don't care if you need your appendix out, you can get it out afterwards."

She was honestly a little bit scary right then, and I nodded reluctantly, eliciting a sudden reappearance of her sunny smile.

"Go find a cute dress," she ordered. I sighed and walked towards my closet like the grim reaper himself was hiding in there.

First college party, here I come.

LOUD MUSIC WAS BLARING from the house in front of us, and I shifted nervously in my chucks. Jenna had almost thrown a fit when I'd pulled them on with my little black party dress, but I couldn't run away from a murderer in high heels.

I'd learned that lesson from The Demon too.

"We could still go home and watch reruns of Vampire Diaries," I whispered to Jenna frantically. Her arm was linked through mine, and I could feel her body trembling with excitement.

"You'd better be joking," she murmured as her friend, aptly nicknamed Cissy, giggled next to her.

What seemed like a monsoon of college students—mostly girls—made their way to the double front doors of the frat house. There were two beefy guys standing with clipboards at the door. Every person was stopped as the guys checked to see if their name was on the list. We watched as three girls ran away from the door in tears, clearly having not made the cut.

"Are you sure we're on the list?" asked Cissy, nervously.

"He said he'd put me on the list," Jenna said before stopping in her tracks. "I just realized he never asked for my name!"

"Oh, that's too bad. Let's just go back to the room. I don't really want to be rejected in front of this many people," I said, trying to sound upset even though I was inwardly cheering at the chance of a reprieve.

"We're going into that party," Jenna said determinedly, latching onto my arm so tightly I would need to check for blood. Jenna...was a little scary.

She marched us up to where the two guys were checking their list. I watched as they sent away two guys whose cologne I could smell from five feet away from them.

Jenna marched us to the doors, no chance of failure in her steps. She had started fluttering her eyelashes and swaying her hips when we were still a ways out. I thought she looked a little possessed moving her eyelashes like that, but the two frat boys were tracking us like we were their next meal, so I guess it was working.

"How are you fine ladies doing tonight?" the one on the left asked, pointedly looking down the front of my dress. I resisted the urge to deck him with a right hook. I was doing this for Jenna. I could be chill.

All bets were off, though, if he did more than look.

"Good now, honey," Jenna cooed as she twirled a piece of hair around her finger. I studied the movement closely, trying to memorize what it looked like to actually be good at flirting...just in case I got the chance. Although, I was still unsure if Jenna was good at flirting or if the fact that she was wearing what resembled a napkin as a shirt was the thing doing the job. Whatever it was, the guy holding the clipboard looked like he was drooling.

A guy who must have been one of his frat brothers walked by, and that seemed to snap him out of the trance he'd been under. Looking a bit flustered, he pretended to look through the list on his clipboard before belatedly realizing that he didn't know our names. A flush hit his cheeks before he cleared his throat and asked Jenna for her name.

"Jenna Parker," she announced confidently, even though her hand was shaking against my skin as she continued to hold onto me. She was making me nervous just being in the same vicinity as her.

The guy glanced at his sheet and frowned as he began to go through the names.

It was clear pretty quickly that Jenna was in fact not on the list.

"I'm not seeing you on this," he said, clearly disappointed that he had to tell his new crush she hadn't made the cut. Cissy threw a frantic glare behind us to where a growing crowd of impatient co-eds were lined up waiting to get in.

"Let's just go," I whispered to Jenna anxiously. It felt like a million eyes were on me. Even with my new face, it was too much attention.

"What about Aurora Hart?" Jenna blurted out, panicked.

The guy nodded and went back to his list. Mr. Pervert who had been checking out my rack this whole time elbowed the guy once he realized there were at least fifty people in line behind us.

"Aurora Hart," Clipboard Guy muttered as he ran through the list.

Please don't be on it, please don't be on it, I chanted in my head.

"Oh hey, you're right here," he exclaimed, pointing to the list like we could somehow see my name through the back of the clipboard. He blushed again when he saw us looking at him.

"Go right in, ladies."

"I'll see you later?" Jenna flirted as she pulled me reluctantly towards the door, and the guy nodded his head fervently like he was a puppy.

"Thank fuck you were on that list, Aurora!" Jenna exclaimed as we walked through the front entryway and were immediately assaulted with the scent of sweat and booze. "Stellan must have put you on there. You are totally holding out on me about what happened in the cafeteria!"

Jenna led Cissy and me to an impressive bar set up in the back of the enormous room that was ten feet deep with people trying to get a drink.

"Well?" she pouted while we waited in line, trying to avoid getting alcohol splashed on us as people pushed by to head to other parts of the house after getting their drink.

I shifted uncomfortably, staring at the scratched wooden floor beneath us. "It wasn't in the cafeteria. He's in one of my classes apparently and needed notes. I didn't think he'd even remember my name."

Liar. The word pulsed in my brain as it did anytime I lied...which was frequently.

Jenna nodded, evidently believing me. Cissy popped up next to us, somehow carrying three drinks full of what looked like fruit punch. I had no idea how she'd waded through the line, but I took the drink gratefully, swallowing down a big gulp of liquid courage as quickly as I could.

Fuck, it tasted like pure alcohol with a dash of fruit juice.

I took another big sip just for good measure.

Cissy giggled, holding her drink above her and sloshing some to the floor like somehow, she'd managed to get plastered in the two point five seconds that had passed since she'd gotten her drink.

"Let's go dance," Jenna yelled as music and the sounds of the crowd around us tried to drown her out.

Cissy and Jenna danced and giggled as we passed through another doorway into an even bigger room. There was a set of stairs off to my left where the DJ must have been set up because I could hear the thumping sound of the bass coming up from the stairway.

I took another sip of my drink as I furtively looked around me, sure that Stellan was going to pop out at any minute. I plastered a fake smile on my lips as I swayed a bit in place as Cissy and Jenna danced around me. The room was packed...really, the whole place was packed.

I blushed when I saw a couple going at it in one of the shadowed corners. I averted my eyes when I was pretty sure I saw the guy's dick. The corner was shadowed...but not that shadowed.

Jenna rolled her hips against me, almost spilling my drink, and I stopped being a creeper and staring at everyone and tried to dance a little too. I felt like a complete idiot as I moved since I had little to no experience dancing, and I threw back the rest of my drink, wincing as the strong burn of the alcohol went down my throat.

But it was working. I was already feeling a bit more relaxed. Jenna and Cissy moved us down to the stairs that led to the basement. The air coming from down there was humid, the result of what could be hundreds of people packed together like sardines. A group of girls passed by us on the stairs. They were sweaty and disheveled, and one of them tripped and almost fell down the stairs as she tried to drunkenly walk.

I shivered thinking about having that little control. It was tempting to think about getting obliterated, allowing myself not to worry...to forget about the monsters that lurked in my past. But as soon as those thoughts crept in, I pushed them away. I didn't have the luxury of escape. I would have done that already.

When you held as many secrets as I did, you didn't get to forget. There was too much to lose.

I shook off my depressing thoughts when we got to the bottom of the stairs. Another DJ was set up on the far side of the room, and Doja Cat was blaring from the speakers. I couldn't hear a word Jenna was saying as she tried to talk to me. Finally, she just yanked me to the bar down there where we all grabbed another solo cup of red punch.

I might not have been able to get messy drunk, but I could do *a little* drunk.

The basement was lit by strobe lights like we were in a rave rather than a frat basement, and it added to the surreal energy in the place. The three of us danced our asses off until I was desperate for water. The bar down here didn't have any, so I was going to have to hunt for it.

"I'm going to go upstairs and find some water!" I yelled in Jenna's ear.

"Do you want me to go with you?" she asked, clearly not wanting to. A frat brother had been grinding against her for the past thirty minutes, and I knew they would be sneaking off to hook up any minute now.

"I'm good," I told her.

I wasn't too nervous about wandering around by myself. The Demon had been good for at least making sure I was dangerous myself. I pitied the frat bro who would try and do something.

I headed back up to the main floor. It was even more packed than it had been before, and a quick look at the bar on that floor told me I'd be lucky to get to the front in the next hour. That wasn't going to work.

Upstairs it was.

Couples were making out on the staircase, and I was sure that some of them were going to fall down it by the end of the night. I was thanking the stars for my Converse as I made my way up the stairs. The first hallway was packed up here too, so I just began to open random doors. The first door I opened got me a good look at some guy's ass as he writhed against a girl who was definitely faking it, but the second door revealed a bathroom that was miraculously empty.

I closed the door and leaned against it, taking a deep breath. I stared at the sink for a moment, tempted to just get water from the spout. But the sink was filthy. I wasn't quite that desperate yet.

I laughed when I saw my reflection in the mirror. My perfectly straight hair was now a wavy, crazy mess and my makeup was smeared from sweating. I grabbed some paper towels from a luckily still full dispenser and tried to fix my face. My hair didn't look half bad like this and there was a flush and glow to my skin from the alcohol and heat. Not terrible looking. Even if it was a stranger's face staring back at me.

I wondered how long it would take for me to get used to this new me.

Somehow I managed to use the toilet without touching the toilet seat, a trick that all college girls needed to master, but one that I had mastered from all the campouts I'd been forced into by The Demon when we were laying low. I opened the door and crept back out into the hallway. The desperation was becoming real. If I had to steal a bottle out of some frat boy's room, I would do it at this point.

I came up empty in a few more rooms after getting an eyeful of things I wished I could unsee. I ran up the next flight of stairs, because these frat houses were freaking huge, and practically threw open the first door I came to.

And immediately regretted every decision I'd made the whole night.

Because *they* were in this room. All of them except for Stellan.

I'd stumbled into a huge loft where evidently the cool kids held court. There was an enormous couch in front of a projector screen. Behind the couch were a few pool tables and another table that had been set up for beer pong. I gulped as my gaze ran across the three other kings of the school who were sprawled out on the couch. Their adoring courtiers were in various spots around the room, obviously hanging onto whatever the guys were saying.

I thought about trying to back out, but it was too late. The whole slamming open the door to their lair had set me firmly in their sights.

A hush fell upon the room as everyone made me the center of attention.

"You lost?" the pretty, dark haired one drawled. I doubted he would like being called pretty, but honestly, that was the best word to describe him. He was so pretty it was ridiculous.

Remington.

I was pretty sure that was his name.

The room was dim, only a few spotlights on along with the light coming from the humongous tv on the wall. Even with the low light, I could still see those startling blue eyes of his, almost seeming to glow from across the room. He leaned back deeper into his couch cushion, his eyes hooding as he let out a low groan that sent illicit sparks dancing through my body.

I belatedly realized that there was a girl on her knees in front of him, her head bobbing up and down over his lap. He was getting a freaking blow job in a room full of people. The people playing pool on the far side of the room weren't even bothering to hide the fact that they were watching. Between Remington and I, we were evidently giving the room quite the entertainment.

But the other two kings sprawled nearby on the same couch just looked bored as girls tried to get their attention.

I had seen people get spliced in every which way, but watching a guy get a blow job in public... well, I was blushing like mad.

"Best run away, little girl. Grownup games might be a bit too much for you in here," the king sitting next to Remington drawled. That one would be Paxton. He had a crazy look in his gaze as he slowly perused my whole body, and a shiver inched up my spine. I knew what it looked like when someone was unhinged. I'd seen that look for years...sometimes I'd seen it in my own gaze. And Paxton Jones was the epitome of unhinged. I lifted my chin and stared back at him, ignoring the low grunts of pleasure coming from Remington. You couldn't show weakness to crazy people. That was Surviving a Serial Killer 101.

Not that Paxton was a serial killer.

I thought.

When I didn't look away, or even blink, Paxton grinned, the smile slipping across his face like a ghost. There one second, then gone the next, like it had never happened.

Honestly, the smart thing would have been to take a step back and run for my life. But I somehow found myself taking steps further into the room, their stares drawing me in. I walked to the edge of the couch, my gaze drawn back to Remington as he finished with a loud groan, holding the girl's head down so he could make sure to finish in her mouth.

There was a grimace on her face when he finally let her up for air, but she quickly schooled her face, giving him what I thought was supposed to be a seductive grin as she struggled to get off her knees.

"Thanks, Remington," she purred, and my jaw dropped. I didn't know that was a thing, thanking someone for fucking your face.

But what did I know?

"Want to go next?" Paxton asked, and I realized my mistake in taking my eyes off of him because he was standing right behind me somehow, his breath tickling the back of my neck.

"I'll pass," I said flatly.

And then Remington was there, standing in front of me. I froze between the two of them, afraid to move a muscle surrounded by two apex predators.

"The ass is probably an eight," Paxton commented, and I bristled in shock.

"Tits are a clear ten though, Pax. At least two handfuls. Cantaloupes maybe?" Remington added.

"Want to comment on my waist to boob ratio?" I spit, ready to junk punch both of them.

"Back off."

The order was soft but threaded with an edge of violence. And it came from the golden-haired angel still sitting on the couch.

Cain.

The room went silent at his order, and both Pax and Remington went still, displeasure clear on their faces as they stared down at me.

I was feeling uncomfortably hot as they both stepped away, albeit reluctantly. "Just having a bit of fun, Cain," Remington said smoothly as he walked over to the bar on the far side of the room and grabbed a bottle of Grey Goose. He slung it back like it was water.

"Come here, new girl," Cain ordered in that same calm voice. Pax was still standing behind me, but somehow I wasn't as worried about him. Because I'd just identified the leader of the kings, and I didn't think Pax would try anything now that I was snarled in Cain's sights.

I hesitated, wondering what my angle should be here. But then I finally took a few hesitant steps towards him until I was standing in front of him.

He was sprawled casually on the couch, his legs wide-spread just as Remington's had been, just with no girl in between them. He was wearing a loose pair of grey sweat-pants and a white t-shirt along with a faded black ball cap that he had on backwards. The sweatpants were the stuff of every girls' dreams, sitting decadently low on his hips, enough to showcase those v lines that looked like they'd been airbrushed; they were so perfect. And...

Holy Fuck.

Talk about Big Dick Energy. Cain's nickname was officially going to be #BDE because I was pretty sure those sweats were housing a trouser snake or something. I quickly flicked my gaze to his face, trying to control the ever-present blush that didn't seem to want to go away.

But his face didn't help. Seriously, how were all three guys so freaking hot? I mean, I'd seen them in the lunchroom, but I'd been intentionally trying not to look at them. I had no choice but to look at them now.

His perusal of me was...erotic. That was the only way to describe it. I might as well have been naked with the way his eyes were caressing my skin. I felt flushed, achy...needy. My breath hitched and he pulled me forward until I was suddenly straddling him, not really having any idea how I got there.

I could feel him there, right between my legs, and it was all I could do not to move...to feel him in that perfect spot.

"What's your name, new girl?" he asked in a gruff voice that had me imagining the feel of silk sheets against my skin as he moved in and out of me...

What had he asked me again?

"Your name," he repeated, sounding amused. I forced myself to look him in the eye. I wanted him to know I wasn't prey. His pretty face was distracting me, that's all.

Why was being a normal girl so fucking hard? Maybe I should challenge him to a knife fight or something. I could be normal then.

"Aurora," I finally answered in a rough voice, getting a little lost in his eyes. They were so...green. Like freshly mowed grass on an early summer morning where the dew was still kissing the blades. I didn't know how eyes could be like that, but his were. I had an actual ache inside of me that had nothing to do with the need for sex as I stared at him, somehow reminded of childhood and early mornings on the playground during the summers in between school...before The Demon had come for me.

"Shots!" Remington suddenly shouted from behind us, breaking whatever moment I'd been having with myself and Cain's eyeballs.

Cain stood up, taking me with him. It was a smooth move and I was impressed, his hands never leaving my hips as he got up from the couch.

"Going to take a drink with us, new girl," he purred, the tip of his tongue dancing around the rim of my ear and making my entire body quiver.

One shot couldn't hurt, right? I'd already burned off the alcohol I'd had earlier, and it would be good to get in with the kings. I could at least get some party invites for Jenna.

"Let's do it," I answered, impressed with how steady my voice sounded. I even sounded a bit...flirty.

Go me.

Remington was at the bar, filling a long line of shot glasses with the Grey Goose he'd commandeered a few minutes before.

He handed me a glass with a cocky wink. "Ladies first," he said, offering me another wink, and I'm pretty sure that all the girls in the room, and guys probably, suddenly needed a change of underwear.

I took the shot and quickly threw it back, making sure not to make a face as it slid down my throat. The expensive stuff never burned as bad, so that was a plus. That punch downstairs was like gasoline.

Fun fact. Although I was always careful about my alcohol intake, it was a sure thing that I could drink everyone under the table here without getting the least bit sloppy.

The Demon had loved vodka. It had been one of his tests to train my body to tolerate as much alcohol as possible. I wasn't sure what he had been trying to teach with that one—maybe he wanted to torture me, but I was sure it would come in handy here.

A girl pushed up against me, reaching out eagerly for one of Remington's poured shots.

"Don't touch, Wendy," Remington hissed at her, and she flinched like she'd been struck.

"M-my name's Katherine," she stuttered.

"Okay, Wendy," said Paxton with an honestly evil laugh.

Poor girl looked like she was going to cry. She backed away from the bar and hurried back to the safety of her friends who looked like they wanted to push her out a window now that she'd been mocked by the kings.

"Another," I said, and Remington slid me another shot.

I threw that one back as well.

There was a pause as Remington studied me, and then a grin lit up his face, fucking blinding me with how incredibly beautiful it was.

Cain's grip tightened on my hips, like he didn't want me to forget that he was there.

"New girl wants to party!" Remington yelled to the room, and everyone there cheered wildly.

It was kind of...weird.

The music began to blast louder, Billie Ellish crooning something about a damn crown. I could get behind that.

Paxton, Remington, and Cain grabbed shots then, and Cain spun me around. He threw back the shot and then his lips were on mine. I opened my lips, completely off guard, and some of the vodka slipped into my mouth from his, followed by his tongue.

He tangled his tongue with mine, and a slight moan slipped from my lips because fuck, it had been so long since I'd had any form of physical affection.

Cain pulled away suddenly, heat in his gaze like he wanted to rip my clothes off. His breathing was heavy like he'd actually been...affected by our kiss.

Remington whooped and everything became a blur after that. Paxton threw open the door and a swarm of people came into the room. The lights dimmed even more and people began to dance. Cain pulled me through the crowd and tugged me close.

"Just relax," he murmured, his voice a caress across my skin.

I could do this. I could dance with the hot guy.

In the darkness of the room, he looked even more dangerous and wild than he had before. One of his hands moved from my hip, up to the base of my neck. I felt his fingertips gently tracing an invisible line from my collar-bone down to the top of my dress and back, igniting a trail across my skin. My breath hitched as his intense gaze followed the path of his finger.

Like he owned everywhere he touched.

His eyes met mine, possessive and hungry, devouring me as he moved behind me. His other hand gripped my hip, yanking back roughly, pushing our bodies together until there wasn't even a breath of air between us.

I'd officially lost my mind. But it felt...incredible.

Cain guided our movements, taking over, and somehow I let him, relaxing against his body, following his lead. It wasn't easy for me to let go, but something about Cain made me want to just give in, let him take the lead.

I'd have to examine that particular personality trait at a later date.

Cain fisted my hair gently and moved my head so that I was positioned with my face against his neck.

"You're so fucking hot, new girl," he growled in a rough voice that sent tingles all the way to my clit as if he had a hand between my legs and was pressing on me. He had me trapped against him, and I expected to feel a flicker of panic at any moment, the need to kick him in the dick or something and make my escape.

It was weird, though. I didn't feel nervous at all restrained against him. I almost felt...comforted, with his hard body behind me. The beat of the music changed, some dark sensual pop song that I'd never heard before. His body curved tighter around mine, and I melted into him even further.

My breath hitched and I caught his scent, orange and spice and some musk that I hadn't ever smelled before. Whatever it was, I was obsessed, wanting to find a way to bottle up the scent, maybe sell it? I'd never have to worry about money again. I resisted the urge to lick his skin, to see if he tasted as good as he smelled.

The song switched to *Lollipop* by Lil Wayne, an old song that I actually knew. I closed my eyes and let the music move through me. Cain was an incredible dancer. He was freaking tall but somehow could move his body perfectly. I could only imagine what he would be like on the field...or in bed.

"Fuck," he groaned in my ear, and goose bumps spread along my skin as I felt his hard cock against my ass. #BDE indeed. It felt enormous, more like an elephant trunk than something that could be attached to a college guy. He chuckled, and I realized I must have spoken out loud.

Fuck.

Cain released my hair and his hand began to move along my body, sliding against my skin, exploring every inch that was showing.

We were surrounded by people; the room had been filled to the brim when Remington had opened the door, but we might as well have been all alone as far as either of us were concerned. A little voice in the back of my head reminded me that he was dangerous, that this could be his M.O. But it was hard to believe he wasn't as lost in whatever spell this was.

He pushed his cock against me and I shivered. My dress felt ridiculously thin, reminding me of how easily he could move under it if he wanted to.

Did I want him to? A thrill pulsed through me thinking about it.

One of his hands moved up my thigh, fingering the hem of my dress and making my breath come out in embarrassing gasps. “I need this,” he moaned.

His other hand moved to my stomach, his entire hand holding me, like he owned me. I let out a gasp when his hand moved under my dress, inching up until he was almost to the lace edge of my underwear. His fingers brushed against my cloth covered sex and I shivered.

Someone yelled nearby, and I was yanked back to the present and to the fact that I almost allowed one of the most popular guys in school to finger me in a room full of people.

"Not here," I whispered, stiffening and grabbing his arm to stop his hand from going any further up.

Cain froze before squeezing my thigh and reluctantly removing his hand from underneath my dress. He whipped me around and stared down at me, a wild look in his eyes as he pressed his bulging length against me. He let out a hungry noise before suddenly devouring my lips; his lips, tongue, and teeth set me on fire.

Cain abruptly pulled away, his eyes scanning the room desperately. He grabbed my hand and began to pull me through the crowd towards a door on the far side of the room. I faintly heard catcalls following us across the room, but I was caught in some sort of lust haze. The annoying voice in the back of my head told me that I was going to regret this later, but my pussy stabbed the bitch with a butcher's knife and all thoughts beyond what Cain's cock was going to taste like disappeared.

He opened the door, revealing a bedroom that looked a little too clean to belong to a frat bro. I glanced at the bed that appeared to have been made with military precision, but Cain was on me and I stopped wondering about the neat freak whose room we had taken over.

He didn't go slow this time; his hand was under my dress and stroking my clit through my underwear.

"Is this all for me?" he asked as he massaged my soaking wet panties.

All I could do was groan.

"Answer me," he growled, and the command in his voice got me even wetter, somehow.

He turned me around, pushing me against the door where I could hear the pulsing music from the party.

Cain dropped to his knees, staring up at me. It was dark in here, only the light from the streetlights outside providing any way to see.

The darkness seemed to only enhance his beauty. The dim lighting showcasing his perfect features. He was staring up at me, what looked like confusion in his gaze as his eyes met mine. I was confused too. I'd barely talked to this guy, but there was energy threaded between us, a feeling that there was something to this moment...something more.

He blinked, and whatever I saw was gone. Without warning, he threw one of my legs over his shoulder, shoved my panties aside, and buried his face between my thighs.

He sucked and licked, his hot tongue moving in and out of me as he thrusted two fingers inside of me at the same time. My hands went to his head, trying to push him away and pull him closer all at the same time. I'd never had someone do this to me before. And while it felt freaking amazing...it also felt intimate. Too much for a stranger I'd found myself in a dark room with.

He pressed his face into me, his mouth and tongue demanding as he sucked at me rhythmically. His hands squeezed my ass, moving me forward until I was straddling his face. I was in a daze as I watched him, his cheeks hollowing out as he sucked. His stubble scratched my inner thighs, and the sensation, along with the crazy things his tongue was doing, pushed all reasoning out of me. I fisted his hair tightly, thrusting my hips against his mouth. The movement only seemed to spur him on and he let out a loud groan that filled up the whole room.

"Mmmmh."

Cain ate me like it was his favorite thing. Like he couldn't get enough. Like he craved it. His moans vibrated through my clit, adding to the sensations spiraling through me. Sounds were coming out of me that I'd never heard before. I'd been possessed, consumed...destroyed.

"Yes, yes," I cried. Everything began to tighten inside of me as his tongue did something crazy to my clit. Pleasure suddenly skyrocketed through me. I thrust my hips desperately, chasing every last bit of pleasure I could get from his mouth. He continued to lick me as the tremors continued to shoot through my body. Cain finally pulled his fingers out of me before giving me one last lick that had me aching for more. His breathing was heavy as he gently lifted my leg off of him and sat back on his heels, breathing heavily with fire in his eyes.

Cain smoothly stood up, pulling me close and sealing his lips over mine, his tongue moving in and out of my mouth. I could taste the salty muskiness of myself on his lips. I wasn't sure what I thought about that, but I was still too blissed out to worry about it too much.

He moved his mouth to my ear. "You taste delicious," he said huskily. "I can't wait to fuck you." Before I could respond, his lips were on mine again, his tongue licking and sucking at my mouth the same way that he'd just done to me on his knees.

Cain started to pull up my dress further, but I put my hands on his chest, finally coming to my senses.

"Not tonight," I murmured, and he stilled against me with a loud groan.

"You're killing me," he said roughly, but his hands smoothed down my dress. He surprised me when he pressed a soft kiss on my lips before stepping away.

"I have a feeling that you'll be worth the wait," he said with a wink before stepping fully away and opening the door that led back to the party. In the light streaming in, I could see that his hair was all over the place. Cain's lips were swollen and pouty from what we'd just done. Some perverse part of me liked that you could see that he'd been with me.

As soon as the people out there saw him, a chorus of catcalls were screeched at him. Embarrassment hit me then, and I knew I couldn't go back in there. My skin crawled just thinking of all those eyes on me. He gazed back at me, a questioning look in his eyes like he expected me to just follow him out.

I shook my head and started looking around the room. There were two other doors in here, and I just prayed that one of them led back into the hallway. It was either that, or I was going to wait in here until the party was over.

The first door I opened was a crowded closet, but with the second one I hit the lottery, the musty air of the hallway rushing over me.

It was time to get back to my dorm.

5

STELLAN

I rose from the bed and dragged my gray sweatpants on, over my still hard dick. I'd been fucking these two girls for the last half hour, and they'd each gotten off twice—so loudly and enthusiastically that I was pretty sure they were trying to win the jealousy of the girls partying outside.

"Stellan, don't go." One of them pouted. She reached over my shoulder, grazing the tip of my cock with her palm. I grabbed her wrist. "You haven't even gotten off."

"I guess you just don't do it for me." I released her wrist, pushing her away.

Anger darted across her pretty features. I didn't really care if I pissed her off, but I was being more of a dick than usual because I couldn't come. Every time I was close, I thought of Aurora's face, and the girls on top of me were so much... not her. Not enough.

I ruffled the blonde hair, winked at the brunette. "Sorry. It's not you, it's me. It's been a long day."

"We can make it better—"

But I was already heading out of the random frat room

we'd taken over, and I let the door bang shut, cutting off her words.

As I headed down the hall and went up the stairs to the third floor, thumping music greeted me. There were kegs lined up in the hallway, and there were girls everywhere in bikinis, gyrating to the DJ's pounding music. Every party that the Gamma Delta Chi frat had was somehow themed to invite girls in either bikinis or school girl costumes.

The frat was boring, but then, they all were after being part of the secret society. The frat life seemed like child's play but at least it was child's play with beer.

I was on my way to the den where the other guys had been hanging when a door off the hallway opened, and Aurora stepped out. She was wearing a tight mini dress that hugged those gorgeous curves. She seemed unsteady on her long, coltish legs, and her long hair cascaded over her shoulders. She glanced toward me, her cheeks flushed and her lush pink lips slightly parted.

When those violet eyes met mine, I saw Delilah. She could change her hair. She could change her face. She was curvier than she had been in high school. But those eyes. Even from across the room they sparkled and caught me: a brilliant shade of lavender flecked with silver.

There was no one else like Delilah, and there was no one else who had those eyes. I'd been debating over and over again since I met her if I could be imagining it. I'd convinced that maybe I was, just because I so badly wanted to get my hands on Delilah and twist her beautiful little neck until I found out exactly what had happened to my sister.

But the way she looked at me, her eyes widening before she glanced away, felt familiar. It was her.

Cain came to the doorway behind her. His big body filling the entryway, one of his hands braced on either side of the doorway. He was watching her with a bemused expression on his face.

He'd just fucked her. The thought shot through me, accompanied with white hot rage.

How dare he fuck the girl who held all the secrets about what had happened to my sister. I was instantly furious, but I held onto a shred of common sense.

I had to know, had to know for absolutely sure, and I couldn't help but think there was one way that I could know. As ridiculous as it seemed, I would never forget what it had been like the first time I kissed Aurora...or Delilah as she'd been known then.

It had been raining, and she'd been over at my house, hanging out with my sister Sophia. She had meant to get started home earlier. When she'd noticed the time and the rain, she freaked out, saying that her father was going to be unhappy. My sister, who needed to get to dance class, had seemed to understand something about what that meant to her. She'd turned to me, asking if I'd drive Delilah home so she wouldn't be late or have to walk home in the rain.

I was always such a fucking gentleman, I'd agreed. Maybe part of my willingness to be a gentleman was based on the fact that I saw the way sweet little Delilah looked at me, all full of innocence and desire mixed together, a dangerous little package.

But I'd always told myself I wouldn't take the bait. It was a bad idea. She was my little sister's best friend, and there was some kind of code against doing that as a big brother, no matter how much I had enjoyed tormenting my little sister in other ways.

When we stopped at a red light on a long country road, she started complaining about my playlist and trying to get to a song she liked, but she accidentally dropped my phone into the crack between our seats. She leaned over, searching for it. I'd twisted to talk to her, warning her that she wasn't going to find any of the bubble gum pop like my sister loved on my iPhone.

She'd looked up at me, our eyes meeting from inches apart. Her lips were soft and pink, incredibly delicious looking with a rounded lower lip and pronounced bow. I had thought about kissing her, then rejected the idea, but she apparently didn't get the memo, because the next thing I knew her lips were on mine.

She caressed my lips with hers, and my cock jumped; I raised my hand to put it on her arm, to pull her close and deepen the kiss, and then I realized what the fuck I was doing.

I pulled away. "This isn't a good idea."

She pulled back, her brow furrowing above her adorable little nose. "I know."

The next minute, she was throwing her door open. The light had turned green and I'd just picked my foot off the brake; the car lurched forward a foot before I mashed the brake back down, and she stumbled but caught herself. The rain pelted her as she stormed off down the road.

"Delilah!" I shouted to be heard over the roar of the rain.

She stalked along the side of the road, her hair now clinging to her shoulders, her t-shirt drenched and almost transparent. I stared at her with my jaw ticking. Was she really going to make me chase her down and throw her into the car?

"Delilah, don't be an idiot!" I wheeled the car over to the right, threw on my hazards and got out of the car myself.

She was ignoring me and the rain.

I stormed after her, with no idea what I was even going

to do. Pick her up and throw her over my shoulder like a barbarian?

"Delilah!" When I reached her, she pretended that she didn't even see me or hear me and just kept marching through the rain.

I grabbed her arm and spun her around. She looked up at me with her violet eyes blazing.

I grabbed her around the waist and kissed her hard. My lips seared against hers in a claiming kiss, and for a moment, even the rattle of the rain around us faded. Her body swayed against mine, her nipples sharp little points pressing against my chest. She resisted my kiss for a fraction of a second, then her lips parted against mine, welcoming me in.

The two of us traded quick, wild kisses. I sucked her lower lip, my thumb sliding across her lip as I pulled away. She was breathing hard as her gaze met mine, her chest rising and falling.

"This is a bad idea," she said, at the exact same time that I was repeating the same thought.

I didn't know if she was mocking me or if she realized it for herself. But she still made me laugh.

"Well, at least we both know it."

Delilah had always made me laugh. She was the only person besides my little sister who could. And I felt like I had given up on anything in the world being funny or bright or decent since I lost my sister. I wished I'd been a better brother to her when I could have been.

But I couldn't help but feel I'd be able to know if she really was Delilah, if I kissed her again. I'd kissed her. Many times, of course, but the time that stuck the most in my memory was that wild, unexpected first kiss.

Because I regretted it like I regretted nothing else in my

life. She was the only woman I ever loved, and she was the devil I regretted.

When I stormed toward her, her eyes widened as if she didn't know what to expect, but she didn't flinch away.

I grabbed her face, my hands cupping either side of her jaw, and kissed her hard.

"What the fuck?" asked someone in the crowd.

I plundered her mouth with mine. She resisted, just for a second, and then her body swayed against mine.

If she'd been a stranger, she should have resisted. Sure, there were plenty of girls who would have lined up for a make out session with me, but she didn't give off those kinds of vibes. It was different with her.

She kissed me back, because she knew who I was, because I felt familiar, like an old friend to her. Even though I definitely wasn't her fucking friend. I'd save that for a fun surprise later though.

For right now, I was really curious about her fake identity. It made sense she couldn't be herself. She'd be hated, just like she should be.

"What is that about?" Pax asked. Oh great, all my favorite assholes had come to this party.

She stumbled back, her lips parting and her eyes wide open. "What was that?"

"I just wanted to taste a little of the same sweet little slut that my friends have apparently enjoyed tonight."

Those kinds of coarse words didn't come easily to my lips. Cain would have been more the expert on how to degrade a girl, but it had the right effect. She staggered back just a stutter step, as if I had physically struck her, her eyes widening. Yeah, that blow wouldn't have landed so hard if she didn't remember me, either. If I weren't her first fucking love, for all the good she'd repaid me with.

"Excuse me?"

"I don't care about you enough to excuse you. Get out of here. I don't want to look at your stupid face." Her stupid, new face, her lips too puffy. She looked too much like every other standard pretty girl at this college who'd had a sixteenth birthday rhinoplasty.

She slapped me across the face, the sound echoing through the room.

I grinned as I turned to the crowd. "What do you think, guys? What kind of score you gonna give her?"

I turned back to her with a grin still written across my face, and she looked livid. "Some girl slaps me across the face pretty much on a monthly basis. It's just one more way you aren't special, sweetheart."

Her face colored, and she turned to race off. I smacked her across the ass as she went. "You don't want to play those games with me, little girl."

She cast a wounded look over her shoulder at me, and then disappeared out the door, running down the staircase. She made good time; maybe she'd worn Converse planning on running the whole time. My friends stared at me with perplexed expressions written across their faces.

"What the fuck was that?" asked Cain. "Even for you, that was a little unnecessary."

"Even for me?" I said. "You're usually the one who fucks up girls' heads."

He shrugged one big shoulder. "Girls know what they're getting into with me. They come here because they like it."

I was sure that was true for some girls, but some girls were just willing to debase themselves any way Cain wanted for the chance to be close to the Golden Boy.

"We need to talk," I said.

"What can't wait till morning? I'm trying to get drunk," Cain groused.

"You never get drunk," I answered. Cain's incredible muscled physique kept him from metabolizing alcohol very quickly. And even though he liked to watch the people around him get drunk, he hated to lose control. I'd never actually seen him tip over into being drunk himself.

I got the guys to join me in the same room that still stunk of arousal. Smelling the scent of her cum in the air made my nostrils flare, but I tried to pretend to ignore it.

"Alright, what's your little temper tantrum about?" Cain demanded. "Don't tell me that you got jealous about me playing with that girl tonight."

"I could care less what you do with other girls," I said. "But not that girl."

Cain was getting a familiar stubborn look on his face that always meant trouble. "Why not that girl?"

"Because that's the daughter of The Demon."

Cain looked bemused again. It was Pax who said, "The Demon, the serial killer?"

"The one and only."

"I followed the case," Pax said, "And even though she was a minor and there weren't supposed to be any pictures of her, a couple of journalists had stalked her and managed to get photographs of her. That's definitely not the girl I saw."

"I'm telling you, that's really her. She's had a lot of plastic surgery. But I would know her anywhere."

"By the way she fucking kisses?" Cain was looking at me as if it were the most asinine thing that I had ever said, in a history of many asinine things.

"Not just by kissing her," I said, irritated, "but it definitely is one more tip off."

"You used to date The Demon's daughter?"

"I didn't know she was the fucking child of a serial killer at the time." I said, "but I think he's the one that took my sister and I think maybe she knows something about it."

For a few long seconds, no one said anything. I felt vulnerable and exposed, and I hated that.

I started to say something, but Cain cut me off. "All right. I don't know if that's really her, but I'll take your word for now. We'll bring her in, keep her close."

"We'll find out her secrets," I said, picking up what he was suggesting.

"And if she betrayed your sister, if she was working with The Demon and she's the reason that your sister's dead..." Cain smiled wickedly. "Then we'll make sure she's punished for her wrongdoing."

The Bible was never creepier than when Cain was referencing it in favor of his own twisted misdeeds.

"Alright," I said, the idea working for me. "Let's do it".

She had no idea what was about to happen to her. And that was just the way I liked it.

6

AURORA

I shot awake in the morning, sitting up with a jerk out of my dreams. My heart was pounding and there was something slick in the back of my throat. I pressed the heels of my hands into my eyes, drawing deep breaths through my nose, then exhaling out my mouth.

My nightmare was already forgotten, but the effect it had on me was slower to fade. My breath was still coming too quickly as I stole a glance at the other bed, wondering if I'd woken up my roommate, or if she'd even come back the night before. Jenna lay on her stomach, one slender arm pillowing her head. She was wearing too much eyeliner, but not as much as her pillow; she was still pretty though, even drooling.

Apparently, she'd had a better night than I had, at least I hoped so. Although when I thought about Cain's hands on my body, it didn't seem like the night had been all bad. Until I ran into Stellan, it had been a lot of fun, no matter how awkward I was.

I was still rattled by seeing Stellan. Just thinking about how he'd strode up to me and kissed me... and then how he'd degraded me in front of the crowd… made my heart race all over again. Not today, Satan. I took another deep breath and swung my feet out of bed, finding the cold tile floor.

I took a long hot shower and scrubbed away every last bit of the scent of the night before, from spilled vodka punch to the faint scent of a man's cologne on my skin, dark and heady.

I came out and began drying my hair with a t-shirt, a little trick I'd read in a magazine. Jenna blinked her eyes open and looked at me. She sat up and groaned, rubbing her hands with her eyes. "Oh, I think I have regrets."

"Sorry I abandoned you last night." I paused, still scrunching my waves in the t-shirt. If I wasn't going to blow dry my wild mane, it was my best bet.

"Oh, I understand," she said, giving me a sympathetic look. Then her gaze brightened. "Good morning, Miss Popular. You had quite the night, huh?"

I groaned. "I have definitely never been Miss Popular."

She fumbled her cell phone, then let out a groan. "Great. I plugged my cell phone in last night. I had enough foresight to do that. But you know what I didn't have enough foresight to do…"

"What?" I rifled through my closet for a hoodie—one of my two options.

"Make sure that it was plugged in at the other end." She held up the dangling end of her iPhone charger.

"Aw, boo." I pulled my black hoodie on. "Do you want me to get us both some coffees? You look like you need it."

"It's almost as if I wasn't thinking my absolute best last night."

"Did you make any more interesting mistakes than that?"

"I think you did, didn't you?" she said with a wink. "Or maybe those weren't mistakes."

"It didn't go that far," I said, although replaying the better parts of the night made me feel a throb of longing all over again. "It really was an interesting night, wasn't it?"

"It really was." She scooted to the edge of the bed. "I'm glad you came out last night."

"Me too." I kept my mixed feelings to myself. It had been an interesting night that I would like very much to leave in my past, joining the litter of dark moments strewn behind me like a trail of trash. I had to figure out a way to stay away from Stellan, because seeing the boy I used to love as a monster was soul-destroying.

She looked at her phone again then jumped up. "Come on. We're supposed to have breakfast with the girls."

"With the girls? What girls? And isn't it brunch at this time?"

She rolled her eyes. "Okay, yes, brunch. And yes, our girls, the ones who live in the dorm with us. Our new besties. We all wanted to get together and rehash what happened last night."

I groaned, but apparently I had been adopted by an extrovert and this was just my life now. She hopped in a quick shower, and soon the two of us were heading downstairs to the cafeteria.

She waved and squealed at some girls we'd met at dinner. I liked listening to their happy banter, even if I sat there quietly, with a big breakfast of pancakes, eggs, bacon and fruit salad piled up in front of me. I mostly just focused on sipping my coffee. I wasn't hung over, but I didn't feel great either. The experience with Stellan had unsettled me. It really seemed as if he somehow saw through what I was trying to be and saw who I'd been. That was pretty scary.

"So let's talk about last night," one of the girls at breakfast said. She made a mock drum roll on the cafeteria table. "Who had the best misadventure?"

I felt like they were all looking at me.

"I wouldn't call it a misadventure," I said, but apparently I was outvoted because they all pressed me for details.

"I really don't know what that all was about with Stellan," I confessed. "That was a really weird night."

One of the girls let out a big sigh, her chin propped on her hand. "With Cain? I'll take that kind of weird."

"Everyone's talking about that weird moment with Stellan." A pretty brunette raked her hair back with pointed red nails. "What brought that on?"

I didn't know what to say. "I don't understand him at all."

"I've never heard of one of the guys acting, like, jealous before," she said. "Like a girl was special."

"I would hope he didn't make a habit of acting that way," I said.

I hadn't enjoyed Stellan's special attention. But strangely, the girls eyed me as if they were almost jealous that I provoked such a weird reaction that Stellan had grabbed me and kissed me. They seemed to forget about the part where he had insulted me afterward.

"Remember the part where he called me a slut?" I asked. "That is not a nice man."

The blonde with pink ends said, "Well, that's kind of their thing with girls. At least, Cain tends to be pretty... like, degrading, from what I've heard?"

"Wow," I said, "and how exactly are they still getting laid?"

The brunette crinkled her nose. "I mean, have you seen them?"

It was almost a valid point.

But no, there was no excuse for that kind of behavior. That was their brand of toxic.

"You all deserve better," I grumbled. "And I deserve better."

Even with my dark twisted past, I knew that I deserved better than men who were bullies and monsters like those guys seemed to be, or at least like Stellan was. I wondered what had happened to him. He had been such a nice boy when we were growing up. Yeah, he was the popular jock, and he knew it. He'd been handsome and cocky and way too charming. But something was different about him now, a mean, vicious side that had been a cruel gleam in his eyes after he kissed me. My heart ached as I thought maybe it was because of what had happened to his sister.

No one was listening to my grumbling now. The conversation had moved on, and the girls were comparing how drunk they'd all gotten the night before.

For a moment, just as I always had when I was a kid, I had a glimpse of how we looked from the outside, half a dozen girls laughing and shouting. For a moment, it was nice to see myself as if I was part of the group laughing with a bunch of fun, cute girls. And the next second just made me feel sad. I felt like I didn't really belong here, that I wasn't really one of them.

"I have a ton of homework to do," I said finally.

"Hey, yeah, me too." Jenna got up from the table too. "But I'm gonna go take a nap."

We all laughed. She went upstairs with me.

As I packed up my backpack to go study, she tumbled onto the bed and stretched out. "Our freshman year is going to be such an adventure."

She sounded so happy, and it was such a jarring contrast

to my jangling nerves about Stellan. "I like your enthusiasm."

"I'll be enthusiastic for both of us, Aurora."

"And I'll study for both of us, Jenna." I hoisted my backpack and headed out. "Later!"

"Later!" She already sounded sleepy. I would love to have her ability to sleep so easily, without any subconscious freakouts.

I didn't actually head off to the library. I realized once I left our room that I felt weird going back there after that strange note. A shiver ran down my spine. If someone knew who I was, I couldn't shake the feeling that knowledge would be followed by violence.

I should have known there was no way I could get an actual second chance. What The Demon had done to me, and what he'd made me do, would haunt me all my life.

But I didn't know at the time just how much it would haunt me that day.

I WENT into a café on one end of campus. I hadn't been there before, so I spent a few minutes looking at the menu before ordering a green tea latte and trying to pick a seat. I found a table by the window where I could sit with my back against the wall.

I pulled out my books and got to work reading, highlighting, and making note cards. If there was one thing I knew how to do, it was to be a good student. Reading and researching had always been my escape, a way to make my mind so busy that I couldn't ruminate over my memories at the same time.

But after a while, I noticed that people were giving me a

second glance. And a third glance, and a fourth. It was my nature to always be keeping an eye out on what was happening around me, no matter how deeply engrossed I was in my homework.

I could have sworn I heard people twittering and whispering and giving me long, dark glances. Was word spreading about what I had done with the guys? And were people really that jealous of my few miserable moments with Stellan, or even the nicer ones before with Cain, Remington, and Pax?

I mean, the guys looked like gods, but they weren't literal gods, no matter how much people treated them that way.

I couldn't stand the weird, dirty glances anymore. The air around me felt charged, so I gathered up my stuff and headed back across campus to our room. I didn't want to risk waking up Jenna, but it had been several hours, so hopefully she was awake by now.

I opened up the door to our room as quietly as I could, trying to tiptoe in so that I wouldn't wake her up. But when I caught a glimpse of red, my heart stopped. Blood! There was blood splattered all over my side of the room.

My heart rate dropped as my reflexes took over, my hands rising to protect myself as I whirled, looking around the room for a fight.

But there was no one else in here. Jenna was still breathing, and drooling.

The red was everywhere. It was all over my side of our room, poured over my bed, over my clothes. I pulled open one of my dresser drawers and realized that every single piece of clothing I owned had been doused red.

It didn't smell like blood. I was intimately familiar with that particular scent.

No, it carried the tang of wet paint. Someone had

doused everything so thoroughly, the carpet was wet with paint, too.

A gasp startled me. I turned to find Jenna, wide-eyed. "What happened?"

"Apparently someone dumped paint all over my stuff," I said, staring at the damage, too stunned to say anything comforting.

"But everything was fine when I went to sleep." She shivered and wrapped her arms around her chest, her shoulders sloping. The look on her face was lost and horrified. "Someone came into our room while I was sleeping."

"Well, it's a good thing you were in your bed." I gestured at her untouched side. "That was how they knew not to mess with any of your stuff. Otherwise, they would've had to use twice the paint."

She stared back at me. "This isn't funny. Someone snuck into our room. What if they'd hurt me?"

"I'm sorry. I didn't mean to suggest it was funny. It's not funny to me at all. It's just that your stuff is all fine. And you're not hurt."

"But I could have been," she said. "Do you know how much it creeps me out to think that someone got into our room?"

She stared at me for a second then blew out a long, slow breath.

"I'm sorry," I said again, because she was obviously mad at me. Even though I was the one that felt like I'd just been hurt. I mean, I was the one who had red paint covering every single possession I owned.

"Don't worry about it." Her voice was flat, and it made my stomach curdle. I'd just ruined my one-and-only friendship, with a little help from my new stalker. "I'll go get our RA."

A few minutes later, she was back with our RA, a peppy 22-year-old grad student with Kramer style hair and a perpetual professional smile, although that smile distinctly froze as he took in what had happened to my room.

"This is very upsetting for you girls," he said. "I don't know who would pull a prank like this. This is so wrong."

"I don't feel safe here anymore," Jenna said. "Do you think someone has a key to our room?"

"Maybe you left the door unlocked," he suggested, although he didn't sound very confident.

She shook her head, her arms pressing harder and harder into her breasts, as if she was going to shrink herself until she could disappear. "I can't stand it."

"It's all right," he said. "We'll figure it out."

I began to gather some of my things into a laundry basket. Even my dirty clothes had gotten the red paint treatment.

Letters in the general red chaos caught my eye. Someone had painted *killer* in red paint above my bed. I stared at it for a few long seconds.

I turned and realized Jenna was staring at it too. For a moment, our eyes met and her lips parted, as if she had no idea what to say or what to ask me.

Then she fled the room.

"I'll go see if she's okay," the RA said.

"All right. Great," I muttered. "Yes. Take care of her."

There was no way I wanted anyone to take care of me. I couldn't imagine what comfort anyone would give me in this situation anyway. But the whole thing still left me feeling rattled. So much for my second chance here. I needed to make a new plan for the rest of my life. I couldn't go through a fresh round of plastic surgery when my face was still swollen from the last one. I didn't want to go full Michael Jackson.

In what seemed like an uncharacteristic fit of optimism, I dragged my laundry basket downstairs and piled everything into a washing machine with an unreasonable amount of Tide. It didn't seem likely, but maybe a miracle would happen. Did girls like me get miracles?

It was only when I had finished feeding quarters into the machine and started to head back through the fluorescent-bright hallways that I noticed the first of the signs.

There were posters hung up everywhere, but at first they just blended in with the decor. There were, after all, tons of signs everywhere. Signs about intramural soccer and outdoors club and study groups and Greek life recruitment. They all just kind of blended together for me because I wasn't much of a joiner.

But the sight of my own face stopped me. My arms were splattered in red paint from my laundry as I reached out and ripped the poster off the wall.

On one side was my old face, Delilah's face. And so was the text from one of the tabloids that had caught me and photographed me that day. But on the right side of the picture was my student ID photo, all shiny blonde hair and bright smiles.

It was quite the contrast to my other photo where I had my hand up, telling the photographer not to take a picture of me, but my hand was still rising, and he'd gotten a good shot of my whole face. I was scowling at the camera. I looked like I might just kill the cameraman. If I could go back in time, I might undo that moment.

I stared at it for long seconds, staring at the arrow sign that had been drawn between the picture of Aurora and the picture of Delilah. Then I dropped the flyer on the floor.

Everything was over.

Woodenly, I went into our dorm room and into the bathroom, where I took another shower. But I felt like I couldn't wash the dirt off.

The dirt on me from being The Demon's daughter wasn't anything that I could ever wash off. When I got out of the shower and got dressed, there was a knock on the door.

I opened it and found my RA there with a new kind of smile: an apologetic one.

"Hey, because there are some concerns about your security and making sure you're safe, you've got a new room assignment." He rattled off the words fast as if he were in a hurry to escape.

"I don't think that's going to help. It seems like I have a stalker." I'd be lucky if it was just one person.

He hesitated, then said, "Aurora, your room has been reassigned. This isn't really an option."

I stared at him until he seemed to cringe, although he kept smiling, then sighed. I didn't really want people to be scared of me. "Fine. Where am I going to have to move? Different floor?"

I didn't really relish the thought of dragging all my stuff into an elevator.

He cleared his throat. "You're being assigned to a whole different building. Here's the address."

He handed over a printout to me. My name was at the top, and there was an address, but no room assignment.

"Great." I shoved it into my pocket. "Fantastic. Thank you so much for your help."

I decided to leave my stuff in the washing machine for now and go scope out my new spot. I made sure to pack up my few undamaged things in a few bags. At least I'd had my laptop with me and some of my most expensive textbooks.

It wasn't as if I hadn't lived most of my life owning nothing really of my own. I'd never been allowed to get attached to things other than The Demon himself. So maybe it wasn't a great loss for me to leave my paint-soaked room behind and set off across campus with nothing but the backpack digging into my shoulders and two bags.

I had to check a campus map to find the right street, and I wandered along looking for the address. I was in a row of frat houses on the edge of campus. I felt a little funny about the location. I didn't see any big dorms out here for freshmen.

Then I saw the castle-like building in front of me. It was the same secret society house that my roommate had pointed out to me with so much enthusiasm.

Why in the world would I be assigned to a secret society? I wasn't a part of this. I think I would have noticed. This had to be some kind of mistake. I looked down at the paper again, then back up at the address. I could go back and talk to my RA, but he didn't seem super helpful.

Maybe I should knock. I was just curious enough that I'd be glad to have an excuse to glimpse the inside of the building.

I climbed the stone steps, glancing up once more at the foreboding stone walls covered in ivy.

I could have sworn that my knees shook just for a second as I raised my hand to knock.

The door was made of a thick, dense wood that muffled the sound of my knock completely.

I fidgeted nervously, just hoping that I didn't have to stand out here with my bags. Students were walking past me on the sidewalk, and the back of my neck burned thinking about all of them staring at me and talking about me. I had somehow convinced myself it was an impossibility that anyone would ever find out.

And yet here I was. Stuck with a face I didn't need, and a name I didn't want.

There was a whirring, mechanical sound nearby, and I frowned as I tried to find the source. I jumped a little when I saw what looked like a security camera peeking out from the ivy, pointed directly at me.

"That's not the entrance," an unfamiliar voice said from behind the ivy right by my head...making me jump again.

I was like a nervous rabbit. *Get your shit together,* I told myself fiercely as I lifted up the ivy to find the source of the voice. It seemed to be my mantra since I'd been here.

Behind the ivy was an old, rusted speaker. I heard laughter from nearby and hunched towards the building as if it somehow had the power to absorb me and make me invisible from everyone.

"Are you going to stand there all day like an idiot?" the voice said again from the speaker, and I glared at it before remembering he was watching me from the camera. So I glared at it too.

"This is the front door. Just open the damn thing," I said out loud, even though I wasn't sure if the speaker worked two ways.

He didn't answer me, and after another minute I sighed, grabbed my bags, and started to make my way around the building to see if there were any other entrances. I walked around the entire thing, dragging my ridiculously monstrous suitcase without seeing another entrance. I would have dropped my bag somewhere while I searched, but I didn't feel like making myself a prime target for some student who wanted to torture me.

What the fuck.

Sweat was dripping down my back and my face was red from a combination of the heat and embarrassment as I envisioned tiny cameras watching my every move as I walked around the damn place.

There was just so much ivy everywhere. I began to pat along the walls, growing angrier and more frustrated by the minute. Why did everyone on this planet seem to be an asshole?

For a second I thought about Cain and the look in his eyes...nope. I wasn't going there. I had imagined things because he'd given my pussy butterflies. That was it.

My nails scraped against the stone under the ivy. I walked down one entire wall before the stone finally gave way to something smooth. I pushed the ivy out of my way, my breath coming out in slight gasps because, motherfucker, it was hot. But I'd found a door. An industrial grey colored door that looked like it could withstand a bomb, but that was beside the point.

My knock was far less tentative this time around. I had no fucks to give. I practically beat on the door, prepared to jump anyone who came out.

It took five minutes of solid knocking, but finally the door swung open, barely missing my nose. An asshole looking guy I'd never seen before stood in the doorway with a cocky grin on his face that I really wanted to slap away. To be fair, he probably wouldn't normally look like an asshole; a lot of people would probably find him attractive, but I was too annoyed to see anything but "punk ass bitch" when I looked at him. Maybe it was the green mohawk he was sporting, or the fact that he was shirtless.

Either way, major douche.

I took a deep, centering breath and schooled my face of

all emotion, something I wasn't sure was that effective considering how sweaty I was.

"Come on in, killer," the guy said with a grin. I rolled my eyes. Zero points of originality for that one, obviously.

I glanced nervously behind him. It was pitch black. It was easy for my mind to go wild and start imagining blood and all sorts of scary, freaky things being performed in the building's depths. What did they even do in a secret society anyways? Was it like a frat on steroids? I was going to be the only girl after all. Would there be hazing involved in living here?

I was in a well, treading water, my arms tied together to prevent me from using them. It was cold, and I was soaked to the bone...my teeth chattering so hard I was afraid they were going to break. But it wasn't the fact that I was exhausted, or that my clothes felt like they weighed a thousand pounds because they were so drenched with water...it was the darkness.

"You can't be afraid in this world," The Demon whispered from somewhere around me. His voice was everywhere at once somehow, like he'd installed speakers in this old, abandoned well he'd taken me to in the middle of nowhere. Which, I guess I couldn't put past him.

He was right, you weren't allowed to be afraid in this world. He'd taught me that. But it didn't change the fact that I was terrified here in the darkness, struggling desperately to stay afloat as various debris floated around me. And the stench, it was so overwhelming I'd already thrown up once. It was the smell of decay and rot, and I had the awful suspicion that this was one of the dumping grounds for The Demon. In the dark, it was easy to imagine skulls and flesh floating around me.

"Are you coming in or not?" the guy said crossly, dropping his easygoing façade as he dragged me out of my past.

"Yeah," I muttered, exhausted from constantly defending myself in the past and present creeping up my spine.

He stepped aside to let me in, but I motioned for him to lead the way. I didn't want that guy at my back.

The door slammed shut behind me as I stepped in, plunging the room into darkness. Panic started to burn through my blood, but I held it back by biting my tongue until I could taste the tang of blood in my mouth. The act immediately calmed me as it had a thousand times before.

It was so dark that I couldn't even see where he was standing. It was only because of my training that I knew how to use his breathing to pick out exactly where he was standing in the room. The Demon had taught me that too. Once you've been trapped in a room in the dark with him somewhere in its depths, you learned fast.

The guy opened a door and light flooded into the room. He walked through the opening, and I hurried after him, afraid he was going to try and lock me inside the empty entryway or something. I found myself standing in a very elaborate hallway with cream walls and gold sconce lights situated every few feet. The floor was made of light, white oak planks, and there were gilded gold frames hung up with black and white pictures of what must have been prior members from the early start of the secret society based on their old-fashioned clothing and hairstyles.

"How many people live in this place?" I asked quietly as I followed him down the hallway. There were tall, black doors every few feet as well, a lot of them, and I was itching to get away from him and explore.

The asshole didn't answer me, of course; he just kept walking as I concentrated on not dropping my two bags that seemed to weigh a thousand pounds now that he hadn't offered to help me with them. He led me down a long staircase covered in heavy, burgundy carpet that looked brand new, and then walked down another long hallway until he finally stopped in front of a set of double doors.

"Is this my room?" I asked as he stepped aside.

"Go on in," he said with a smirk, gesturing to the door.

I hesitated but didn't want to look afraid, so I tried to stride confidently towards the doors.

I turned the knobs and threw them open and...

What the fuck.

The doors opened into a dark room, red light beaming from tinted spotlights.

And there was a girl, dressed in nothing but some black lingerie, on her knees in the middle of the room, her arms tied behind her back with what looked like cable ties. A guy dressed in nothing but a pair of loose black sweatpants held a long horse whip in his hand, and I watched in horror as he struck it against her back repeatedly, her loud screams filling the room as flecks of her blood flew all over the room. Long open wounds crisscrossed all over her back, signaling he'd been at it for a while.

I was faintly aware of others in the room, but I paid them no mind as I ran at the torturer and jumped on his back, my arms going around his neck as I began to choke him out. He let out a muffled shout before I pressed tight enough to cut off his oxygen supply. His arms began to struggle against mine, but I held onto him tightly with my left arm before stabbing two fingers at a pressure point on the other side of his neck that made him immediately pass out. I dropped his dead weight and ducked down as a humongous guy, also shirtless, lumbered to grab me. I placed a drop kick in his gut, and when he bent forward with a groan, I angled my shoulders underneath him so I could flip him over my back.

He crashed to the floor with a shout just as another guy grabbed me by the hair.

How many were in here?

I gritted my teeth as he ripped out some of my hair, and then I reached back and grabbed at his face with my nails, feeling around for his eyes and pressing my thumbs right into them.

He screamed and let me go, dropping to his knees in pain.

My breath was coming out in gasps as I whirled around to look for my next threat. Suddenly, a strong pair of arms decked out in a myriad of tattoos wrapped around me and pulled me against a hard chest. I bashed my elbow backwards into the guy's stomach, eliciting a soft "mmph" of pain from him. His arms tightened around me. I tried to wrench one of my arms back into the person's gut again, but he was holding me so tightly now I couldn't move an inch. I lifted my leg to stomp on the guy's foot, but he wrapped a leg around both of mine until I was completely helpless. Fear shot through me at being incapacitated. Despite the fact that I knew I should try and keep a cool head, I began to struggle against the person's hold, desperate to get away. My shoulder blades pressed against the cold surface of the wall, but it was his hard body against mine that felt inescapable.

"Hello, little devil," a familiar voice whispered.

7

AURORA

Cain seemed to glide out of the shadows. Suddenly, I realized that all of the guys from the other night were in here now.

Pax was the one who had me pinned against the wall. Stellan was staring slack jawed at me, and Remington was sprawled on the floor, his tattooed arms spread.

"Did she really knock Remington out?" Pax sounded amused, nay, delighted. "Who knew this little thing could do that?"

He crooned into my ear, "I knew I liked you, sweetheart." Cain stopped and glanced down at Remington, looking a little bit perplexed. Then his gaze swept up to me, a frown written across his handsome face.

Fuck, now these guys would see me as the threat that I was. I had to fight my way out of here before things escalated even further and I turned into the girl on the floor. I glanced at her and saw her looking up at me with a derisive sneer, which was strange for someone tied up on the floor.

Cain nudged Remington's shoulder with the toe of his

shoe. "Wake up. You're going to want to get started on living this down as soon as possible."

Pax laughed, his grip on me loosening slightly.

I could correct Pax's amusement. He'd given me just a hair's width of room to move, and that was all I needed. I threw myself suddenly into motion, propelling my body against his, slamming the two of us into the wall. I slammed my head backward into his face, felt his head jerk. I was already twisting. I grabbed his shoulder and dragged him down, slamming my knee into his face.

He was quick though, grabbing me around the waist so I didn't manage to slip out of his grip the way I'd planned. The two of us struggled, but I found myself slammed up against the wall again, this time with my face and breasts shoved into the drywall. His elbow planted in my back, digging into my skin.

"That wasn't very polite," Pax scolded, sounding far less perturbed than I'd ever heard most men about being kneed in the balls.

"Victoria," Cain said. "Why don't you explain to our new friend here exactly what was going on? I think she might have assumed you were in distress."

Pax yanked me away from the wall, his arm circling my throat, so that I could see her. The edge of his arm pressed so tightly against my throat that black spots danced at the edge of my vision.

"Yes," I said, "It's easy to see how you're the good guy and this is totally explainable when you're holding me hostage."

"Let her go, Pax," Cain said. Even though the words were benign, there was something about his voice that was dark and domineering. There was a subtle threat in it, as if it didn't matter if they let me go. I wouldn't be able to run far enough to escape.

Pax turned his head and pressed a quick kiss to my temple. I wanted to push him away, but he was already laughing and letting me go. "Thanks for the snuggles, Aurora," he said, patting my shoulders as he released me.

Victoria was still staring at me as if she hated me. Her red lipstick was smeared down her face, her mascara was a wreck, and some of her long, dark hair clung to her scalp with sweat. I'd come out of a weekend trapped in a storm cellar with a serial killer looking fresher than she did at the moment.

"Any day now," Cain prompted her. "Or did so much cum shoot down your throat today that it ruined your ability to open your mouth for any purpose besides our cocks?"

I winced at his crude language. I couldn't believe he would talk to her that way. Cain's gaze caught me. He looked at me as if he was always assessing me, and I'd given him one more way to torment me.

She gazed at him for a second, adoration lighting her eyes, then turned to me. "Cain and I were just playing before you interrupted."

She pouted at me as if I'd ruined something for her.

"That wasn't any kind of playing," I responded. "He was hurting you." I mean I'd heard about BDSM, but I'd never seen it in action...The Demon would have freaked if he'd caught me watching porn. Was this it?

"Only in the best of ways," she purred.

I was unconvinced that she wasn't just lying for the sake of the men around me. They were smirking. That could mean that she was telling the truth, or it could mean, they knew they had the upper hand in this situation, as they seemed to have in almost every situation.

But there was a spark of life in her eyes. It really did seem as if she'd been having fun.

Her chin rose as she stared at me. "Who do you think you are, anyway? Do you think you can just come into the Order of the Sphinx and ruin our—"

"Shut up," Cain cut in. "I don't want to hear anything more from your greedy little mouth, slut."

She just smiled up at him, pressing her breasts against his thigh, as if she were eager for him, but he didn't even bother to look down at her.

"It's funny that you seem to think we're villains, Aurora, when it certainly seems we could learn some things from you."

The words struck me deeper than they should have, maybe because they were accompanied with a sudden flash of almost certain knowledge. These guys somehow had found out who I was. And they had been the ones to reveal it to the entire campus. They had ruined my second chance.

Underneath the sudden pounding sense of loss, I felt a constant thrum of rage.

Remington stirred on the floor, then sat up, rubbing his face with his hands. "Fuck. That didn't just—fuck no."

The other guys all laughed. Cain offered him his hand and boosted him easily to his feet. "This is definitely a special day, Remington. You're buying tonight."

"I'll buy every night if you promise never to bring this up again."

Victoria let out a sharp burst of a giggle. Cain turned a look on her that made her wither slightly before he picked up the whip again. He let the tail tease over her thighs, and she rolled her hips forward as if she was desperate for him to beat her more.

Although he didn't look my way, I still knew Cain was talking to me when he said, "We only play with willing participants, little girl. You should be so lucky."

Remington's gaze fixed on mine. His eyes seemed to burn right through me. I took an involuntary step backward that just slammed my shoulder blades into the wall again.

"No hard feelings, new roommate," he said, his voice dry. It didn't make me feel any better.

"I'll take her to her room." Pax gestured for me to go ahead of him.

No one had to ask me twice to head to the door. I moved quickly, afraid that it was just a setup and I wasn't going to be able to make it out. But I escaped into the hallway, grabbing my bags from where I'd dropped them.

I should give up on college entirely. Hit the road and run. My identity was already burned.

Remington was behind me, closing the door just as there was a whip crack and a scream from inside. There was a breathy note to it. She and Cain had begun their game again.

He was studying me in a way that I couldn't make sense of. As if I were an interesting puzzle he was curious to figure out. I didn't like the idea of these men figuring out anything about me.

"She was indeed having fun," Pax said. "But chin up. No need to be too embarrassed by the way you just floundered in there."

"Floundered?" I shot back. "I thought she was getting hurt."

"She was. She just happens to like it. Are you some kind of prude?"

I never thought I was until today, but maybe I was, maybe that was where I drew my line in the sand because the degrading way that Cain had talked to that girl, and the way she practically writhed in pleasure at every degradation he had to offer, had left me feeling a little bit uncomfortable.

Pax opened the door to the next room. "Sorry, there must have been a slip up," he said, giving me a devilish grin.

He held it for me, pretending to be a gentleman. I peered warily under his arm, convinced that there must be some new nightmare waiting inside. But the room seemed to be just another large bedroom beautifully furnished with a big window looking out onto the campus lawn and trees beyond. No sign of the dungeon—had that been one of the guys' *bedrooms?*

Should I run or should I stay?

There was a terrifying part of me that was riveted by Cain and the others, that was curious what might happen next. That thought I could beat them at whatever game this was, convince them I was sweet and innocent...make them want me.

But given that I'd been bottle-fed trauma from infancy, maybe I didn't have the best instincts.

"So, where did you get those moves?" he asked me.

I studied the room, ignoring him for a moment. There was a big walk-in closet to one side and beautiful modern furniture. There was a fireplace across from the king-sized bed and a vase of roses on the bedside table. It seemed cozy. If I hadn't seen the torture chamber next door, I might've felt at home.

When I turned around, he was rubbing his jaw. It must have hurt when I'd kneed him in the face.

"What moves?" I didn't want to be drawn into conversation with Pax. Something about him was unnerving and sexy. Dangerous and disturbing all at the same time.

"Bullshit," he said. "You're not getting off to a very good start. First you knock me in the face, and try to murder my bestie, and then you lie to me."

"Did I hurt you? I just must have gotten lucky."

"That's very strange." He moved closer to me, dominating me with his size. I breathed in his clean soapy scent with a hint of cologne. "Because I happen to know that particular pressure point you used on Remington."

His fingers stroked over my throat, then found that particular nerve. He rested his thumb on it lightly, his other fingers curling around to caress my skin. A tremor of fear and desire ran through me all at once. The sensation of his fingers seemed to race across my skin, lighting it on fire.

As his gaze met mine evenly, there was a strange heat between us that kept me from knocking him on his ass again.

"Your pulse is going two hundred beats a minute."

"No, it's not." Pax wasn't remotely the scariest thing that I had encountered.

"I'm really curious why a girl like you ran in to protect a total stranger."

"A girl like me? Exactly what kind of girl do you think I am?"

Pax didn't bother to answer me.

There was a heavy knock on the door, then Cain pushed it open. He seemed to fill up the whole doorway, and the room seemed to shrink when he walked in. But as always, when his gaze met mine, heat flooded my body—wayward, wanton heat.

Cain always seemed like he couldn't stop looking at me, even when he was talking to someone else. "Pax, why did you take our little playmate away? She seemed to really be enjoying the show."

"You're a monster," I said.

"Thanks." Cain didn't smile or react besides that blunt word. "Now get dressed. You can't wear that to my football practice or to dinner after. I'd rather you didn't embarrass me."

"Thank you, but no," I said.

"Pax." Cain's voice was quiet, yet everything he said sounded like a command.

Pax gave me a peck on the cheek, leaning in so fast that by the time my hands rose, he was already dancing backward. The scent of his cologne seemed to linger on my skin, or maybe that was the scent of his body.

He winked at me. "Stay alive. Aurora. I have a feeling knowing you is going to be very entertaining."

"Fantastic. I am so happy that I can entertain you."

Cain stepped into the room to allow Paxton room to pass, and somehow that seemed to bring him far too close to me for comfort.

"What are you going to wear?" he asked.

"Are you kidding me right now?" I demanded. "You want to have a chat about fashion? I'm not going to your football practice."

"I think you are. I want to keep an eye on you. And I know that you like keeping an eye on me." There was an arrogant flare in his eyes that made me resolve to never check him out again.

"I don't need anyone to keep an eye on me."

He leaned close. "I don't trust you, and if you want the privilege of walking around this campus, you'll have to convince me you're trustworthy. You can begin today."

"I don't need to convince you of a goddamn thing, except to take a step back." I put my hand on his chest, ready to shove, but I didn't bother yet. I knew that I wouldn't be able to move him without it coming down to a full fight. He had a good eight inches and ninety pounds of muscle on me. I was very capable of taking down larger, more dangerous opponents, but I knew the risk.

"I don't think you understand your situation here. None of the other students want you here. None of them trust you."

"I wonder why," I shot back.

"Oh, I think we both know why," he said.

"If you want to have your professors read your papers, maybe even grade them, you'll have to convince me. If you want to eat in the dining hall without anyone putting poison in your food or knocking your tray out of your hands...if you want to have a chance to pretend to be a normal student, despite what you've done, then you have to convince me."

"Why do you think you're in charge of everything?"

"I never said I was in charge of everything, Aurora." He gave me a slow, maddening smile. "I'm just in charge of you."

There was no way in hell that I was going to play his little game. That was my first impulse. And then I thought better of it. Cain had an obvious need to be in control. His strengths were pretty obvious. He was popular. Rich people seemed willing to do almost anything to appease him, but he had to have weaknesses too. And he'd invited me to get close to him, after giving me a good motive to murder him. One of those weaknesses appeared to be a slightly faulty intellect, because here the man was claiming I was dangerous and not realizing that he was setting himself up for a whole lot of pain.

"I would love to watch your football game," I purred, trying to dig down deep and channel just a little bit of Victoria.

He didn't look convinced.

A little while later, the two of us were headed across campus to the football stadium.

"You can sit in the stands," he said. "Don't go anywhere else."

"Like I'm your girlfriend?" I couldn't help but notice how many people had stared at me like I was the luckiest girl on earth because I was walking by Cain's side.

"Definitely not like that," he answered.

It was kind of interesting to watch the football team practice. And let's be honest, it was always kind of interesting watching Cain. I propped my chin on my hands, leaning forward with my feet on the bleacher ahead of me, feeling the sunshine warm my hair and shoulders.

All the while, my mind was spinning.

Running would be the safe choice.

But I couldn't risk plastic surgery again so soon. I was stuck with my current face, which meant maybe there was nowhere to run—not truly—at the moment.

Cain had suggested that maybe I could still have my second chance here—if I won him over.

Maybe I could beat these assholes at their own game.

The bleacher vibrated under my ass, and I jerked my head up.

Two men were walking down the bleachers toward me, coming from my left.

My gaze snapped toward the right where I saw another man making his way up toward me from that side.

Dear lord, please don't make me hurt anyone today.

But they all had that smug air and the quick, predatorial gazes of men who probably deserved to be hurt.

8

AURORA

"Well, look who we have here." One of the men sat down next to me, sliding his hip against mine. "If it isn't The Demon's daughter."

"I don't know who you think you're talking to, but my name is Aurora and I think you should leave me alone."

"Oh, is that right? Well, I bet your father's victims wanted to be left alone too. Or are they just as much your victims?"

"I don't know what you're talking about."

One of the other men sat down on my other side. They were trying to pin me in. The third man moved behind me, and that was what really worried me, hearing his slow footsteps move down the metal bleachers.

"You know my name, what's your name?"

"You don't need to worry about our names. We're some of the people who are coming for you."

"My girlfriend's been scared ever since she heard you were on campus. She's worried that she'll find herself splayed open somewhere with superglue sealing her eyes shut just like so many of your father's victims."

The images that reeled through my mind at those words would have made bile rise in my throat if I didn't have so much practice coping with adrenaline coursing through my body. My heartrate was dropping, my mind growing cooler, quicker.

"Well, your girlfriend can rest assured that she'll be just fine. I assume you think that I'm The Demon's daughter because of that stupid prank, but I'm not. And The Demon is locked away in prison."

That was the thought that made it almost possible for me to sleep at night.

"It's funny that you look just like her."

"It's funny that you think I look just like her. It sure seems like you've never cracked a book or a newspaper. You see one *poster* and you're convinced it's the God's honest truth. People that gullible are going to be the death of this whole nation."

"Do you think it's wise to talk back to us?"

"You just made it clear that you think that I'm dangerous, right? So I'm not understanding why you would think it's wise to talk to me to begin with unless you know that this is bullshit and you're just seeking a reason to bully a young woman, like you're any better than The Demon himself."

Maybe I shouldn't rile them up, but I was about done with humanity today.

"I was reading about the things that your daddy would do to girls." The man on my right leaned toward me.

I had the sense that he was trying to distract me from the one behind me, and I twisted subtly, trying to keep two of them in my sight at all times while I used my instincts to look out for the third. My skin prickled, and I knew that the second I got up to move away it would turn into a chase, so I needed to pick my moment carefully.

But even though I was trying to keep my eyes on all three of them at once, something pulled my gaze down to the field, a sensation crawling up my spine as if someone were watching me. I looked down to find Cain staring up at all of us, his eyes blazing with fury.

"Really, that seems remarkable. I didn't get the vibe that you read very much. I'm very excited for you. Maybe you can earn a free personal pan pizza if you keep up the good work."

My childhood had been a nightmare that seemed relentless where I'd careened from one terror to another, but there had been brief pleasant moments, and some of them had been provided by Pizza Hut's "Book It!" program.

"I read that in the early days he used to steal girls out of thin air, or so it seemed."

"I think you're mixing metaphors. Girls don't come out of thin air, the unlucky ones *disappear* into thin air." And I hated how often that happened to them. Not that these men would believe that. "Also, you can't steal girls. They're people, not toaster ovens. You *can* steal toaster ovens, like if you have a lot of bagels that you need to toast."

The guy on my left looked bewildered. "Why the fuck are you talking about toaster ovens?"

I started to shrug. I didn't know why I was the way I was sometimes.

Suddenly, the guy behind me burst into motion, grabbing my shoulders and yanking me backward. My head slammed into the metal bleacher, stars bursting in front of my eyes. The two other guys scrambled over the bleachers toward me, trying to pin me down, but it was the knife thrust against my throat hard enough to draw blood that had me suddenly pausing.

"I read about how your dad used to cut off pieces of girls one little bit at a time."

"Maybe," I said, my breath coming out thin even though I didn't want to sound afraid. "But at least my dad wasn't an idiot who murdered girls in public."

"Who said we were going to do it in public? This is just a start. There's a whole Internet forum dedicated to who's going to be the one to take you off the streets. You might have gotten off a lot better than your father, but everyone knows what you did, and someone's going to make sure that you pay. If it's not us, it might be someone even worse...someone who will make it take even longer."

Suddenly, Cain loomed into view. He'd moved silently until he was here, but now he definitely was two hundred and twenty pounds of pissed-off muscle and blazing eyes. He grabbed the guy nearest me and threw him. The guy went flying. He slammed on his back on one of the bleachers and then tumbled over, his legs folding over his head before he toppled off the bleacher to the ground. It would have been comical if there hadn't still been a knife to my throat.

Stellan, Paxton, and Remington were there too suddenly. I wondered if they'd been watching or if Cain had sent some kind of SOS to them.

The four of them had moved so quickly to come to my rescue.

If I needed Cain and his buddies to rescue me, then I was in a sad state indeed.

It was Pax who suddenly knife chopped the man who held the blade to my throat. The blade went flying and

Paxton caught it out of the air. He grabbed the guy and pressed the knife against his throat.

Pax murmured into his ear, "If you cut her, I'm going to cut you."

"Easy," Cain warned him. "I'm sure these gentlemen had the best of intentions. They just didn't realize that we're going to take care of her."

The guy with the knife to his throat was wide eyed as he began to stammer. "I didn't know. I didn't mean to get in your way."

"It's all right," Cain promised, giving him a smile that didn't reach his eyes.

The guy with the knife to his throat couldn't see, but Pax stuck out his lower lip as if he were pouting at Cain. Cain just shook his head, apparently unimpressed as Pax mouthed, "But can I just cut him a little bit?"

Pax was growing on me already. It was too bad I couldn't trust him not to murder me any more than I could trust the others.

"I want you to make it very clear to everyone," Cain said. "The girl is someone we'll take care of. We'll keep her from being a threat, but no one's to interfere in what we're doing to her. No one hurts her."

"Or they'll have us to deal with," Pax said darkly, before he finally pulled the knife away from the man's throat.

"You can go," Cain prompted impatiently.

The men didn't need a second invitation. They took off, scrambling over the bleachers and jumping off, disappearing into the rest of campus. I caught a brief glimpse of the one who held the knife to my throat fleeing and realized his jeans were soaked dark with his urine.

"I'm a little disappointed in you, Blondie," Pax said. "I know you could have killed those men if you wanted to."

"I still don't know what you're talking about. I don't know what those men were talking about." I was going to find that Internet forum later. I needed to assess just how big the threat was that I was dealing with.

Cain locked eyes with me, stepping close, dominating me with his eyes and the power and heat of his body like he always did. He caught my chin in two of his fingers and tilted my face up to his, his eyes smoldering. He almost looked as if he might kiss me, strangely enough.

Then he muttered darkly, "That's the reason you need us, sweetheart. Because on your own... you'll reap everything you deserve."

9

AURORA

Dinner was torture. Which was saying a lot because I'd actually experienced torture many times in my life. I sat at an over-the-top table in the banquet hall of the Sphinx, the fifty-person table completely empty besides Cain, Remington, Pax, Stellan, and myself. The fact that this secret society had a full-on banquet hall in its depths shouldn't have been surprising, considering what else I'd seen in this place this week...like the indoor swimming pool, theater room, and game room... But my mouth had still dropped open when I'd walked in and seen a room that would fit right into Versailles with its chandeliers, gold painted walls, intricately carved table, and fine leather chairs. As would befit the room, our place settings were the fancy kind, the ones that had three forks and five hundred spoons next to the plate and you had to somehow figure out what the difference was. Who were these guys, that they sat down to fancy meals like this in college? It was super weird.

People dressed in full suits were bringing out dinner to the table like we were in a palace, or at least a fancy restaurant. I tried to catch their eyes a couple of times, but they kept their gazes levied intently on the floor. If some of them had been working for the Sphinx for a while, they could possibly know something about the assholes I found myself surrounded with. I filed that away to think about and plan around later on.

A salad filled with different, brightly colored vegetables was placed in front of me. I bit my lip, wondering what fork I was supposed to use while at the same time wondering why I even cared. I just hoped that we were having actual food at this meal since rabbit food wasn't my first choice on any day.

Remington sat next to me, and he picked up a small fork on the far side of his long row of utensils, a small smirk on his mouth. He knew I was watching him, the bastard. I grabbed the same fork and began to eat, begrudgingly admitting to myself that the salad was actually pretty good, even if it could use some ranch.

"You have a fight this weekend," Stellan said from across me, his attention directed towards Pax. I pretended not to be interested in the conversation as I stabbed a purple carrot and pointedly refused to look at Stellan. Out of the four men, Stellan was the only one who hadn't spoken to me since that night at the party. Any time our eyes met, he would just gift me with an infuriating smile that didn't match the calculation in his gaze.

"Did you get someone actually good for me to fight?" Pax drawled as he sat back in his tall, leather high back chair.

Hmmm. I had heard that he did some underground fighting. I wondered if he was any good. A hand reached forward in front of me to take my plate away, and I dropped my fork on the glass plate in surprise, the sound seeming to echo around the enormous room. All four of their predatory gazes were suddenly on me, and I sat perfectly still, like I really was prey and trying not to keep their attention by moving an inch.

"It's Kaplan," Stellan finally answered, drawing their gazes away from me.

"Mmh, that will be a good one," answered Pax, sounding delighted. I couldn't help but look over at him. I'd never heard him sound so...alive. He was the most monotone of the four of them, seeming to go through life like he was above everything. Like he found his existence on earth all together boring and everyone around him beneath him.

Pax met my gaze, and for a second I was trapped in his hazel eyes, eyes that looked gold under the twinkle of the freakishly large chandelier hanging above us. "Going to come to the fight, princess?" he purred. For a second I imagined him in a fighter's ring, the light dim above him, droplets of sweat sliding down his body as he pounded his opponent over and over again with tape wrapped fists. I could almost hear the grunts of pain, the beads of blood flying from skin as he tore the other guy apart. My breath hitched just thinking about the violence of it all.

I wasn't going to examine closely why that was.

I pursed my lips and looked down at the orange-colored soup that had just been placed in front of me by another silent worker...or servant. I wasn't sure what the right term was for them.

"Of course, she is. She wouldn't miss it. Isn't that right?" Cain answered with a smirk.

"Is this where I say, yes sir?" I asked them in a bored tone.

Cain threw back his head and laughed, and something inside my stomach wiggled around at the sound of it. "You can call me "sir" any time you want," Cain answered with a wink.

I rolled my eyes and picked up a random spoon, shoving

soup in my mouth just so I could pretend to ignore them as they all laughed at me, as though Cain had just told the most hilarious joke known to man.

The soup was pretty good too. Once again, I wasn't sure exactly what was in it, but for soup, it was good. Much better than all the options at the cafeteria at least.

There was a knock on the double doors behind me, and I craned my neck to see who was there.

"Come in," Cain drawled, like he was king of the castle. The door opened and the same guy who'd been such a gracious tour guide of this place peeked his head in, his gaze immediately going to me.

"Don't look at her," snapped Pax abruptly, and my gaze immediately went to him. The other three were looking at him with matching frowns.

"What do you want, Drew?" Remington asked.

"The entertainment is here," Drew answered, his gaze steadfastly averted from mine like he was afraid that Paxton was going to pound his face in.

A nasty grin crossed Cain's face, and I knew that whatever the entertainment was, I wasn't going to like it. Stellan shot me a smirk for good measure, and I contemplated just walking out. But that was what they wanted. They wanted to push me and see how much it took before I broke. I was stubborn. It would've been easier just to lay down and lose, but my pride wouldn't let me do it. Dread splashed through my veins when four beautiful girls walked in, wearing nothing but skimpy, expensive-looking lingerie and high heels.

There was a girl for every taste. The first girl had blonde hair cut in a sharp bob, with wide brown eyes and dark red lipstick that contrasted perfectly with her milky white pale skin. Her body was encased in an ice blue bra and panty set.

Another girl was Asian, her perfectly smooth black hair falling almost to her waist, so shiny that it looked like glass. She was wearing a crimson lingerie set that was practically see-through, showcasing her small, pert breasts and rounded nipples. The third girl had light tan skin and could have rivaled Gisele in the looks department. She had on a black thong that displayed her rounded ass, and her breasts were so large they had to be fake. The final girl was a redhead with bright emerald eyes. She was wearing a green babydoll style nightgown with sky high matching heels.

I felt like I was going to be sick.

The girls stood there proudly for the guys' perusal. "You can leave now," Remington commented, and I realized that Drew was still standing there, drooling at the ladies. Drew's face fell, and he stomped from the room, slamming the door behind him, which just made the guys laugh.

"Ladies, looking good," said Remington mockingly as he shot me a smug grin. My fists clenched under the table as a waiter came around and set what should have been a mouthwatering looking slice of chocolate cake down in front of me. There was no way I was going to be able to eat it, though. As it was, I was slightly afraid that I was going to throw up the contents of my stomach all over the table.

I kept my face perfectly blank, though, and just stared straight ahead as if the women weren't even in the room. The lights dimmed, and a sultry beat began to play out of speakers in the wall. The women began to dance expertly, leaving no doubt they'd done this before...in a professional setting. The redhead and the blonde stepped close to each other and began to stroke each other's skin, their lips brushing against each other. Their gazes went to the guys every so often, expertly monitoring the room to see what would get the best reaction from their audience. The redhead slid her fingers into the blonde's underwear and started to finger her, the blonde's cries of ecstasy filling the room. I sat back in my seat and acted bored. I somehow managed to pick up a fork, and started force-feeding myself bites of the chocolate cake, even though it tasted like ash in my mouth.

"Enjoying the show?" Paxton murmured to me.

I shot him a wide grin. "Who doesn't love a show? They're very lovely," I told him mockingly. Paxton's eyes flashed in surprise at my response, confirming that at least part of the display was to make me uncomfortable.

Just as I had that thought, the Brazilian looking model began to walk towards Cain, hunger in her gaze as she swung her hips back and forth. She sank to her knees in front of him, and my eyes widened. Were they really going to take it this far?

Cain turned his head towards me as the girl's hands slid farther up his legs until they were stroking his dick. I clenched my jaw and focused on keeping my breath steady, not letting myself think about the fact that I wanted to rip her hands off his body.

At the same time, though, there was heat building in my core, an aching, illicit desire. Part of me wanted to be that girl. Part of me wanted to be on my knees pulling down his zipper like she was, pulling out his hot, thick cock. My tongue licking drops of the pre-cum beading at his tip.

My breath hitched as I watched her grab him with both hands, her pink tongue darting out to taste him. I was vaguely aware of the fact that my breaths were coming out in gasps, and my chest was heaving as she took him into her mouth, not even coming close to being able to fit it all in. Cain's gaze never went away from mine. He groaned, and I ripped my eyes away from the sight, only to look over and see that the Asian girl was now straddling Remington and the redhead was eating out the blonde on the floor. This was actual hell.

A small gasp slipped from my mouth as I saw that Paxton had his pants open and was fisting his enormous dick as he took in the show. He must've felt my gaze, because he looked over at me. "Want to take over?" he asked cockily as he squeezed himself tighter and let out a low moan.

Stellan looked over at me. "Join them," he ordered. He gestured where the redhead and the blonde were moving together on the floor. "Get on the floor and let them make you come," he commanded.

"You like this, don't you, little whore?" Cain remarked mockingly as the girl continued to work on his dick. "You think we can't see the flush on your cheeks, hear your little gasps of breath, see how you're struggling to not touch yourself. Go ahead, slut. We won't mind."

I wasn't sure what to make of Cain's dirty talk, and I certainly wasn't going to acknowledge how it made my panties wet. I kept my face blank. "You should tell her to use her tongue on the tip of it more, and really move her hands in alternating directions. That would make the experience much better for you," I remarked, gesturing to his lap.

There was a brief flash of surprise in Cain's gaze, followed by desire, and just the right side of his mouth twisted up.

I had a momentary feeling of victory, but that soon went away when Remington abruptly stood up, holding the girl, and pushed aside the plates that had been in front of him on the table. He threw the girl onto it with a loud thunk, and then he grabbed the chocolate cake, spreading it all over her stomach.

Locking eyes with me, he dragged his tongue from the

top of her underwear to right under her breasts. She moaned loudly, and I rolled my eyes at the fakeness of it. Did guys really like that sort of thing? The fake moan that usually was only found in pornos? At least I was pretty sure that it was fake. Although, as Remington's finger slipped inside her underwear, I got the feeling that he really knew what he was doing. As the four girls' cries filled the air, I decided I'd had enough. I stood up, and all four of the guys' gazes went to me.

"Where do you think you're going?" drawled Stellan. The redhead and the blonde looked towards him hungrily, and an absurd flash of hurt pulsed through me. I'd love to say that I wouldn't care if he fucked a million girls in front of me, but I hadn't gotten myself to that level of numbness yet.

"I think I've had enough entertainment for tonight. And girls aren't really my thing, if you know what I mean," I said. "Not that you aren't all very beautiful," I told the girls, most of them shooting me death glares because none of the guys they were trying to work on were paying them any attention.

"Sit your ass back down," growled Cain, pulling the girl off his dick and onto his lap. He began to kiss down the side of her neck, and for a moment I remembered what that had been like... What that felt like.

I'd been through a lot in my life, the sort of stuff that wasn't even featured in horror movies because it was so dark and twisted that the audience probably would've fainted dead at the sight of it. But this? This I had no experience with beyond what I'd done with Cain... And Stellan years ago. I didn't know what it meant, but I'd survived all of that, and being in this room was making me sick.

"Too much for you, sweetheart?" purred Remington. I bit the side of my cheek so I wouldn't react like I knew he wanted me to. The blonde and redhead were beginning to crawl towards Stellan, and I realized that Paxton was still fisting himself, the only one a girl hadn't approached. Was there a reason for that? I filed that away to look into later and rolled my shoulders back. The redhead chose that moment to push Stellan's shirt up and began to nibble at his skin. The blonde was playing with the redhead's breasts at the same time, and I watched as the redhead's tongue slid around Stellan's nipples at the same time the blonde's tongue slid around hers. My face curled up in disgust, and I knew that I had messed up and let a flicker of hurt show in my eyes when Stellan's face lit up with victory.

"Don't look so sad, darlin'," Stellan said mockingly. "I'm sure the girls wouldn't mind you tagging in. I bet they could teach you a thing or two; I doubt you've improved very much from your last performance."

I lost my mind at that moment and picked up my wine glass, still filled to the brim with red Cabernet, and splashed it all over him. The blonde and the redhead yelled out indignantly, pushing away from him as wine dripped all over them as well. I set the now empty wine glass back down on the table before I threw the actual glass at him, my hands trembling as I did so. I left the room without looking back.

I didn't think I'd have trouble playing games with all of them, but I hadn't come close to anticipating that. If that's what I had to be subjected to... there was no way I was going to deal with that for the rest of the semester.

As I walked back to my room, some of the other members' doors to their bedrooms were open, and laughter followed me down the hallway as I passed by. Evidently, they all knew what was happening in that room. Hell, I wouldn't put it past any of them to have cameras in there so they could watch the show as well.

I slipped inside my bedroom and locked the door

behind me, leaning against it and struggling to get my emotions in check. I wouldn't cry. I couldn't. I grabbed the skin in between my thumb and pointer finger on my left hand and squeezed, trying to center myself like I'd been taught, creating a mental wall between my emotions and the rest of me so that they couldn't leak out.

Once the urge to cry went away, I let go and stalked to my bed, throwing open my laptop and logging into my email. I wrote a note to the Dean's secretary, requesting an urgent meeting for tomorrow morning. I'd explain everything to him. They'd find me a room somewhere else. I wouldn't have to put up with this.

I should have felt better as soon as I sent the email, but I didn't. I still felt dirty from what just happened, from listening to the girls' fake moans, the panting breaths from the guys, the smell of sex and desire in the room. If I could have ripped off my skin I would have.

I ran to the shower, turned on the water, and waited for it to reach a scalding temperature. There was a connecting door to another room, Paxton's room unfortunately, so I locked both.

Then I stepped into the blazing-hot water. I lifted my face to the water, pretending that it was possible for all of the sins coating my skin to be washed away.

I tried not to think about it, tried not to picture what Cain's hand had looked like wrapped around his huge dick. I tried not to think about what Paxton had sounded like as he'd watched.

But I couldn't help it.

The images were burned into my mind. In my fantasies though, the other girls hadn't been there. It was me on my knees in between Cain's thighs. It was me crawling on top of

Stellan's lap. It was me spread across the table while Remington's tongue slid up my skin.

As if someone else was controlling me, my hand slipped down my body, sliding over my erect nipples, moving down my soapy, slick skin until I was leaning back against the cold tile, dipping my fingers in and out of my wet heat as I pretended that it was someone else touching me there. I slowly circled my clit as I remembered what Cain's lips had felt like as they danced across my skin at that party. My breath came out in gasps as I fell down the rabbit hole into a fantasy that never should've entered my head. Heat built inside of me, spiraling higher and higher until my orgasm was a breath away.

And then the door that connected Paxton's room to the bathroom, the door that I had locked, flew open and crashed against the wall right as I fell over the cliff, pleasure surging through me.

My shriek was mixed with a moan as I dove for my towel to cover myself.

But it was too late.

Paxton was standing there in the doorway, his gaze dancing all over my skin. I could feel it everywhere, like it was actually his hands caressing every inch of me.

"Have a good shower?" he asked mockingly, making me feel naked even though the towel covered me down to my knees. "No need to cover up on my account. You don't have anything special."

He was such a liar. Even now I could see the hunger in his gaze. I deliberately dropped my towel, and that hunger turned into a living, breathing thing, threatening to scorch both of us as he looked at me like he wanted to eat me alive.

"Nothing special, Pax?" I asked with a smirk. "Your dick thinks I'm special."

He opened his mouth and then closed it again, a tic in his cheek like he had a million things to say in response but was holding them all back. I slowly and deliberately reached down to grab the towel, making sure that my assets were in perfect display with every move I made. I winked at him and then sashayed my way out of the bathroom. It was only when I was safely behind my locked door that my bravado dropped, and I sank to my knees as adrenaline coursed through me.

Had I really just done that? This place was making me lose my mind. Morning, and my meeting with the Dean, couldn't come soon enough.

I quickly got up from the floor and got dressed, slipping on a pair of sweats instead of the tank top and short pajamas that I usually wore to bed. I needed an extra layer tonight.

But as I slid underneath my sheets, I knew it was going to be a long night. It was obvious that the guys wouldn't stop until they'd ruined my nights just as much as they had started to ruin my days.

Mission accomplished, I whispered to myself as I closed my eyes and tried to think of anything but the look Paxton had in his eyes tonight.

THE NEXT MORNING, I marched across the enormous grass lawn that sat in the middle of campus, determined and ready to do anything to get a new room assignment. I was not leaving the Dean's office until I'd gotten him to help me. My stomach dropped as a group of girls all holding steaming cups of coffee saw me and deliberately went down another path to avoid having to walk by me.

It was funny, but last night's events had almost made

me forget how much I was hated on this campus. I didn't let myself start to spiral downwards though. Sure, it would've been nice to have some friends. That was obviously one of my goals I'd had when I endured the months of recovery after my surgery, a surgery that I really should get my money back for since my cover had been blown almost immediately. I could do this though. I could get a room somewhere, keep my head down, not go anywhere for the next couple of years. I would get that degree and then I'd get the hell out of here. None of it would matter again.

I continued this pep talk all the way to the large stone steps that led to the administration building. I took a deep breath, wishing I'd been able to grab some coffee before coming here, but I hadn't wanted to risk being seen and questioned by one of the guys. I could stop after this by that coffee shop I'd seen two blocks off of campus the other day. It would be my reward.

With that bright thought, I opened one of the huge double doors that led into the building, the cool air caressing my skin as I walked into the entryway. It was completely empty except for an enormous desk where a very tired, very perturbed looking woman sat. We were the only two people in the room. I guess at least I beat the line.

I walked toward the desk, my shoes clicking across the ornate tile, echoing around the room. I stood there awkwardly once I got there, waiting for her to look up at me. After a minute passed and she hadn't even acknowledged my presence, I cleared my throat, wondering if there was a little bell somewhere I was supposed to ring.

The woman sighed and finally looked up at me from her seat, like I was the biggest inconvenience she'd ever experienced. I tapped my fingers against my thigh, reminding myself that I needed to be polite even with all the attitude she was throwing me.

"Do you have an appointment?" she barked.

"I sent an email last night. But it's an emergency. I need to see Dean Worthington."

She let out another long sigh and shook her head. "The Dean only sees people by appointment. Get an appointment and *then* come see us." She looked down at her desk, typing away at her computer and going back to pretending that I didn't exist.

I put my hands on her desk and leaned forward, determination surging through me. "I don't think you heard me correctly. This is an emergency. I'll wait here all day if I have to in order to get even five minutes of the Dean's time. Surely he has at least a minute to spare."

I hated begging. Hated it more than almost anything, actually. I had The Demon to thank for that, as he'd made me beg more times than I could count. But I'd do it if that's what it took to get that meeting, and to get that new room assignment.

"No, I don't think you heard me. The Dean only sees people with appointments, and you aren't on the list," she snapped as she held up a paper filled with a long list of names.

I gritted my teeth. "How would you know if I was on that list or not? You haven't even asked for my name."

"You think I don't know that you're The Demon's daughter? I can't believe you would have the nerve to step on this campus with all the pain you've caused the world. You should be locked up right along with your father!"

And there it was. I knew it was too much to hope for, that who I was hadn't spread to everyone. Obviously, the whole administration knew who I was now too. I didn't bother trying to correct her, or tell her that I didn't have anything to do with my father's sins, because that would've been a lie. All of my previous determination rushed out of me, and my shoulders dropped. Maybe there was a bridge I could live under for the rest of the semester, because I was pretty sure that no matter how many emails I sent, I wasn't going to make it on that list.

Just then, the telephone on her desk rang. She stared at it unhappily before finally answering it.

"Yes, Dean Worthington?" she asked in a light, breathy voice that was a far cry from the snide rude tone she'd been giving me. "Oh. I see. My apologies, sir. I'll send her right in."

She hung up the phone and pursed her lips before looking back at me. "Apparently, you're a lucky girl. The Dean will see you now." She gestured to the door that sat behind her and then looked back at her computer, stabbing at her keyboard like it had personally offended her.

I frowned, wondering how the Dean even knew I was here. Maybe there were cameras in here, or maybe our voices had carried into his office. It was weird, but I wasn't going to look a gift horse in the mouth.

"Thanks," I told her insincerely as I began to walk towards the doors.

"You should leave if you know what's good for you," she hissed at my back. But I just ignored her as I finally got to the doors and prepared myself to face the Dean. I knocked twice on the heavy wood, and a loud voice quickly yelled out for me to come in.

I had a whole speech I was prepared to launch into as soon as I saw him, but the words all disappeared as I walked into the room and saw Remington sitting behind an enormous wooden desk, his hands behind his head and his feet sitting on top of the desk on a pile of papers.

There was a nervous looking older man sitting in a chair in the corner of the room, his gaze darting between Remington and myself like he was afraid that one of us was going to attack at any minute. I recognized the man from the handbook they'd given everyone at orientation. Dean Worthington looked like he was about to shit himself. There was an obvious twitch right under his eye that was either there from nerves or anger, it was hard to tell.

I felt like I was going to throw up as I surveyed the scene. How had they known I was going to be here? How was he sitting in the Dean's chair like he owned the place?

"Surprised to see me?" asked Remington with a big grin.

There were two leather bound chairs in front of me, and I gripped the top of one of them, squeezing it so tight I was sure I was going to break it.

"You could say that," I answered through clenched teeth.

"Imagine my surprise when I saw your email come in last night trying to set up a meeting. You wouldn't be trying to get a room change now, would you?" His grin widened, and I was tempted to launch myself at him, tear off that smug smile, and light his ass on fire. They were monitoring my emails. Of course they were. Why hadn't that thought even crossed my mind?

Oh, because it was psychotic. That's why. I'd obviously underestimated these guys, which I shouldn't have, especially after last night.

I wouldn't make that mistake again.

"I'd like to speak with the Dean," I answered, my nails tearing into the leather as I worked to keep myself in place.

Remington sat back in the chair, his boots crunching the papers underneath him, and I saw the dean flinch out of the corner of my eye. "Go right ahead, the Dean's right there," said Remington mockingly, gesturing to the cowering man to my right.

I shifted uneasily but turned my attention to the dean, even though I knew now that it was futile.

"Dean Worthington, I need a new room assignment. I'll stay anywhere. There has to be somewhere on campus that's available," I begged, feeling like I'd never done anything so useless in my entire life.

The Dean just looked at me with pity, but before he could say anything, Remington responded. "I'm afraid that your request is denied," he said cockily, flashing me a brilliant grin. "But please feel free to check back another time, the office is always open."

He smiled again, but this time it looked more sharkish, like you could see the predator that lurked beneath his skin.

"I have to say, Aurora, I'm quite disappointed that you aren't showing more gratitude for the accommodations you've been given. Anyone on campus would love to be where you are. That's something we're definitely going to have to work on."

This time I squeezed the chair so hard that it actually did crack underneath my fingers.

I shot the dean a pleading glance, but the coward wouldn't even meet my eyes.

"Worthington, you can leave the room," ordered Remington as he pulled his feet off the desk, making sure to take the papers with him so that they littered the ground underneath him.

Without a word, the dean got up from his seat and left the room, closing the door quietly behind him and taking away any hope I had of getting out of this situation.

I turned my attention back to Remington, taking my time to really look at him. Who were these boys that had this kind of control? This university was one of the best in the country, if not *the* best in the country. And here he was, ordering the head of the school around as if he was nothing but an errant schoolboy. It was scary.

Remington leaned forward, putting his elbows on the desk as he stared right back at me. "Are you understanding the situation a little bit better, princess? There's nothing you could do at the school that we wouldn't know about, that we wouldn't have control over. It will be much better for you to accept your fate with a pretty little smile. You can't run, and you can't hide. We control everything that happens here, and that includes you."

I was tempted to lunge over the desk and punch him. That's probably what I should have done, but instead, I crossed my arms in front of me and gave him the same look of cool indifference that he'd been giving me.

"Have anything to say?" he asked, raising an eyebrow, something I'd always been jealous that people could do for some reason. It figured that he would be able to do that. They probably all could. But why was I thinking about that?

"I think you've made yourself very clear... Sir," I added, watching the glimmer of heat in his gaze at the word and wondering what it would feel like to choke it out of him. It was errant thoughts like that that kept me up at night sometimes, wondering if I was closer to The Demon than I thought.

It only mattered if I followed through with them, I always told myself. And so far I'd succeeded in controlling myself. I turned around and began to walk towards the door without another word, knowing that the battle I had on my hands wasn't going to be won this morning, obviously. I'd have to pick apart all of their weaknesses, find the things that could give me back control.

Or I could always try transferring to a different school.

As if he could read my mind, Remington's voice trailed after me. "You're not going anywhere until we say you're allowed to, Aurora," he warned, and the threat in his voice was clear. I wouldn't be allowed to transfer, they'd make sure of that.

I walked out of the room before I lost control. The dean was sitting on a bench outside the door, the secretary standing beside him and stroking his shoulder inappropriately. I was pretty sure that the dean's wife had been at orientation with him. I think he had a couple of kids as well. Maybe that was something that Remington had on him, an affair. I'd have to look into that sometime.

As my shoes clicked against the tile, the dean glared at me, all the pity that had been in his gaze before completely absent. Evidently, he was blaming me for the embarrassment he'd just experienced in his office.

I looked away from him and his maybe mistress. Dean Worthington's feelings about me were the least of my concerns now that I knew he was nothing but a glorified puppet.

I hurried through the still student free lobby and practically flung open the doors to the outside, taking huge gulps of the fresh air in like I'd been without oxygen this whole time. I wanted to scream, destroy something, pick a fight with someone... But all I did was drag my ass to class where I endured hours of the students whispering things about me and giving me dirty looks.

It was still better than before though. I'd still escaped *him*. It was the silver lining that I would have to keep telling myself to survive all of this.

When classes were finally done, I headed to the women's locker room in the gymnasium and changed into running clothes, carefully putting all of my things away and locking the locker so that no one could get my stuff. I didn't go run around the track though. Knowing my luck, someone would probably try to trip me intentionally.

Instead, I ran outside, setting off down the road that circled the lake. I'd heard during orientation that it was a two-mile loop around the lake, and I ran around it six times until my legs threatened to give out. Running had always been a sort of therapy for me, a way to push my body so hard that all my problems could disappear for a little bit.

Surprisingly, The Demon hadn't tried to ruin it for me. At least a few times a week he let me out of the house to run free, like I was some sort of caged animal that he was giving some exercise. Whatever his intentions were with it, I hadn't tried to look too closely at them. I'd used running to transport my mind somewhere else, somewhere that was free.

I had a feeling that I'd be needing to run here quite a bit as well.

The sun was setting, and I reluctantly headed back to the gym to get my stuff before making my way to the Sphinx. I would've hung out at the library until it closed, but then I probably would be having to find that bridge to sleep under since the school still hadn't given me the combination to get into the secret society. If I headed back now, I'd at least have some chance to catch someone as they were going in.

It was just my luck, I only had to wait around twenty minutes before some member I hadn't met yet came back and let me in with him. He didn't mock me or say anything stupid, but he didn't give me the combination either, so I put him firmly in the asshole column with everyone else I'd met in the place.

I was starving, everything I'd eaten for lunch long gone after my run, but I didn't have it in me to go sit in the dining hall with my four torturers, or even to try and raid the kitchens. Instead, I slinked back to my room, thinking that if one of them did come and try and drag me to dinner, I really would start throwing fists. I was so done with the day.

Once safely in my room, I started my homework, and the hours flew by, blissfully free of any of the guys. After finishing up, I decided it was a good idea to wash up before bed since I was covered in dry sweat.

I locked myself in the bathroom, frowning at my appearance. When I'd started up at the school, what seemed like forever ago now, I'd looked in the mirror and seen a stranger. But at least it had been a hopeful stranger, with a whole new life in front of her. The person looking in the mirror now was still a stranger, but one that looked beat down...desperate.

I hated her.

I wrenched my eyes from the mirror and jumped in the shower, hurrying through the process just in case Paxton decided to make another appearance. I'd put a chair under his doorknob so that I'd at least have a warning before the door flew open, but I knew it wouldn't stop him if he really wanted inside. Just another thing they'd ruined for me.

When I was able to shower without anyone coming in, I started to get suspicious. I would've thought one of them would be lurking around, wanting to gloat about what happened this morning.

But the place was completely silent. I haven't even heard anyone walking down the hallway. It was weird. I didn't want any of them to bother me, but it also made me uneasy being alone in the place. I still hadn't seen most of the building. And it was a secret society. Who knew what things they got up to here?

I checked every nook and cranny in the room...just in case.

Satisfied that no one was hiding in the room, I slipped under the covers, making sure that the light was on in my closet before I did so. I was hoping to get a good night's rest after my run, and sure enough, I soon found myself slipping into dreamland.

Which was never a good thing.

I was cowering in the corner, trying to keep my gaze on anything but what was happening on the table in the middle of the room. Bach was blaring from the speakers, so loud that my eardrums were about to explode. It was Bach's Toccata & Fugue in D Minor tonight. I knew the music would be embedded in my brain for the next month after this, which was not a good thing, since the piece was the stuff of nightmares. Of course that was why The Demon liked it so much. He could play it as loud as he wanted down here. We were so deep underground, with so much soundproofing around us, that there wasn't a chance of being overheard.

A woman's tortured cry cut through the music, and I couldn't stop myself from looking over to the table where The Demon was working. I wasn't sure where he'd picked this one up. All I knew was that she was a prostitute who'd made the mistake of getting into his car. He'd injected her with something that paralyzed her, and now she was laying there on the metal table, trapped in her body as she stared at him pleadingly.

He'd just started with the scalpel. He'd drag it down her chest, just deep enough that he could pull away the skin, but he wouldn't hit any major organs. The Demon considered himself an artist, and his victims were his canvases, his beautiful sacrifices to the devil he worshiped.... himself.

I wanted to look away from the scene, but I felt paralyzed as I watched the scalpel move down her chest, and her stomach, stop-

ping right on top of her pubic bone. He made two perpendicular lines on each side and began to peel away the skin, showcasing the muscle and fat underneath.

Tears ran unbidden down my face...and hers as he worked, her cries coming out in garbled, tortured gasps since he'd cut out her tongue to start the process.

"Aurora," a voice seeped into my subconscious, crowding away the dream that held me captive.

"Aurora," the voice called again. It sounded so familiar, but my nightmare was holding on fast; blood was starting to pour off the sides of the metal table in a way that I knew somehow was impossible yet seemed so realistic in my dream.

The room started to shake suddenly, and then I felt hands on my body as I was lurched out of the dream. I sat up with a gasp, my forehead hitting something hard. Not something, I realized. Someone.

"Fuck," a gravelly voice said, and it took me a second to realize that it was Paxton. He'd just woke me from my nightmare.

A mix of shame and embarrassment cycled through me. The last thing I wanted was one of *them* to see me at my weakest, and that's what had just happened.

Something wet hit my hand, and I looked down only to realize that I had tears streaming down my face from the horror of the dream. I frantically wiped at my face, as if he hadn't seen them already. t I hated that I was afraid of the dark. With the light coming in from the closet, you could see everything. He'd probably gotten a perfect view of me thrashing on my sheets.

"Why are you in here?" I asked, my voice coming out hoarse and broken.

Paxton shifted on the bed, but I realized he looked

uncomfortable. “I heard you screaming,” he said roughly. “Even with all the doors closed, I could hear you."

That comment had my head jerking towards my now open bedroom door that led into the bathroom that I knew I had locked. The door didn't look broken either, confirming that I couldn’t count on it to keep anything out at all.

Belatedly I realized that Paxton's thumb was softly caressing my leg, and I involuntarily shivered from the sensation. He didn't seem to realize that he was doing it though. He was staring at the wall above my head, lost in some deep thought. Or maybe it wasn’t something deep, maybe it was something dark. There was something in his gaze, something tragic, like he’d seen some horror for himself and was still trying to escape it.

But of course, that couldn’t be it. That was just me romanticizing something, trying to find the silver lining in an embarrassing situation.

“I have nightmares too,” he suddenly admitted, still staring at the wall. His gaze flicked to me, and he stared at me like he was really seeing me for the first time. "What do you dream about?"

I opened my mouth immediately to tell him to fuck off, to tell him he was crazy to think I would bare my soul to him. And then I closed it. In the dim light, he didn't look as fierce as he did during the day. In the shadows, he looked almost... Haunted.

"Truth for truth?" I whispered, and he held my gaze, his amber eyes burning into me like he could see straight to my soul.

"Okay," he said after what felt like the longest minute of my life.

He got up from the bed abruptly and walked over to the closet, shutting off the light before closing the doors.

"I need that," I told him sharply as I watched his shadow walk back to the bed.

Paxton didn't ask why I needed it, and I guess the answer would've been obvious to anyone. He simply crawled into the bed and pulled me against his body.

I laid stiff against him, wondering what he was going to do.

"You first," he murmured. I couldn't keep back the shiver as his breath danced across my neck.

I'm not sure why I said my next words. Maybe it was the darkness that surrounded us, or the way I felt with his arms around me. For the first time in a while, I felt safe, like it wasn't really Paxton behind me, but someone I could spill secrets to. Maybe it was temporary insanity, but despite my best efforts, sometimes my weaknesses slipped from my lips.

"The rumors... Some of them were true," I began. Paxton's arms tightened around me. But he didn't say anything. And maybe that was why I kept going.

"The Demon wanted me..." I paused, trying to look back at that time in my life and be honest about it, for maybe the first time. "The Demon wanted me to be some sort of protégé. When I would refuse to participate, he'd force me to stand in the room and watch. Somehow he thought that if I watched, I'd develop the same cravings for blood and pain that he did."

Paxton was perfectly still against me.

"I saw unimaginable things. Things so dark they'd never be in a book. They'd never be in the scary movies that everyone seems to love so much. They're unfathomable, because to commit those crimes, you would've had to lose every part of yourself. And no one wants to think about that. What it would really be like if we all were just empty, dark voids set on lighting the world around us on fire."

Paxton's fingers were stroking the skin where my shirt had ridden up. The act was soothing, not sexual in nature at all… just soothing. Which was what I needed right then.

"Sometimes, when he'd taken me out to where there weren't any people, the desire to destroy, or whatever it was that was inside him, would start to surface. And there wouldn't be anyone around us. There would just be me. So, sometimes I dream about that too," I said quietly.

He was quiet for a long time. "Did you always refuse to participate?" he finally asked in a gruff voice. Of course, that question brought out all the demons in my head, the imaginary ones my father had created in me.

"You said a truth for a truth," I told him quietly, unable to give that answer to him.

He pulled me closer and tangled his legs with mine, until it was hard to tell where I began and he ended.

"That's fine, little devil. You don't have to tell me all your secrets tonight." There was another long silence, so long that I thought he wasn't going to tell me anything. But just when I was getting up the nerve to kick him out of my bed, he spoke.

"My nightmares are about my mother. Of seeing her dragged to the floor in front of me and raped before she was shot in the head."

My breaths came out in shocked gasps. I'd seen flashes of pain in his gaze, but I never would have guessed that it was from something like that. I had a lot of questions. But no words came out.

"Seems like every time I close my eyes, I'm back in that room, listening to her screams. Listening to the grunts of the man that took her. I'd do anything to be able to cut those memories from my mind." His strokes across my skin quickened, like he needed the touch to center himself. "But it sounds like you would know all about that, wouldn't you?"

I didn't answer, but I didn't need to. It felt...nice, to talk to someone else with trauma...as bad as that sounded. Everyone around me had always seemed to flit about their lives, escaping the darkness that had followed me since that fateful day as a child. You couldn't take comfort from someone made of sunshine when you had always been in the storm.

Behind me, Paxton's breaths lengthened, until I knew that he had fallen asleep. And I know I should've pushed him out of the bed, but I couldn't bring myself to.

Just for tonight, I whispered to myself. *Just for tonight.*

I found myself slipping into sleep despite my best efforts, wrapped in the warmth of his embrace.

And this time, I didn't dream.

10

AURORA

The next day, I woke up in an empty bed. I wondered if I'd dreamed my night with Paxton.

I showered, dressed, then sat around doing homework, nervous to leave my room until I had to get to class. What kind of misbegotten orgy might I wander into this time?

A servant knocked on the door to offer me breakfast. When she told me to follow her, I did, and she led me to a smaller dining room with a fireplace and a view of the campus. It was blessedly empty. I sank into one of the mahogany-and-crushed-velvet dining chairs and set up my laptop on the table. "Thank you so much. What's your name?"

"What would you like to eat?" the woman asked, ignoring my question.

Operation Make Friends in this house might take a while.

"What are my options?"

"We can make anything you like."

I wondered if they would bring food over from one of the cafeterias or if anything I wanted was really made fresh here. I'd order something they'd have from the cafeteria just in case. "A bacon and cheese omelet, fruit salad, and orange juice, please?"

She nodded, then headed back out the door. A few minutes later, as I was searching for my name on the internet and squinting one-eyed at the search results, trying to find what I needed without reading too much I didn't, she returned and set my plate and glass on the table. Everything was hot and fresh and better than in the cafeteria.

"Thank you," I started to say, but she was already gone. Friendly. With a groan, I clicked on the internet forum that I thought was most likely responsible for my attackers at the football field.

Sighting reported – campus green. Wearing a black hoodie, jeans, black Converse. Platinum blond hair now. Think she's looking for a new victim?

Mod here. You guys, stop reporting the same sightings! Scroll the thread! If you have details about the SAME sighting, add it as a nested comment under the original!

When I get my hands on that bitch, I'm gonna to do the same thing to her that she and her daddy did to Penny Gottman.

Can't believe she's walking free.

And dared show up to college with a new face like nothing ever happened! None of her victims get to go on with their lives. Why should she?

Where's she living now?

I scrolled through the internet forum that was tracking my movements and making plans to rape and torture and murder me, trying to stay focused on the important details and not get distracted by how gruesome it all was. I was usually good at erecting walls in my mind, but right now those walls were crumbling under the weight of all my lost dreams.

I'd never be able to convince anyone of what had really happened with the Devil.

I looked up as I felt someone approaching, just in time for Remington to loom over me. His tall, lean frame was dressed in a tight-fitting t-shirt and dark jeans, his tousled hair looking as sexily imperfect as always. He pushed the lid of my laptop down with two fingers.

"What are you up to, Aurora?"

He asked as if he already knew.

"Nothing."

"Oh?" Quicker than anyone should be, he spun my laptop around, pulling it off the table. I would've grabbed for it, but it was already too late.

His gaze roamed the screen, then darkened, his pupils reflecting the glowing blue light of the screen.

"Enjoying reading about what those men want to do to me?"

Maybe I'd just imagined the darkness in his eyes, because he was back to his usual lighthearted self as he closed the laptop and handed it back to me. Remington scared me just as much as the others, and the fact that he seemed to be a morning person didn't endear him to me anymore.

"Come on," Remington said. "I've got your class schedule, and you've got to get to American Lit."

"Are you on babysitting duty?"

"Consider it more like corrections."

I focused on putting my laptop and books back into my bag, throwing it over my shoulder. I could barely stand to look at him after what had happened with the dean's office...then there was what happened at dinner the other night. I hated that he was standing so close to me, so confident that he had the right to *take care of* me like Cain had said the other day. I hated that he looked so clean and untouchable and cheerful after what he'd done, and the debauchery of their evenings. Most of all, I hated that part of me still felt drawn to him. Heat seemed to crackle between us even when I despised him.

The two of us left the building through that weird side door again. "Why don't you use your perfectly good front door?"

"Because I'm walking with you," he said with a wink, "and I don't want anyone to see me. I do have *some* standards, you know."

I glanced over my shoulder at the door, at the camera angled over it. There were cameras everywhere in this house and outside it.

Was the danger to me inside the house greater than the danger outside?

If I ran, there were going to be dozens of self-appointed bounty hunters on my tail, all eager to hurt me.

Walking across campus with him was surreal. Even though people lobbed looks of hatred at me, they looked at him with respect and even adoration. I caught flashes of jealousy from a few girls who looked at me then tossed their hair, chins raised. *Girlfriend, you don't want any of this mess.*

Remington seemed to know my schedule flawlessly. He led me into my classroom for Lit, then plopped down into one of the seats beside me.

"Are you staying?" I hissed as he sank down in the seat, his legs spreading slightly in those dark jeans. He looked sexy even with his face propped on his hand, waiting for class to start.

"Where you go, I go."

All morning, I struggled to concentrate. Schoolwork had always been an escape for me, a way to calm my busy mind, but now I couldn't stop noticing Remington being so close to me—the way his elbow occasionally brushed mine, the way he moved, the way his aftershave smelled dark and spicy. Every tiny accidental touch for some reason stirred up memories of that dinner, raising a thrill of unexpected lust.

He didn't seem to be listening, just working on something on his laptop, his fingers flying over the keys and his attention focused there, but no teacher bothered him.

I had a break after my first two classes of the day. "I can go to the library to do homework," I said, even though my heart sank at the idea. The private carrels of the library would mean I'd need to watch my back the whole time.

"Not a chance," he said. "You can sit in on my Quantum Physics class."

I assumed he was fucking with me. *Quantum Physics* sounded like something he'd make up. But once we were sitting in the lecture hall with all of a dozen other students—all of whom looked at me quizzically—and the professor started talking about *probability amplitudes,* I started to believe him.

Remington seemed to come alive, too. When he raised his hand, I stole a glance at his face, finding it hard to believe he was actually going to answer a question. Remington had seemed too cool for school.

The professor smiled at him, his eyes crinkling above his white beard. "Yes, Remington? Do you think amplitudes are physically significant?"

"Yes, absolutely. The mathematical scale for probability on the quantum scale is just hard for us to wrap our heads around. And of course, it makes interference effects possible, and that ultimately does impact the physical world."

I was used to being the smartest person in the room, and I couldn't help but steal a second glance at Remington as the teacher said he was absolutely right, then continued with his lecture. For once, though, Remington didn't even look cocky; he was taking notes, a look of concentration written over his handsome features.

When the class ended, I asked, "Why? Why are you taking this?"

"Because a rigorous math and Physics background will make it easier to design my own algorithms for stock trading and take over the world," he said with a smile.

"Why am I not surprised that would be the end goal?"

At lunch, I opened my laptop to pull up the internet forum, feeling a sense of dread.

Only to receive a *Page Not Found* error. I tried other search terms, but nothing could bring up that website or any of the similar ones that I'd found.

When I thought about how Remington had been busy on his laptop during class, I had a sneaking suspicion that he was somehow responsible, but that was ridiculous, wasn't it?

"Remington," I said uncertainly.

He tilted back into his chair, staring at me smugly. "Nobody gets to hurt you but us, baby doll. But if you run, I'll put it all back up."

"Run?" I asked, my heart pounding, as if I'd never thought about it. "Why would I run when you and I are having so much fun?"

He let out a short laugh. As we headed to the rest of his classes and mine, I realized that despite the admiration everyone gave him, people skirted around him as if he were a predator that might lash out at any moment.

"Everyone seems scared of you."

"Wise of them."

"They must not know how easy you are to knock out."

He glanced at me, a little smile on my lips, and I wasn't sure what he was going to say. I'd been surprised to find Remington was smart as fuck, and I was curious to talk to him more, if I could ever get him to open up to me. Remington felt like he was all façade, and I wondered who the real man was behind the act.

"Come on, let's get some homework done," he said suddenly.

I assumed we were going to the library, which I had very mixed feelings about after that note. Had the note really come from Stellan?

After experiencing how many other ways these men had to torment me, I doubted they'd bother with a silly little note. So, where had it come from? It was one thing to know I had enemies out there who wanted to hunt me down because of what my father did.

It was another thing to know one of those enemies had been able to recognize me after thirty thousand dollars' worth of plastic surgery. The Demon had friends, and those friends worried me far more than the keyboard warriors bragging about how they wanted to torture me.

I realized we were walking in a different direction than the library and stopped abruptly, concerned he was taking me someplace secluded. "Where are we going?"

"The cafe. I need coffee to deal with your suspicious nature."

I scoffed, but he was right that I didn't trust him. "You can hardly blame me."

"Come on, Aurora, aren't we having fun?" He turned wide, innocent eyes on me before reaching around my shoulders and tucking me into his side.

I breathed in the intoxicating scent of his aftershave as my shoulder collided with his warm, hard muscle. He tucked me under his arm, the two of us staggering a bit to walk together before we fell into step.

I happened to meet the gaze of a girl walking toward us and caught the shock and jealousy on her face. I lifted my chin, slipping my arm around Remington's lean waist as if I belonged here with him.

He followed my gaze. "You should really read that self-help book, *How to Win Friends.*"

"I don't think it's going to help."

"Oh, I don't know, I kind of like you."

"I'm still not convinced you're not going to murder me."

"Probably best to stay alert," he agreed amicably. "But not today. You can relax for once. What do you like to drink?"

Could I really relax for once?

He unwound from me to open the door to the cafe, and I walked in ahead of him. "Grab a table while I get our drinks."

I went looking for my usual kind of table, a four-top against the wall at the back of the coffee shop. I was pulling out my books when Remington started toward our table. He was carrying both our drinks and a paper bag, his hair falling over his high forehead in a way that made him look like a teen heart-throb out of a movie, and I bit my lower lip. I couldn't relax around him, no matter what he said. But it was hard not to, because he was fun and flirtatious and made me feel... normal.

A girl intercepted him, touching his arm, smiling up at him. He smiled back at her and said something, and jealousy twisted through my stomach, surprising me. Then he headed toward the table. His eyes met mine and seemed to crinkle in amusement, as if he could read my face, and I forced myself to turn stony.

The Demon had taught me to hide my feelings: fear, disgust, cunning, manipulation. But I wasn't used to feeling jealous.

Remington reached the edge of my table, and the girl followed him, a look of smiling determination fixed on her face. He plunked my iced coffee down on the table and started to say something, but she interrupted, grabbing his wrist and pressing herself against him.

"I was hoping you could tutor *me* today," she purred.

"I already have plans." He pulled his wrist out of her grip, although his tone was light. He settled into the chair across from mine and glanced at me. "I see you put my back to the door."

"People seem to like you better than me."

"True," he admitted.

She slid onto his lap, and his brows rose. Danger seemed to tinge the air around him, but she didn't notice as she smiled at him. "You know there's no point in trying to help her. She's going to fail out of school if she doesn't get the hint that she's not wanted here anyway."

He shifted, his hands rising so he wasn't touching her, but the way he moved subtly still unseated her. She fell on her ass on the floor and looked up at him in shock.

"Aurora doesn't need my help," he said coolly. "And anyone trying to give her any *hints* will answer to me."

Her cheeks had gone very pink. She half-stumbled to her feet and ran for the door.

He raked his hand through his hair and blew out a slow breath. "God, the girls around here get tiresome."

"I promise not to fawn over you," I assured him, taking a sip from my iced coffee.

"Let's not make any promises you might not be able to

keep," he said with a wink. He pushed the paper bag over to me. "I bought you a cookie too. You're skin and bones."

"Just how The Demon liked me." The Demon had endless rules to govern my appearance, my actions, and most of all, my purity.

His face clouded, but he let the mention of The Demon pass. I couldn't believe I'd just said that, so casually. I usually kept everything that happened with The Demon a dark secret, a fist closed around my heart that no one else could see.

The two of us studied in peace for a few moments. The silence felt companionable, just the blurred chatter of others in the cafe beyond us, the sound of pages turning and pencils scratching. He propped his chin in his hand. Remington was always sexy, but the way he focused drew my gaze to study the lines of his face, the softness of his lips.

"Have you ever sat in anyone's lap?" he asked suddenly, without looking up from the page.

"What?"

"She tried to sit in my lap, and you didn't like it."

"I was definitely not allowed to sit in any man's lap."

"Would he have hurt you or them?"

He asked the question so matter-of-factly that it startled me, made me feel seen. "Both."

He nodded. "Well, you're free to do what you want now, aren't you?"

"I don't know."

My voice came out in a whisper.

He rose suddenly and swung around the edge of the table, taking the seat beside me. He patted his thigh, his look full of challenge.

I shook my head. "Really, Remington? Here?"

"It's just sitting in my lap. It's not life or death."

Not anymore. But it had been.

"I can't," I said in a whisper.

He leaned close to me, his intoxicating scent washing over me, his lips sweeping gently against my ear in a way that sent a shiver of lust down my spine. "You can do anything you want when we're together, Aurora. No one will stop us."

"Must be nice," I muttered.

He patted his thigh again. I happened to glance out at the rest of the cafe and saw a girl staring at us, jealousy and loathing written bare across her face. She glanced away when she saw me.

Between the way she looked at me and the teasing expression on Remington's face, I couldn't resist. I swung into his lap, planting my ass on one thigh as his hands settled on my hips. It felt awkward, like I towered above him like this even though he was so much taller than me. "I feel ridiculous."

He adjusted himself, the back of his hand brushing my ass. "I don't." He turned his face toward me, his lips skimming my throat, and my breath hitched.

"You're so innocent," he murmured. "How have you seen so much and you're still so innocent?"

"I'm not."

"Liar." His hand glided up my thigh, and I pressed my knees closed, a throb of lust sparking between my legs that I tried to ignore. His touch felt good on my skin. "How did I find the one good girl on this whole depraved campus?"

"How did you *find* me? You practically kidnapped me to make me live with you," I answered drily.

He chuckled, and the vibration of his chest warmed my back. I leaned against him, feeling slightly more comfortable as his hand kept stroking across my thigh.

He said into my ear, "You should start wearing skirts, little devil."

"I don't love that nickname."

"I don't care."

But even through my jeans, his heated touch was stroking desire through me. His fingers found the seam between the legs of my jeans, and I gasped and sat up, trying to wiggle away. His arm tightened around my waist, holding me there as he continued to tease me. The way he rubbed me through my jeans made me want to writhe against his lap, and it took everything I had to stay still, to pretend I felt nothing.

His gaze boldly met the eyes of anyone who dared look at us, and everyone turned away, busying themselves with something else.

"You like making them scared of you," I said softly.

"No, that's more Cain's department," he said. "I just like giving you what you want."

"I don't want this."

His hard cock pressed against my ass, as if he wanted to finger-fuck me in front of all these strangers no matter how much he pretended this was out of the kindness of his heart. "New rules, little devil. There are consequences if you lie to me."

I shook my head, rejecting the 'rules' he was making up on the fly.

"You might like the consequences," he murmured into my ear, and my back arched despite myself, pushing my throbbing core down harder onto his waiting fingers. His teeth caught my earlobe and pinched it, and I bit my lip, holding back the moan that came to my lips. "If you pretend you don't want me, little devil, if you try to hide how you feel in public—well, I'm going to make sure everyone knows."

His hand swept up the front of my jeans, working against my button and fly. As much as I wanted him, I shook my head. "You're going to get me in trouble."

"Yep." His lips grazed my throat again, alternating between pressing kisses and sucking my skin hard enough to bruise.

I glanced down at the table, which had to block my jeans from view. People were pointedly not looking our way now, as if they were afraid to earn Remington's ire, too. They'd seen what he did to the girl who pushed herself on him.

His hand delved into my jeans, into my panties, and his warm fingers pressed against my clit. I let out a gasp, wiggling helplessly against his grip as he continued to stroke me. Heat washed through me, my core melting into liquid warmth, my toes curling inside my sneakers.

"You've got an exhibitionist streak," he murmured into my ear. "Ohh, we're going to have so much fun together, Aurora."

I pressed my lips together, holding back both my denial and the moan that came to my lips. I had a feeling if I pushed Remington, he might very well just throw me down on the table. His hand rested against the bare skin of my waist, pushing my t-shirt up, and his lips kept teasing against my throat. I tossed my head, feeling my hair lash against his face, finding myself squirming hungrily against his fingers.

"That's my girl," he murmured. "Come for me right here."

I shook my head, or maybe I was just tossing my hair. I certainly wasn't trying to escape him anymore. His fingers worked steadily against my clit, then two of them plunged inside me, pressing against my g-spot, and my hips jerked. I almost came off his lap before he yanked me against him, reeling me in.

"Come for me," he whispered, and I couldn't help it anymore.

I let out a long low moan as I shattered, grinding down against his fingers, my thighs opening wide. My head found his shoulder as my back arched, his long, deft fingers playing me like a violin as the world around us blurred, as pleasure flooded every part of my body.

I collapsed against his lap, breathing hard. He turned his face into mine and pressed a kiss to my forehead. "Good girl."

I blinked as if I were waking up, coming back to life. Everyone around us was staring fixedly at their books.

"Ohh, Remington," I groaned, and he grinned. "I can never come back in here again."

"Bullshit. You'll be fine. Who cares what the sheep think." He withdrew his hand and popped his fingers into his mouth, absently sucking my juices off his fingers. "Come on. Let's go use the library at the society house."

I bolted off his lap, my clit still sore and aching from that orgasm as I fastened my jeans again. "Why did you bring me here, then?"

He gave me a sunny smile that was all innocence before he stood and took my hand. "My own amusement."

Remington was a terrible person.

But the ache between my thighs suggested that my body didn't agree with my mind.

11

AURORA

I was drowning. Water flowed constantly over my nose and mouth, and I choked and sputtered.

He finally peeled back the cloth covering my face, and the world brightened. I tried to draw in long, desperate, gasping breaths, then rolled over and vomited. It still felt like my lungs were full of water and my sinuses were burning, filled with water themselves. I covered my face, pressing the heels of my hands hard into my eyes, trying to fight back tears. I'd just come so close to death, I could feel it.

"Stay calm, Delilah. You're so ugly when you cry."

My father was obsessed with calm, with molding me into the perfect predator who never faltered, never felt fear. My shoulders shook once, then relaxed, as I finally mastered myself. I dropped my hands and turned to face him.

"So what do you think?"

My throat felt so swollen, and my voice came out in a rasp.

"Very interesting."

My father rewarded me with a smile. "Now you're ready to try it on someone else."

I hesitated, and he said, "Come on, Delilah. You know what this man did to other little girls... we only hunt the bad ones..."

The knock on my door came as I was settling into bed with my book. When I pulled it open, Remington leaned in the doorway, all boyish good looks and casual cruelty.

I noticed that Stellan never came around, which was a blessing. I'd loved the boy once, so seeing him act cruel was devastating.

Remington's gaze roamed my baggy sweatshirt and duck-printed sleep shorts. "You cannot wear that."

"I think I can." I tried to close the door, and he caught it easily, pushed it aside, and sauntered into my room.

"You're not going to bed. We're going to a party."

I noticed he was dressed casually—board shorts and a white t-shirt that clung to his powerful shoulders and the taper of his waist. He was a thing of beauty, even if he was a cruel thing.

"I don't swim."

He flashed me a smile. "Stellan told me."

My heart sank. But he said, "You don't have to swim, sweetheart, but we're all going, and we're not leaving you in this big house alone. You can come with us and hang out on the boat."

"I don't have anything to wear." I wasn't exactly running out to buy a swimsuit.

"That's where you're wrong." He snapped his fingers, and the door, left half-open behind him, swung open all the way.

The half-dozen servants who worked in the house filed in, all carrying bags and boxes from expensive stores. They put them down on the floor, the bed, in the closet, then filed out and returned with more.

"What's all this?" I demanded.

"We don't want you to keep embarrassing us. If we're going to be seen with you, you can at least look respectable."

I poked open one of the bags and pulled out a strip of red lace with two strings attached, the purpose of which I could not immediately identify. "Respectable? Are you sure?"

"Be downstairs in ten minutes. I've got to go, but Cain is waiting for you."

"Terrific." Cain's name alone stirred something in me, a sudden pulsing heat that reminded me of his fingers between my thighs, his hard muscular body against mine.

Remington blew me a kiss goodbye, then he was gone.

Maybe I could stay the hell away from Stellan tonight. He'd been staying away from me after that crazy—then humiliating—kiss. The worst part was the memories that kiss had stirred, memories I'd locked away to protect us both. The memory of Stellan sliding his hands through my hair, the way his lips felt on mine, the mischievous light in his eyes... that light seemed to have faded since those days.

I rummaged through the bags and pulled out a dozen different options. Red bikini. Black bikini. Tropical-print bikini. One-piece... with the sides all but missing. I didn't own a swim suit--I'd had no plans to go anywhere near the water—but the guys had certainly provided options.

Skimpy, skimpy options.

I picked out a black bikini and checked that my door was locked, given the tendency of the guys to just walk in. If they wanted to buy me clothes, fine. I certainly deserved something for the shit I was putting up with.

There were a dozen boxes filled with shoes, all with unhelpfully tall heels. I pushed them aside and slipped on my favorite black sandals. I wasn't wearing heels on a boat.

The odds were already too high someone might push me overboard.

I let myself out of my room and rested my fingertips lightly on the doorknob, wishing I could lock it. All the other doors in the hall had locks; mine had a lock, but no key. I wouldn't trust any key they gave me anyway.

If they wouldn't let me hide anything from them, then I wouldn't let them hide anything from me, either. Remington had given me a reason to stay... and it was time I figured out why they wanted me here.

I headed down the sweeping stairs that led to the two-story entrance hall. Cain was facing away from me, his hands shoved in his pockets. There was always a crackling dark energy around him that seemed out of place with his board shorts and the t-shirt clinging to his powerful body, as if Lucifer were on his way to a pool party. The power of his presence—and the way it immediately flooded my body with heat—almost made me miss a stair. I slid and caught myself, grabbing the railing.

He turned at the sound, but by the time his gaze found me, I was head up, shoulders back, dignity on. He didn't need to know what he did to me.

His gaze swept up and down my body, and instead of feeling intimidated, the sight of how he drank me in hungrily made me feel powerful. These men thought they had the upper hand, that they could control me.

Silly boys.

"Evening, Cain." My voice came out sultry. "I heard you're my ride."

Desire flared in his eyes. He slid a finger under the strap of my black bikini. "I like seeing you wear the things I gave you. I guess I can take it back any time I want."

I reached up to pat his cheek, the movement bringing

the two of us as close together as a kiss. Maybe that dark energy should have scared me, but instead it seemed to speak to my soul, and my soul seemed to answer in kind. I felt lighter, reckless, free when I was near Cain. "It became mine when you gave it to me, buddy."

He caught my wrist with his hand, pulling me taut against his body. My nipples, suddenly sharp, collided with the hard planes of his chest. "I like it better when you call me sir."

"Then I guess you'd better earn the title." My voice came out in a purr that surprised me, and Cain's gaze sharpened.

He suddenly spun me around, his hand drifting up my spine to cup the back of my neck. His fingers squeezed just faintly, controlling and sexy at the same time. "Come on. I'd better get you in the car before we end up any later."

I tried to ignore the thrill that shot through me every time Cain touched me. "You know, normal men offer a lady their arm."

"I'm not a normal man." His voice was a growl in my ear, and just like his touch, I felt it all down my spine, felt the heat of his words pooling low in my stomach. "And you're not a lady."

I knew it was a dangerous game that the two of us were playing. I knew I might get hurt.

And I knew that might be why I liked this so much.

Maybe The Demon had broken me in ways I hadn't even seen yet, or maybe—like him, but in entirely different ways —I was born broken.

Cain steered me out the door to his waiting car, a low-slung McLaren Speedtail, the cockpit a sleek glass bubble as if it were a fighter jet. He opened his door for me and nodded his chin, making me climb in over his gear shaft. Maybe I should've walked around, but instead I obeyed, watching the way his eyes heated as my thighs spread to climb over the shaft.

I settled into the narrow leather bucket seat and pulled my seatbelt over my lap. The way he jetted off forced me back in my seat, but I didn't mind the speed, or watching his competent, broad hands on the wheel.

"Where are we going?"

I almost expected him to refuse to answer, just to fuck with me, but he said, "The Elder Pointe Yacht Club. We're taking out Remington's yacht."

"Remington has a yacht?"

"Doesn't everyone get a yacht when they turn eighteen?" Cain's voice was light. "Oh, right, you probably got a bone saw for your birthday."

They already knew who I was, there was no point in pretending. "I got my first bone saw long before eighteen."

I flashed him a bright smile, and for the first time, there was a flicker of thought in his eyes that I couldn't quite read.

We pulled up at the yacht club, and he checked the glovebox was secure before he handed the keys to the valet. What did he have in there? A gun?

We walked down the damp dock under sparkling fairy lights strung along the way. The dark water made a lump lodge in my throat, but I ignored it, focusing on the details around me. Yachts and sailboats rocked up and down on the soft waves which lapped against the shore with gentle sounds. It was almost relaxing, if not for the bright lights of the party on the yacht at the end of the dock.

Cain grabbed my elbow to steady me as I stepped onboard, his grip firm and commanding. But I didn't need him—that's why I hadn't worn heels. I stepped lightly onto the deck, and away from the peace of the night into the crowd.

There were a few dozen people wandering around on deck, plus several crew, wearing white, who walked around offering drinks and snacks. I was very interested in snacks. But everyone had stopped to stare at Cain and me, and I froze at the sensation of their eyes crawling over me.

I moved away from them, trying to get the layout of the yacht so I'd be prepared for anything that happened tonight. I did a quick circuit around the deck, keenly aware of Cain prowling behind me. Even with some distance between us, my body seemed to tense when he was watching me, always waiting for his warm palms to press against my skin. There was a lounge area in the front of the yacht, with a hot tub full of giggling girls spilling champagne and white sectionals where several people were making out, having decided that even bikinis and board shorts were too dressy for this event.

I turned away from the tanned, writhing bodies and made my way below deck, where I found a big lounge space being used as a dance floor. Beyond that was a hallway with bathrooms and the doors to what were probably two bedrooms; I heard the moaning and decided I was done exploring.

I turned back from the hallway toward the dance floor and my gaze met Cain's, even across the throb of music and gyrating bodies and roaming lights. I licked my lips, wishing I could press my body against his and dance with him, that we could move together—without it being another step in some game.

A man stepped in front of me, blocking my view of Cain. He stared down at my breasts, a lascivious grin spreading across his face. A prickle of disgust raced across my skin, as fast as his gaze.

"Hey there, beautiful," he said. "You want the grand tour?"

I stared up at him. Remington owned the yacht; who was he to offer me a tour? "Who the hell are you?"

His gaze colored with anger. "Watch your mouth, slut."

He raised his hands like he was going to grip my shoulders, and my hands rose subtly, preparing to snap his grip loose and drop this asshole to the ground. I wasn't in the mood to be touched... at least, not by anyone but Cain.

But his hands never landed.

Cain suddenly grabbed him and threw him into the wall. Girls in bikinis and heels screamed and ran—it's hard dressed like that, huh, girls?—as Cain looked down at him, pummeling the man with short, sharp punches around the head and shoulders. The man folded up like a paper doll, dropping to his knees in front of Cain.

"Apologize to her." Cain's voice came out in a growl.

"S—sorry," the man all but sobbed, not even looking up at me.

"Don't you ever fucking look at her again." Cain grabbed the nape of my neck--did the man have a kink or what—and steered me ahead of him toward the stairs. "Someone clean that up and get him off the boat."

Two crew members moved toward the man and the blood smear Cain had left on the floor.

"So protective," I noted.

He laughed in my ear, his body pressing against mine as we reached the top of the stairs. His hard cock and abs pressed against my ass and lower back. "No. But I walked in here with you tonight, and I'm not going to be disrespected by that little trust fund bitch."

The memory of his degrading words in that dungeon

scene rose in my mind. "Oh, so you're the only one who can call me a slut around here?"

His lips brushed the shell of my ear, sending a ripple down my spine. "You haven't earned your way up to *slut* yet."

His voice was dark and sexy, and suddenly, some wanton part of me understood why some girls didn't mind the dirtiest, cruelest phrases when they were spoken in that voice.

"What are you two up to?" The deep voice was deceptively casual, and I turned to find my ex-boyfriend staring at us with his arms crossed over his powerful chest.

The only thing that could make my bizarre night even more... interesting.

Stellan.

12

AURORA

"I was just rescuing our wayward girl from yet another admirer," Cain drawled.

They must all know, then, about my fan club—and how Remington had used that fan club to anchor me to them all. Great.

There was the purr of an engine constantly underfoot, and I looked over the side to realize the lights on the horizon were steadily falling behind. We'd started out to sea while I explored below decks. I was trapped.

The only way to escape these men for now was through that vast, dark sea, and the thought made nausea squirm in my stomach.

"She's pretty good at rescuing herself." Stellan's gaze found mine, pinned me. "Aren't you?"

My mouth had gone dry. When I was around Cain, it felt as if I fed off his dark energy, became more like him. But Stellan... Stellan undid all that. Stellan made me feel like an off-balance teenage girl with her first crush again, vulnerable and tender and exposed... and hopeful.

It had been that sense of hope that had been my undoing, when I let myself care about Stellan and Sophia.

"Maybe." My voice came out cool, and it gave me the confidence to go on, even if it was an act. "But I don't think you know me as well as you think, Stellan."

"I certainly made the mistake of thinking I knew you before."

Cain's gaze swiveled dramatically back and forth between the two of us before he pronounced the conversation, "Boring," and walked away.

The yacht had come to a stop and was rocking gently on the waves. Cain jumped onto the railing surrounding the yacht, then jumped off, doing a flip in mid-air before he disappeared into the black water. Everyone else cheered, but my stomach tightened, and I couldn't resist the urge to rush to the side to make sure he came up. As Cain broke the surface, grinning, others rushed to fling themselves over the railing, none with his grace.

Stellan chuckled darkly behind me. I spun to face him, but he was already gone.

I angled myself in a spot where I could watch who came up behind me, then leaned on the railing, watching them. Cain was floating lazily on his back, sexy as hell with his powerful arms spread and his back arched slightly. Remington did a flashy dive into the lake, and Pax sat on the railing and shook his head at them, a faint smile playing around his lips as everyone cheered for him to jump in. He finally pushed off the railing and jumped in without any of their splashy fanfare.

I wondered where Stellan had gone... partially because I felt a strange pang when I thought of him, and partially for self-protection.

But for now, I watched the other three swimming

around. Technically, I was watching all three dozen people in the water, but I was only drawn to those three. Girls kept swimming around them, flirting with them, kissing them and touching them. They flirted back, and jealousy clutched my stomach. Everyone in the water seemed to be laughing and having fun.

"Do you want a drink?" A guy stepped up to the railing next to me, already carrying two beers.

In the water, Cain's gaze suddenly found me and sharpened as he treaded water. A girl slid her hands across his shoulders, pretending she was going to jump on his back, but he had suddenly lost interest.

So they were watching me just as much as I was watching them.

"I don't think you want to do that," I said, still watching Cain, never bothering to look at the man who had just approached me.

He followed my gaze, and even from the corner of my eye, I could've sworn I saw him blanch.

I should make out with someone in front of them. Someone dangerous enough to push them back.

But I didn't think anyone like that was on this yacht. For some reason, those men who hated me had also marked me as theirs, and I got the distinct impression Cain would beat anyone to at least a quick glimpse of the pearly gates if they paid me too much attention.

A few other folks approached me and received an equally cool reception. After a while, they left me alone. I didn't want the attention of any guys who just saw me as a fun story to tell later, about how they'd dared to get close to The Demon's daughter.

Instead, I soaked up the glimpse of a life I'd never have. The fairy lights strung over the yacht twinkled, and everyone seemed to be laughing and having fun. It seemed like a magical moment straight out of some teenage drama about rich kids' existential angst—which happened to be my favorite kind of television. I would've liked to have been a part of it, actually a part of it, for tonight.

It seemed like I always belonged on the edges, pretending to be normal but never fitting in.

I'd passed on any drinks because I needed to be clear-headed around these men. But it was probably a good idea I'd passed on the booze too, because I'd probably have been crying into my champagne.

People began to climb up the ladder and emerge onto the deck, where crew mates draped white towels over their shivering shoulders. Cain climbed up last, his bowed head and big shoulders appearing first. His gaze found mine, then he looked away as if I was nothing, speaking to another girl.

The worst thing about being The Demon's daughter was the loneliness. I'd had a moment when Stellan's sister was my best friend, when Stellan was my first kiss and my butterflies, when Stellan's mom would make me tea at her kitchen table... that was when I'd had the briefest brush with normal life.

I usually didn't get myself lost in my memories in the daylight. It was bad enough that they swallowed me at night.

And there was a good reason for that, because the past was a distraction from surviving the present.

"Whatever did happen to my sister, Delilah?" Stellan said abruptly in my ear.

The next moment, he was scooping me around the waist. I kicked out, smashed my elbow into his jaw, and heard him grunt in dismay. I flailed against him, trying to make him drop me.

And he did.

Right after he heaved me over the railing.

I plummeted toward the dark water. It rushed up toward me, and then I slammed into it so hard it seemed like I lost my breath. I tried to draw a frantic breath only to have icy cold water rush up my nose, burning its way through my nasal passages just like when I was waterboarded.

"You have to calm yourself, Delilah. It's only death. You and I walk with death all the time. Why are you so afraid when it's your own?"

I lashed out, trying to claw my way up to the surface. I drew a long, ragged breath.

Up above me, on the deck, people had gathered at the railing. I caught glimpses of laughing faces. Now the beautiful scene I'd glimpsed earlier seemed distorted, ruined.

I swam blindly for the ladder where the others had come up, only to hear a *clunk* above me. I looked up the sleek, steep side of the yacht to see Stellan pulling the ladder in.

"Where is she?" Stellan demanded. "All you have to do is answer. Then you can come up."

There was something wild that broke through Stellan's carefully controlled demeanor, that leaked into his voice. Remington and Pax exchanged a glance. Cain still stood there beside Stellan, his arms folded across his chest. Then Pax and Remington began to clear the decks, sending everyone away from the railing.

"Go drink my champagne and ignore the pathetic girl," Remington said cheerfully. "We'll let you know if she drowns or not."

I focused on my breathing, trying to ignore the way my throat felt ragged and swollen once again, as if I'd never draw in a full breath. My heart was racing so hard my chest ached, as if it were about to burst. My arms and legs were wind milling through the water frantically, keeping me upright but exhausting me, and I tried to slow my pace even though it felt as if I was going to die.

"I don't know!" I shouted up at Stellan. "I never would've hurt her!"

"Bullshit!" Stellan shouted back at me.

He was completely unhinged. I looked over my shoulder at shore, but down here, I could see nothing but the dark waves rolling toward me. I couldn't see a glimpse of the shore's bright lights. I tried to swim around the ship, but there was no way up. The guys strolled along the railing, pacing me. Only Stellan seemed to care; he was wild-eyed and frantic. The others were talking, making jokes. Pax began to whistle to himself.

I was exhausted, and my lips kept sinking below the water. My body had shivered so hard my muscles ached, but now I felt warm. Sometimes my toes brushed something underwater —bones, maybe—but the glow coming over me meant I didn't care.

Some part of my brain knew I was dying, but I didn't even care anymore. Rest was so close.

"He took her because of you!" Stellan yelled at me.

Was that true?

"She ran away!" I called back, my voice coming out weak in a way that scared me. I wasn't sure Stellan could even hear me.

She'd always hated her stepfather. As warm as her mother was to me, she'd come to hate her mother too, for staying married to him.

"She didn't run away!" His hands knotted into fists. "That's what everyone believes, that's why no one looks for her. But he took her, I know he did."

The image of my best friend, screaming, tied down to his table while he cut her open surfaced in my mind...

It was so strong, so detailed, that it felt like a memory.

It jolted me, and I swallowed cold water, coming up spitting and sputtering.

Had that happened?

Had I just blocked it from my mind?

There was water in my lungs again, and I kept trying to spit it out, but then I couldn't manage anymore.

The warm glow blurred things, even the panic that maybe I was the reason The Demon had hurt her.

I was slipping under the waves.

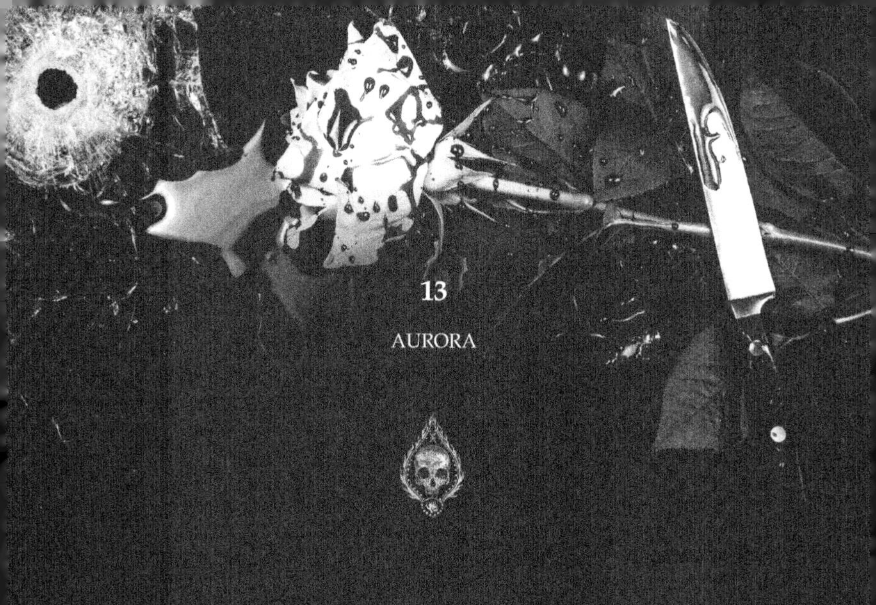

13

AURORA

There was a splashing sound, distantly. Then I felt strong arms circle my waist, drawing me against his body. His legs moved with big, powerful strokes. I was in and out, but then he was passing me up the ladder, and someone caught me, lifted me, laid me down on the hard deck.

Pax rolled me onto my side, and hammered my back hard enough to bruise. I vomited out a burst of water that made my head explode with pain.

Then I was coughing. I was alive.

Cain crouched in front of me, beads of water gliding over his body. His eyes caught me, held me.

"You can't get away from us that easily, little girl."

I made it up to my knees, the hard deck seeming to press painfully against my skin, and swayed. I felt sick and light-headed.

Cain scooped me up again. "Move," he growled at someone who dared to get in his way, then he was carrying me below decks. I caught blurry glimpses of the dancers scattering to get out of his way. Then he deposited me on the bed, his touch surprisingly gentle as his hand cradled my head down to the pillow. I wouldn't have thought Cain would be capable of gentle.

I shouldn't have been able to sleep so soon after that dose of fear and adrenaline, but my head felt heavy as if panic had exhausted me. Even my bones felt as if they'd all turned to lead, weighing me down. I found myself drifting into sleep, leaving Cain's gaze behind.

I jerked awake some time later, my mouth tasting like the bottom of the lake. All I wanted was to go back to sleep, but the urgent pressure in my bladder finally forced me to swing my aching legs out of bed. I'd swallowed too much water.

How had I fallen asleep? That occupied my groggy thoughts. Even after wearing out my body swimming frantically around the boat... I was in the lion's den, so how come I'd curled up with my pillow and slept deeper than I ever had?

Blearily, I stumbled into the bathroom and launched my butt onto the toilet.

It was only when I stood up and yanked my bikini bottoms up that the sound of water running next to me fully registered.

I turned in horror just as Cain pushed open the glass door, revealing his blond hair soaked to his head, the spray of water still colliding with his powerful frame.

"Awfully comfortable with me already," he said drily. "I've never known a woman who cared so little about impressing me."

"I'm never going to care about impressing you." I made a valiant attempt to keep my eyes on his face, but I was all too conscious of the blur of tanned skin, tattoos, and muscles that my peripheral vision picked up. I bit my lower lip, feeling a familiar stir of lust.

"No?" His voice was a casual purr, his bicep rippling, and I realized he'd gripped his cock in his hand. I couldn't help stealing a glance at it as he began to work his long, hard cock back and forth, his forearm corded. A silver piercing winked at me under the lights, and I couldn't help staring at it. What would that feel like, deep inside me?

For a second, my brain short-circuited, then I cleared my throat. "Are you taking me back to land?"

"You don't care about land right now."

"I definitely care about land. I don't want to be trapped out at sea with you—"

His eyebrows had risen, and suddenly I wasn't sure I wanted to call him any names, not when I was trapped in such close confines.

"Bullshit," he said, his voice dangerously soft. "You know what you want."

I shook my head.

"I thought you were so brave. But apparently, you're not brave enough to take what you want." He dropped his dick and stepped out of the shower, leaving it still running. He rested his hands on my shoulders, his big body towering over mine, and leaned down and *sniffed* me.

"You are so weird. But then, I knew that from the time you had a girl gyrate on your lap in between bites of your steak." My words came out off-handed, even though the truth was no matter how glib both of us sounded, something dark and dangerous seemed to float in the air between us.

"You smell like the lake bottom. A little more dead-fish than I'm used to from girls who are sleeping in my bed."

"I'm pretty sure there are plenty of girls who sleep in

your bed who smell like dead fish, at least somewhere," I shot back.

He let out a faint huff of a laugh, one that surprised me and stroked a sudden glow in my chest. "Get in the shower."

I took a step back. "Thank you, no. I'll wait."

"Get in the shower, Aurora."

I shook my head, only to have him sweep me around the waist and push me under the water. I shoved back at him, only for him to grab my wrists and pin them above my head against the cool white marble as he pressed me against it, his body securing mine. His hard cock pressed against my stomach.

I should have been terrified, or at least angry. But Cain's bruisingly hard grip on my wrists hurt in a way that just flooded more depraved heat through my body.

His lips pressed my ear. "I'm being generous if I ask twice."

"You're a fucking monster."

His eyes smoldered down at me. "Takes one to know one."

Then his lips were on mine. He kissed me hard, his lips hot and claiming, his cock brushing between my thighs. He nipped my lower lip, trying to force my lips to open against his. My hips swayed toward his, even as I turned my head away, breaking the kiss.

His finger slid under the strap of my swimsuit and tugged. "Take it off."

I met his gaze. "No."

Why did it feel like a game to make him make me?

A dangerous game, sure, but that was the only kind I'd ever known all my life.

This was the first time I'd wanted to play.

He didn't hesitate this time, his fingers tightening

around the cord. For a second, it cut painfully into my skin. Then it snapped.

The hot spray of water ran over us both, beads of water trickling down his shoulders. His eyes were intense as he stared down at me. This time, he didn't bother to ask. His fingers found the waistband of my bikini bottoms and shoved them down, his thumb gliding over my cleft along the way, and the smallest gasp of desire escaped my lips. He watched my face as he pushed my swimsuit bottoms down my thighs, his hands hot against my bare skin.

He caught the back of my neck and pressed my head forward under the hot stream of water. I gasped, my back arching, every instinct sparking in panic. But then my face was out of the water, and I drew in a shaky breath as his fingers ran through my hair, the sweet, creamy scent of shampoo suds hanging in the air.

For a moment, with his fingers massaging against my scalp, his hot, hard body pressed against mine, I relaxed into him. I knew better. But for someone who had spent my whole life fighting every moment, there was something surreal and relaxing about Cain taking control.

He rinsed my hair out, the hot water streaming down my stomach and between my thighs, then said, "Turn around."

I didn't bother to respond. He grabbed the back of my neck and turned me into him, and I let out a gasp of surprise.

He was already kneeling in front of me, his hands stroking up my body, rubbing soap up my calves, my thighs—my knees pressed together in anticipation, but his thumb only seemed to graze between my thighs by accident, and yet a needy throb ran through my body. From the glint in his eyes as he rose, towering over me again, he saw it.

"You like having someone take care of you. You like

being told what to do," he said. "Even if you pretend you don't like to obey."

"I'm not pretending. And you're not—"

He cut me off, his lips pressing mine fiercely. I pushed him away, my hands gliding ineffectually up his wet shoulders. His knee stroked between my thighs, pushing them open as deftly as his tongue coaxed my lips open.

The Demon would've wanted me to kill him.

He grabbed my thighs, yanking my legs up around his waist. My fingernails bit into his shoulders as I clung to him, keeping myself from falling. And no matter what reason and logic screamed at me, I dragged him even closer with my thighs, grinding against him, wanting him inside me.

He carried me into the bedroom and tossed me down on the bed. Those keen blue eyes were intent on mine as he slid his hand between my thighs, his thumb gliding over my clit again, and my entire body responded to his touch.

"Just as I thought in the shower. You're all wet for me."

I shook my head, and a smile twisted his lips. "Fine, then. *Not* for me. I won't touch you, then."

"I don't want you to." I whispered so the lie wouldn't be as easy to hear.

He leaned over me, his lips so close to my ear—but not quite touching—that his breath teased my ear. "Bullshit."

This man was going to destroy me and maybe, after everything I'd been through, everything I'd put other people through, I wanted to be destroyed.

I turned my face, almost brushing my lips against his, but he pulled back faintly, his gaze smoldering.

Whatever he was going to say next was lost as the door flew open.

Stellan stood there, his face cold and beautiful as a statue's, only a flicker of rage lighting his eyes.

"What the fuck do you think you're doing?"

14

AURORA

For a few long seconds, Cain and Stellan stared at each.

"I know you're not talking to me," Cain said, his tone ice. "Because I love you like a brother, Stellan, but I'd still bury you."

The air between them seemed to crackle with dangerous energy, and I felt frozen between them, unable to move.

"Of course not," Stellan said, his voice equally cool. "I was talking to her. She and I have unfinished business."

Cain glanced me over, then said, "Well, you didn't want me to touch you, little devil. Looks like Stellan here is your savior."

He sauntered toward the door, and Stellan stepped aside. I hastily grabbed a blanket and dragged it around my shoulders, cinching it around my body.

Cain glanced over his shoulder, his eyes colliding with mine, and he had a look that I couldn't read. Then Stellan closed the door between us and leaned against it.

"Exactly what unfinished business do we have?" I demanded crisply. "Are you going to try a little harder to murder me this time?"

"I wasn't trying to murder you. I was trying to shock the truth from your lying lips for once." He stalked toward me, cocked his head as he studied me. There was a glimmer in his gaze that I couldn't read. "Somehow you're bringing even our resident psychopath under your spell."

"I thought you were all psychopaths." I leaned back on the bed, cocking one arm to pull a pillow under my head. I was good at reading people, and he didn't bleed *dangerous* tonight. Not anymore.

Maybe after tonight, he was beginning to realize I wasn't his enemy.

"Likely," he admitted. "But Cain is the worst of us."

Not for me. For me, Stellan was the worst.

His accusation that *I* was the reason The Demon took Sophia still lingered.

One night, The Demon had called me down to dinner. I'd walked into the dining room to see him sitting at the dinner table, bowls of fettuccine and salad greens on the table, a glass of wine in front of him. Strains of Vivaldi filled the air. There'd been a dinner guest to his right, a bound and gagged man who begged me with his eyes to help him, even as I turned away.

Those types of men were how he'd first introduced me to his work. He said they were serial killers and child rapists. He said I was making the world a better, safer place for kids like me when I helped him.

Later on, though, there came others.

The Demon had toyed with a cell phone, and my heart had stopped when he pushed it toward me.

It was my *real* cell phone, my secret, not the one he'd given me.

Sophia's last message glowed on the screen. *I can't believe you would kiss my brother! He's so gross! :p*

"I don't want to fight in front of our guest," The Demon had said, "but you have a lot of explaining to do, young lady."

I'd convinced The Demon that Stellan meant nothing to me, and I'd helped flay our dinner guest so The Demon wouldn't hurt Stellan and Sophia. I'd convinced The Demon to move not long after.

They'd been this brief, bright spot in my life, and I'd left them behind even though it tore my heart out. My best friend and my first love.

"Hello." Stellan snapped his fingers in my face. "Are you still with me, Aurora?"

"Unfortunately," I said. Sometimes a good dissociative episode was all a girl had, but that wasn't happening tonight. "I'd never have hurt Sophia. If The Demon had... I would've killed him."

I should have killed him instead of setting him up to finally be caught. I'd been stupid, sentimental, just because he was my only family.

Stellan stared at me, something flickering in his gaze, as if his warring feelings were playing out in front of me. I held my breath, hoping he'd believe me.

I could tolerate everyone else believing the worst about me.

But I couldn't stand for Stellan to believe I'd hurt Sophia.

Some of the tension relaxed from his shoulders, and relief spiked in my chest. He believed me.

"What are you doing with Cain?" There was a raw edge of jealousy in his voice.

"I don't know." Honest answer. There was something raw between Cain and me that seemed to bring me back to life.

But when I looked into Stellan's eyes, I felt the same

butterflies in my stomach I had as a stupid lovestruck teenager. He sat on the edge of the bed, a frown dimpling the space between his dark eyebrows.

"Why'd you leave without saying goodbye?"

"I thought I was protecting you."

"You weren't."

I bit my lower lip, right before he leaned over and kissed the corner of my mouth. His fingers gripped my chin as he pulled away, his gaze burning into mine.

"You're mine," he said. "Not Cain's. Mine."

I couldn't say a word. I didn't think he'd wanted me, and I didn't want to ruin the spell between the two of us. Tonight felt like a pause on whatever else was happening between us, a return to the past that I'd thought I could never get back. My breath froze in my chest.

Then his lips crashed into mine. He pressed me back against the bed, kissing me until I was breathless, and not stopping then either. His mouth was hungry, and his hands swept down my body, pushing the blanket away from me.

His heated touch swept over my skin, igniting me, and I let out a gasp as his hands delved between my thighs. "Stellan, you can't."

The Demon would've killed him for touching me. The Demon had always had people who worshipped him. What if his reach was so long that even from prison, he could hurt anyone who dared to love me?

"I can," Stellan breathed against my lips. "Say you're not mine, Delilah."

"I don't want you to get hurt... that's why I ran."

"I'd say my chances of not getting hurt went to zero the moment you walked into my life anyway." He grabbed my thighs and yanked me toward him, pulling me lower on the bed. His grip on my thighs was bruisingly hard, but my thighs still tightened, squeezing greedily on nothing, wanting more of him.

"The Demon would never let me..." I shook my head, trying to push him away even as I wanted to pull him closer. "Let go of me, Stellan."

"He took that away from me too," he said. "And I'm taking it back. You were always supposed to be mine, and I was supposed to be your first. Not fucking *Cain.*"

I struggled against him, pushing against his chest...but he didn't move away, he didn't even pause.

"Stop," I begged, a flicker of uncertainty strumming through me. He would stop, right?

"Mine," he murmured, as if to himself.

His head dipped between my thighs. He licked down my pussy, sensation flooding my core, and my thighs shuddered around his head. He settled in, his tongue thrusting inside me, his mouth working against my clit.

I froze, overcome by the sensation, by the vulnerability of being spread in front of him like this, no matter how much I wanted him, but he wrapped his powerful arms around my thighs, preventing me from pulling away no matter how much my legs began to shake and my hips buck.

As his mouth worked against me steadily, I fell apart, the beautiful room around us fracturing. My back arched, my fingers gliding through my hair, and I could feel him watching me. I could've sworn for a second that it was my dark, silky hair that I was touching, not the white-blond I was sporting now. I could've sworn for a second that we were back in the grass where we used to kiss. Then it was gone, and I was snapping back into the present moment, moaning his name as my orgasm crested.

Stellan straightened, one hand still gripping my thigh, his gaze on mine. His jaw worked angrily, as if he'd just come back to reality, as if he'd realized what he'd just done.

Maybe he got lost between the past and the present sometimes too.

He turned and strode abruptly from the room, letting the door slam shut behind him.

I turned onto my side, pulling the blankets up to cover me again, my clit still swollen and tender. When I squeezed my eyes shut, I couldn't stop picturing how The Demon had obsessed about my virginity. Once a man had stared at me on the street, cat-called me and made lewd comments. I hadn't realized The Demon was watching me then until he brought me down to the basement and the man was there, and The Demon made me punish him.

I'd known he would do the same thing to Stellan if he knew.

And yet, I couldn't stop myself from imagining what it would be like to have Stellan and Cain and Remington and Pax, to lose myself to their hands and mouths.

There was a knock on the door. For once, it didn't fly open immediately, either.

"Are you ready to go back?" Pax asked quietly through the door. "We docked."

"Yes," I said. The night had been a blur, and I needed space to begin making sense of it.

"Some of your clothes are in the closet," Pax said.

In disbelief, I stood and went to the closet. A few of the new things the guys had bought me were hanging there, including a frilly pair of lace underwear and a bra that was not substantial enough to be much help.

"What were you guys planning tonight?" I asked, but there was no answer from the other side of the door.

I wasn't sure how much they were scheming or how much they were winging it, just like me.

15

AURORA

"Get up." The command roused me from a deep sleep, but instincts had me shooting up in bed, looking manically around me for whatever threat was in my room. Something else The Demon had taught me.

I didn't know how I'd fallen asleep in the first place. I'd been laying on my stomach working on homework and then...

I relaxed only slightly when I realized that it was Cain who'd given the order. He was leaning against my door with his arms crossed, his eyes caressing my skin and all that was showing as a result of the boy short underwear and tank top I'd been sporting while studying. I would've started covering more skin, in case of instances like this when they barged into my room unannounced, but it was so freaking hot in this room. Part of me suspected that they'd done something to the air in here, because it was the only uncomfortable room in the whole building. But my pride had kept me from saying anything.

Hence why I was practically naked at the moment.

"Get dressed," Cain ordered, throwing something at me. I

looked down at the clothes in confusion. There was a pair of leggings that looked like they were made out of leather, and then some kind of scrap of cloth that I assumed was supposed to be a top.

"What is this for?" I asked, pulling the blanket at the end of my bed over my lap to try and cover myself up at least a little bit.

"I don't think you need to bother covering up anything. Is there anything on your body that I haven't seen yet?" he commented with a grin.

I threw the clothes back at him, ignoring his comment. Because he was right. "I'm not going anywhere with you. I have a math test that I have to study for. Thanks to Remington following me around all day, I've had a little bit of trouble concentrating in my classes."

"Not my problem, little devil. Now get dressed. We're going to be late."

I folded my arms in front of my chest, lifting up my chin defiantly in a way that brought sparks to his eyes. Despite the fact that he seemed to love when people obeyed him, I think he got off more on forcing them to.

"I know you're dying to see Paxton fight. You're getting your chance tonight."

Something inside of me did perk up at that. Those unbidden images of fist hitting flesh, sweat and blood flying around the room, the grunts of pain...they completely filled my head.

I got up off the bed, still holding the blanket in front of me, trying to act disinterested even if I was anything but.

"I'll meet you outside the hallway after I get dressed," I told him primly.

Cain didn't make any attempt to move. He continued to lean against the door like he was in no hurry to go anywhere. His confidence was overwhelming. It flooded the entire room, like you could breathe it in, be suffocated by it. Its effect on me varied from day-to-day. Some days it pushed my confidence even higher, while other times it was all I could do to keep from feeling inferior. I'm sure he had that effect on everyone based on what I'd seen around campus.

Cain was dressed in dark jeans that had been artfully torn in that way that made you know they cost a pretty penny. He was wearing a fitted black Henley that showcased every muscle on his body, and made his golden features stand out even more. His hair was pushed back perfectly, and I had the insane urge to drag my hands through it, to make him look a little bit less perfect so that people could at least have a hint of the imperfection lurking inside of him.

"You have two minutes," he drawled. "Probably not enough time for you to waste it on continuing to eye fuck me."

He threw the clothes back at me and I let them fall to my feet. In a rush of ridiculous defiance, I dropped the blanket and slipped off the flimsy tank top that I was wearing, despite the fact that I wasn't wearing a bra underneath. He shifted against the door and my eyes flicked downward to where I could see the hardening outline of his dick. There was no hiding that monster in his jeans.

I bent down and picked up the top first, inwardly gulping when I realized it was basically just a bra with underwire...not that I wasn't being extremely bold with my body right now.

Keeping eye contact with him, I slid it on, sliding each strap up slowly in an effort to torture him like he tortured me every day.

I didn't know who I was in moments like these. I've never been particularly body self-conscious. I'd been so busy surviving that I hadn't had time to think about things like if I was skinny enough or if I was pretty enough.

But I'd definitely never acted like this before. The Demon would have killed me.

After I put on the bra/halter top... or whatever it was I was wearing, I grabbed the leather pants and slipped into the bathroom to finish changing, ignoring Cain's soft laughter that followed me inside. The leather jeans were so tight I felt like I should've slathered my skin with oil in order to get them on, but somehow after a combination that consisted of hopping around and pulling, I did it.

I looked into the mirror and was a little shocked at my appearance. The clothing I was wearing fit me perfectly, showcasing every asset I had. My boobs looked good, I had to admit that, and the top provided just enough coverage that I wasn't going to have to worry about a nip slip the whole night. My hair was wavy from being up in a bun for a couple of hours, but I thought it looked pretty good.

For the first time in a while, I almost looked alive. There was a flush to my cheeks, I'm sure from the impromptu strip show I'd just performed, and a liveliness in my gaze.

"Not bad," I whispered to myself.

"You've got one second," Cain's voice called out to me. I rolled my eyes at my reflection, before reluctantly heading back into the bedroom.

Of course, Cain was no longer against the door; instead, he was lounging on my bed. I'm sure that intoxicating scent of his would be embedded in my sheets. I really needed to find where the laundry room was in this place, because the last thing I wanted was to be drenched in Cain's scent when I went to bed.

Cain's hot gaze licked at my skin as he took my outfit in.

"You'll do," he commented dryly, but he couldn't hide the heat in his gaze. We both knew I looked good.

Cain hitched himself off the bed effortlessly before strolling out the door without another word, apparently expecting me to follow him... like a dog.

We walked down the long hallways, and as usual, a shiver ran down my spine. I rarely saw the other members of the society, which I wasn't complaining about, but this place felt old, and sometimes it felt like I was being watched. And not just by the cameras that seemed to be everywhere.

I've never really liked old buildings. I could appreciate their history, but as usual, my past made it impossible for me to ever feel comfortable in them. For a period of time, The Demon had owned an old house in a quiet village in England. The cottage was apparently three hundred years old, not ancient for England, but old enough to have stories imprinted in its walls. Three hundred years of pain and loss combined with what The Demon had done while we lived there had ensured that I slept very little.

I quickened my steps so I was right behind Cain, and either he didn't notice or he decided not to comment on my pace since he was silent until we got to a door in a hallway I hadn't explored yet. He opened the door, and all I saw was the top of a few steps and then nothing but darkness. He began to go down the set of stairs, but I didn't follow, shifting uneasily instead as I willed myself to not be afraid.

Cain stopped a few steps down before turning to look at me.

"What's the holdup?" he asked, annoyed. Then recognition flared in his gaze, and he grinned cruelly. "That's right, Paxton said you were scared of the dark," he commented.

For some reason, hurt flared through me at the idea that Paxton had told them about that. Had he also told them about our conversation that night? A conversation that seemed so hazy and unreal in my memory, I wasn't sure if it was real.

"Come on, little devil. There's nothing down here scarier than me." He eyed me again, and his grin widened. "And maybe nothing scarier than you as well."

I felt a little sick as I followed him down the staircase, knowing that there was definitely a light switch somewhere around here and he was just intent on torturing me.

I kept a few steps away from him, just in case he decided to do something like push me down the stairs, but after what seemed like a million steps, we made it to the bottom, where a light immediately clicked on, showcasing an array of cars that all belonged in one of the Fast and the Furious movies. It honestly made me a little bit sick how decadent this place was. What did college students, even *rich* college students, need with a secret underground garage filled with luxury vehicles that I wasn't even sure some celebrities could afford?

We passed an Audi R8 that gave me major *Fifty Shades of Grey* vibes to where Cain's McLaren was waiting. I wondered idly what kind of cars the others had.

He unlocked it and I opened up the passenger door immediately, remembering how annoying he'd been the last time we'd gotten into the car. Cain grinned at me like he was remembering the same thing.

Asshole.

"You ever going to let me drive this thing?" I asked, only a little bit joking.

Driving was one of the few things in life that had ever given me... joy. Strangely enough, even though I'd been taught to drive by The Demon, he hadn't been able to taint it with all the bad memories he'd tainted everything else with. I'd actually learned to drive when I was ten, which sounded crazy even just thinking that, but it had happened.

The Demon was determined not to get caught, and even though he was meticulous in covering his tracks, he always had getaway plans ready for us, just in case. And so he taught me how to drive as early as he thought possible. I still remembered what it felt like as that little girl to put my hands on the steering wheel for the first time. Even with The Demon sitting right next to me, it tasted like freedom, or at least the possibility of freedom.

It was one of the only times that it felt like The Demon had actually been proud of me because I'd taken to it like a fish in water. He'd taught me to drive stick first, making manual a no-brainer. Sometimes he'd taken me to roads so out in the middle of nowhere that it was next to impossible for a cop to spot us. And I'd drive so fast it actually felt like I was flying.

"In your dreams, little devil," I belatedly heard Cain say. And I realized that I'd gotten lost in my thoughts once again.

"I'll let you touch my stick, though," Cain said, and it was almost embarrassing how long it took for me to get what he was saying.

“That was bad, even for you," I told him. "You really need to work on your lines."

"That wasn't a line, Aurora. There's not a girl who's been in this car who hasn't desperately wanted to touch my stick... wanted to lick it. You can do that too, you know. Might help you feel like you were getting in with the student population."

I immediately wanted out of the car, because the idea of all the sex acts that had probably been done in this car made me a little bit sick. Or really sick actually.

“What's the matter, princess? It doesn't turn you on to

think of some girl sitting in the same seat as where you're sitting now, drooling over my dick?"

I shifted uncomfortably in my seat, not wanting to even think about how heat flared to life between my legs whenever he talked like that. I already knew that there were a million things wrong with me. I didn't want to add one more thing to the list.

"Tell me about the fight tonight," I ordered, wanting to push the conversation as far away from the current topic as possible.

Cain had finally started the car and driven forward until a panel in the wall opened up like we were in some sort of spy movie. He started down an enclosed road lit by soft lights embedded in the rock around it, taking a few twists and turns before we made our way to the surface where the road popped out into what must've been the woods right outside of campus.

He pressed a button on the steering wheel and the dark, erotic sound of Nine Inch Nails started to pour from the speakers. He didn't bother answering me, and I didn't try again, just content that at least we weren't talking about sex. We were on the unpaved road in the forest for just a couple of seconds until it popped out onto the main road I recognized as being just south of campus.

The town was quiet, just a few couples walking down the sidewalk here and there, and all the stores had closed already. As you would expect in a sleepy college town like this. We were out of town soon enough, driving down the highway at a speed that would get most lowly mortals pulled over, or even thrown in jail.

Something I suspected that Cain and the others didn't have to worry about.

I closed my eyes, enjoying the sensation of going so fast.

We drove for at least a half an hour, and Cain didn't say a word to me.

It was probably the only time I'd almost enjoyed myself in his presence.

Well, except for that first time, a voice reminded me. *And the shower...*

But I didn't think about that. Or at least I tried not to.

The car began to slow down as we entered a town that had seen better days. It seemed like it was mostly made up of dilapidated industrial buildings, and I was debating if now was a good time to pull out the knife I'd hidden at the top of my pants. This looked like the sort of place where you bury dead bodies.

And, obviously, I was an expert on that.

Rocks pinged under the car as Cain turned into the empty gravel parking lot of one of the buildings, and he grunted in displeasure at the idea of his precious car getting dinged. He kept driving through the parking lot until he turned down the side of the building where one other car was parked.

There was no one around, and I frowned, suspicion beginning to churn in my gut.

Without a word, he shut off the car and got out.

16

AURORA

This was it. This was where he was going to kill me. Or maybe they had a plan to try and torture me for information about Stellan's sister. Either way, that shit wasn't happening tonight.

I grabbed my knife from where I'd stashed it in the top of my pants and then opened my car door, keeping Cain in my sights at all times while looking around to make sure no one else was going to jump out of the shadows to grab me.

Only problem was, there were a lot of shadows to watch out for.

Cain stared at me, a little smirk on his face like I was amusing him. "You're making me late."

I scoffed and walked around the door, stopping whenwas a few feet away. "Lead the way," I said, gesturing forward.

He moved fast. Before I could blink, he'd grabbed me and pulled me against his body.

"A little cliche, don't you think? If I really wanted to kill you, I wouldn't do something as expected as take you to a place like this. I'm offended you think so little of me. I told you what we were doing tonight," he murmured in my ear as his hand tightened around the back of my neck.

I slid the knife up until it was resting right on his hardening dick. I pressed in, just enough so he could feel exactly what I was threatening him with.

I had to hand it to him, the slight widening of his eyes was the only tell he gave that I had surprised him.

I couldn't help but be shocked that the motherfucker's dick was getting harder. I'd have thought he'd be a shrinking violet with his appendage threatened, but the violence of the situation seemed to be turning him on. I pressed the knife in further, just so he would understand that I wasn't joking.

"Forgive me if I don't trust anything that comes out of your mouth," I told him sarcastically, but there was no missing that my voice sounded suspiciously breathy as well.

Like I was being turned on as well.

I was disgusted with both of us.

Cain pulled me closer to him, pressing the edges of the knife into both of us. "You may have stumbled onto my new favorite kink," he said, before licking the side of my face.

"Ugh," I hissed before pulling the knife up so it actually sliced into the skin showing between his shirt and his low-slung pants.

His nostrils flared and his eyes heated, but that was all I got. I pushed away from him and, surprisingly, he let me go. "I'm sure I could make it hurt for you, kink or not," I threatened.

Cain slowly slid a thumb across the drops of blood trickling from the superficial cut I'd made and then stuck it into his mouth, licking the blood off seductively.

I resisted the urge to squirm. I wasn't going to admit to

anyone, not even myself, that a part of me wished I'd been the one sucking the blood off his finger.

Cain just laughed before he grabbed my arm that wasn't holding the knife and began to pull me forward. I wrenched my arm away from him just for the heck of it and followed a few steps behind him with my chin up in the air.

He led me down the side of the warehouse and around the back of another, and that's when I heard it, the faint pulsing beat of music coming from within the enormous warehouse in front of us. We turned another corner and I saw a guy dressed in all black leaning against a door while he smoked a cigarette. There was graffiti sprayed all over the wall behind him, a giant skull with a gaping mouth...and a cock.

Because graffiti artists were, for the most part, nothing if not predictable when it came to their penchant for dicks.

There were still no cars around, but you could clearly hear the beat of music from within. The guy spotted us and immediately became alert, pushing away from the wall and throwing the cigarette on the ground frantically like he was afraid that Cain was going to push it down his throat.

Which was actually a good probability now that I thought of it.

I heard the sound of footsteps, and I looked around to see three others dressed in black emerging from random spots around the building. I tensed, wondering if they were going to ambush us or something before Cain gave them all a chin lift that sent them scurrying back to wherever they'd been hiding.

"Everything good?" Cain growled.

"Yes-ss, sir," the guy said excitedly, like he was hoping that Cain would pat him on the head like a dog now that his cigarette was safely stowed away.

Cain grunted in response, and I watched in disgust as the guy's whole demeanor crashed.

The guys' gaze flicked to me and his eyes widened as he took in the outfit that Cain had put me in.

"Want to keep your eyes?" Cain asked cruelly.

A little squeak escaped from the sniveling peon in front of us and he quickly averted his gaze, staring at the ground like it held one of the wonders of the universe.

Cain pulled open the door and then grabbed my arm again, dragging me into the building behind him. We entered a small room, not unlike the entrance to the Sphinx, and there was another door across from us where another guy dressed in all black had been standing. This guy looked a bit more formidable than the one outside, but he reacted the same way, standing at attention and watching Cain closely like he could attack at any moment.

“Everything’s good. Pax’s about to fight,” the guy hurriedly said before Cain had to ask anything.

Cain nodded and pulled me towards the door. The door opened up, showcasing a giant staircase comprised of metal stairs that had been liberally painted with what appeared to be black tar. The music was blasting up to us and there was literal steam wafting up as if the gates of hell were just a few feet below us. It sounded like it was packed; people were screaming and yelling. Despite the fact that I’d had no intention of being here tonight, I couldn't quell the curl of excitement in my gut.

"Ready, little devil?" Cain asked, holding out his hand. And even though I hated that name—loathed it, in fact—I put my hand in his and started down the stairs with him.

The metal door slammed behind us and I jumped, adrenaline coursing through me because of the unexpectedness of the night. I knew how to flay a man into a hundred pieces...but I'd never really lived.

I wasn't sure if an illegal underground fight exactly constituted "living," but it sure as hell felt like it at this moment.

The music and the crowd grew louder and louder as we got down the steps.

My jaw dropped when I saw all the people in this place. It said a lot about the organizer of this event that I hadn't had any idea anyone was even around while standing on the outside of the warehouse.

People of all ages were compacted like sardines, writhing against each other as a DJ spun a heavy, thumping club beat. There was a large roped off ring in the center of the room where I assumed fights took place. Above the ring someone had built glass-enclosed rooms where you could see people walking around there.

Probably for the high rollers. If that was a thing in real life. It had at least always been a thing in the books I'd read.

"Who organizes this?" I asked as we stood there at the bottom of the stairs just taking everything in.

"Who do you think?" Cain responded with a smirk as he began to walk through the crowd without a look back.

Of course *they* were in charge of this thing. I don't know why I hadn't considered that before. I watched, half in awe, half in annoyance as the swarming masses of people parted for Cain, like he was Moses parting the Red Sea.

He didn't even have to say anything. The combination of his reputation and the magnetism that came off of him in waves was enough. No one stood a chance.

The crowd closed behind him and I belatedly realized that I needed to hurry after him or I was going to be lost in here.

I began to make my way after him, and unfortunately for me, the crowd had no intention of moving aside like they had with Cain. It took an elbow to the head before I realized I was going to have to get aggressive to make it through the crowd alive. I ducked and dipped and elbowed my way forward until Cain was in my sights once again. He came to a stop, and for a moment I thought that he was waiting for me, but of course that wasn't it. I watched as some girl wearing what looked like an actual American flag wrapped around her threw herself at Cain, wrapping her arms around him and beginning to pepper his face with kisses that he did nothing to stop. My gut clenched and I turned, not wanting to watch.

Just then, the lights began to flicker and the music changed to a heavy club remix of "Enter Sandman" by Metallica. The song began to blast through the speakers. I hadn't thought it was possible for the crowd to get louder, but they did.

I felt a hand grab my arm, and out of instinct I yanked it away, only to realize that it was Cain.

"Stay by me," he growled grumpily, the girl nowhere to be seen. He looked perturbed like I was the one who had gotten distracted by a mini dress. He glanced over my shoulder and gritted his teeth in a warning glare. I looked backwards and saw a group of guys looking suspiciously at the ceiling, their faces drained of all color.

I sighed and rolled my eyes, because really, this was getting ridiculous. I'd literally watched this guy get a blowjob in front of me, and now he was getting annoyed by some creeps staring at my ass.

Fucking hell.

He began walking again, this time holding me tightly so I couldn't get lost even if I wanted to. Cain wasn't paying any attention to the ring as we walked past it, but I sure was. A man dressed in a sparkly black blazer, bright red Doc Martens, and a bright green Mohawk that stretched out farther than seemed possible thanks to the existence of gravity had stepped out into the center ring, holding a diamond encrusted microphone.

"Are you ready for tonight, assholes?" he screamed loudly into the microphone. The crowd's shouts intensified, and I winced, convinced I was going to be deaf after this. I held my free hand against my ear like that would somehow block out the sound.

"I can't hear you," he screamed again.

The crowd was deafening in its response, and he grinned wickedly as he gazed out over them like they were his loyal subjects.

The ringmaster proceeded to announce that someone nicknamed "The Skull Crusher" was about to fight someone named "Fury", obviously not the headliners of the show with names like that, as Cain led me up the staircase on the opposite side of the warehouse where we'd come in. The stairs led up to the glass-enclosed rooms that I'd noticed when we'd first come in, because of course Cain was going to be one of the *high rollers*.

We got to the top of the stairs and Cain opened a heavy glass door, stepping inside the room, dragging me right behind him. For a second there was blissful silence, and I closed my eyes and almost moaned with relief at having a second of peace and quiet.

But then I opened my eyes and immediately began wishing that I was back down with the crowd when I saw who was in the room.

Remington and Stellan were there, of course, along with some of the guys I remembered from the party at the football frat house. And some of the guys I'd seen walking in the halls at the Sphinx were there, too. Of course, there was also what looked like half of the cheerleading squad draped in the laps of the various guys.

Basically, most of my least favorite people from the school were in the room.

I told myself it wasn't relief I was feeling when I saw that Remington and Stellan didn't have any girls hanging over them despite the longing and desperate glances being thrown their way.

Remington shot me a smirk when he saw me looking, but Stellan pretended that I didn't exist.

Which was fine, I told myself.

"Why did you bring The Demon's daughter?" a guy named Jake, I think, called out to Cain.

"Hoping she'll get annoyed at one of you assholes and stab someone," Cain responded with a blank face.

Uneasy laughter filled the room. Obviously they weren't sure if he was joking or not. And I wasn't sure either.

Noise from the crowd made it into the room, and my attention went to the ring right below us where two fighters dressed in tiny shorts had just entered. I had to admit that the view from up here was amazing. Down there I would've been struggling to see even a glimpse of the fighters. Up here, I could see everything.

Plus, there were snacks.

Thinking I had a second before the fight started, since the two guys in the ring seemed to be much more interested in peacocking around each other in front of the adoring crowd than actually throwing fists, I went over to the bar on the side of the room that was loaded down with all the snacks a girl could want...

Or at least a girl like me.

My mouth watered as I looked over the trays loaded with buffalo wings, Texas cheese fries, and fried pickles...which were the shining stars of the snacks, obviously.

I was in the process of loading a plate when a girl sidled up next to me. I glanced at her out of the corner of my eye while simultaneously going for an eggroll. She looked too perfect to be real. Long black hair that hung in a shiny curtain behind her, a red bandeau top and black leather miniskirt that showcased a perfect body. Her lips were painted a bright red color, and when I looked over at her, she gave me a smile that didn't reach her eyes, showing teeth so perfect they couldn't be real.

She grabbed some carrot sticks and put them on a plate. It was pretty obvious that she'd just grabbed them to try and have an excuse to talk to me. I decided to throw her a bone and smiled at her. A little smile, though.

"Hey," I said, because a brilliant conversationalist I was not.

"I wasn't expecting to see you here tonight," she said in a sweet voice.

I cocked an eyebrow at her, not sure why she would or wouldn't be expecting me to be anywhere. I'd never seen her before in my life. The only reason I even knew she was on the cheerleading team was because of the bright red cheerleaders' jacket she had draped over her arm.

"Here I am," I responded with another tight smile, picking up my plate and turning to walk away.

She grabbed my arm, her bright red nails—or should I say talons—digging into my skin. I sighed and rolled my eyes, for a second missing Jenna even though she'd dropped me the second the news had come out about my father.

I didn't blame her for that. It's not like I had gotten plastic surgery for nothing.

But still, it had been nice to have one girlfriend who'd seemed genuine. I hadn't had one since...

No. I wouldn't think about her right now. *I couldn't.*

"So which one are you fucking?" she asked through gritted teeth, bringing me out of my dark thoughts and into the present. Of course I wasn't surprised by her question. I knew every girl in the room was wondering that, judging by the mixed stares of loathing and curiosity I'd been getting since the moment I'd stepped into the room.

If they only knew that the guys were more likely to torture me then fuck me, I'm sure they wouldn't be feeling so territorial.

"None of them," I told her. She scoffed and rolled her eyes.

"Why would you even lie about that? I fucked Stellan and I'm still talking about it a year later." She laughed like she'd just told the best joke ever.

But I just felt sick. Unbidden images of her perfect features wrapped around the boy I'd once loved filled my head, and suddenly, not even the perfect fried pickles on my plate held any charm.

"You wish you'd fucked me," Stellan's voice interjected from behind me.

I watched as the girl flushed so red that she almost matched the color of her lips.

"Stellan," she responded in a breathy voice. "I'm not sure what you heard."

"Chlamydia isn't my thing, Vicky. I suggest you stop telling people we've fucked," he told her in a smug voice.

"Vicky" burst into tears and ran towards the door, throwing it open and barreling down the stairs so fast that it was a testament to her heel walking abilities that she didn't fall head over feet.

I popped a pickle into my mouth, suddenly feeling ravenous again.

"You shouldn't let them walk all over you," he remarked, and I gave him a hollow shrug, looking out the window to where the two fighters had started to tear into each other.

"Whatever," he snapped before stalking away.

Sighing because I'd somehow made it safely from both of them, I grabbed a couple of delicious looking brownies and walked over to the window so that I could watch the fight.

"Watch," a voice murmured, and I jumped, spilling a few cheese fries. I snarled at Remington, who was standing far too close for comfort, and he grinned a perfect smile before pressing a button on the wall.

The roar of the crowd immediately assaulted my ears, and I watched in amazement as the top part of the glass began to retract up, giving us a completely unfiltered view.

“Wow,” I said, impressed, certainly not expecting that in a warehouse that, from the outside, looked like it was going to fall apart at any moment.

“So easily impressed, princess,” Remington purred, and I sighed as I put some more food in my mouth, moaning softly because of how fucking good it tasted.

I winced as the guy wearing a tiny pair of red shorts leveled a shot right at the mouth of the other guy, the guy who called himself "Fury" if I was remembering correctly. I saw actual teeth fly out of his mouth, and then he fell face forward into the mat. "The Skull Crusher" guy began to dance around as the announcer jumped into the ring. I watched in shock as he picked up his foot and then slammed it down on the back of the fallen fighter, a move that stirred the crowd into a frenzy.

"Jack has always had a thing for the dramatics,"

Remington said with a bloodthirsty grin, obviously enjoying the show.

Two guys dressed in black jumped in the ring and dragged the guy off while the victor continued to dance around.

Mohawk guy—Jack, apparently—let him celebrate for a moment more before shooing him away. "The Skull Crusher" jumped off the ring and the eager crowd caught him, dragging him away from the ring.

"Thomas is going to be pretty good someday," Remington interjected, like he'd taken it upon himself to be my own personal fight guide for the night.

"Hmm," I responded non-committedly.

"What?" he asked.

"Nothing."

"No, tell me. You obviously have something on your mind."

"Can you just go away?" I moaned as I tried to enjoy my last fried pickle.

"No. That wouldn't be fun at all," replied Remington, stealing the pickle before I could put it into my mouth.

I scowled at him.

“He's sloppy,” I finally commented with a sigh. “He's right hand dominant, so he obviously made no effort to do anything with his left. Any good fighter is going to destroy him as soon as they figure it out. I mean, did you see his form when he tried to hit with his left? A child with one class would have better form than that.”

I glanced at him, a little embarrassed about how passionate I'd just sounded. Remington was staring at me inscrutably. He was probably the easiest to read of the four of them, wearing his feelings on his sleeve much more often. But I couldn't read him now.

"Noted," he finally answered, and I shifted uneasily, wondering what he was thinking.

Just then, Jack announced the next fight, and I pulled away from Remington to settle into the far side of the comfy looking couch that abutted up to the open window. The couch shifted, and I looked over to see Remington settling in next to me.

"Don't you have a chick to go fuck?" I asked, gesturing to the eager girls behind me. There were three currently wrapped around Cain because he apparently couldn't go five seconds without getting his balls caressed, and I was wondering if I could get away with dumping the hot queso on them.

At least he didn't look interested in any of them.

Not that I actually cared though.

"Looking a little green there," interjected Remington, and I blushed, embarrassed that he'd caught me staring at Cain.

"Don't worry, little devil. I won't tell Cain about your little crush. Just as long as you stare at me the same way," murmured Remington, leveling me with a look that was far too sexy.

"I don't know what you're talking about," I responded haughtily, shoving a brownie in his mouth so I could get him to stop talking.

Remington snorted and took the brownie out of his mouth right as the crowd roared again. I looked down at the ring and realized that I'd missed the start of the second fight. One of the guys was already laid out on the mat, his left leg twisted back at a grotesque angle that left no doubt it was broken.

"Fuck," muttered Remington as he jumped up from the couch. "He just lost me $20k."

My mouth dropped thinking about having the type of money to just throw $20k around like it was nothing on some fight.

"I'll expect a wire by tomorrow morning," Stellan called from across the room.

I looked over at him, and of course that was a mistake. He was grinning, and Stellan's smile...it had always done something to me. Something big. He'd never been one to gift it freely, so when you got a glimpse of it...you treasured it.

I was sad to say that the effect of his smile hadn't faded with time. Even after everything that had happened.

Our eyes clashed and his smile dropped, because that was all I did now...dragged happiness out of everything around me.

I turned my attention back to the ring where the loser of the fight was being dragged out roughly despite the fact that he obviously needed urgent medical attention.

The announcer stepped back into the ring, a bejeweled bowtie added to his ensemble for what I assumed was the start of the main event. He smoothed his mohawk back dramatically. "Should I give you peasants what you want?" he called out.

Evidently the crowd had no aversion to being called peasants. Their screams were so loud that the half of the glass wall still up in front of me shook so hard that I was afraid it was going to shatter.

"Come now, surely Paxton Jones deserves more than that, ladies and gents!"

A rush of excitement and adrenaline coursed through me, like I was the one about to fight. I watched as men dressed in black walked through the crowd, swiping cards and grabbing cash from the eager betters.

"I'm afraid our boy might have met his match tonight," Jack purred, and the crowd immediately started to boo, earning them a cheeky grin. "You don't think so? Not even against Kaplan Dale?"

The crowd appeared split on this one. Half seemed to boo as loud as they possibly could while the other half cheered like the Kaplan character was their god.

"Let's get our fighters out here!" Jack screamed, and the lights began to flash a myriad of colors while Nine Inch Nails began to play. I couldn't help but shoot a glance at Cain, remembering the charged car ride.

Cain didn't seem to be walking down memory lane like I was though; he was listening to a story that one of the guys from the Sphinx was telling him. He threw his head back and chuckled at whatever was being said. I squinted my eyes and really studied him.

Did everyone else not see it? Did they not see how his movements almost looked...rehearsed. Like he'd mastered the perfect response that he was supposed to give in social situations, but he didn't really mean it. The laugh had sounded right, and the relief in the other guy's face who'd been telling the story certainly seemed like he'd bought it. But if you really studied Cain, you'd see that there was a blankness in his gaze. There always was. Cain was always just going through the motions. And I couldn't help but wonder, who really was Cain? What was actually going on in that head of his?

All my thoughts about Cain disappeared as smoke began to pour out onto the ring and Paxton appeared. I was sure that I was drooling, along with every other woman and perhaps every man in the room. I'd seen him in the dim lighting the other night, and he'd been shirtless on the yacht party from hell, but I hadn't really *seen* him, not like this.

I'd felt his body pressed against mine, felt his hardness, heard the beating of his heart, but nothing could have prepared me for the perfection in front of me. He exemplified the human form, every muscle was perfectly outlined. I know that they said an eight pack was impossible, but Paxton clearly had one. Part of me wanted to jump over the glass wall and see if he'd let me lick them. He was wearing a pair of black shorts that basically amounted to glorified boxer briefs. And even though he was wearing a cup, there was no missing how huge Paxton was.

Various girls in the room were screaming, "Fuck me, Paxton." "Have my babies, Pax!" "I want you!"

Paxton didn't seem to be affected by the adulation being thrown his way. He surveyed the room like he was bored, like he was doing everyone a favor by being present. Which let's face it, he was, since he was giving everyone a view of that body.

He looked up just then, and our gazes met. He held eye contact with me, uncomfortably, long enough that people started to look up into the glass box to see exactly at who or what he was staring. He raised his massive hand and pointed at me before finally breaking contact and turning his attention back to the ring where his opponent had just appeared.

Nervous butterflies took flight, knocking around my insides as I pondered what had just happened, and what he'd just meant by pointing at me.

"Working your way through the ranks?" Stellan said coldly from beside me and I looked at him in confusion.

"What are you talking about?"

"He just dedicated the fight to you. Are you really that unobservant?"

I kept my face blank, my cheeks thankfully getting the

memo that now wasn't the time to blush. They were certainly testing my self-control, or maybe at this point Stellan had said so many mean things to me that I was becoming numb to it.

It was probably wishful thinking judging by the way my heart actually seemed to hurt from his cruelty.

I looked at Stellan wearily. When was he going to get tired of holding on to so much hate?

"Whatever you say, Stellan," I muttered, standing up from my seat and inching closer to the glass to make sure I didn't miss a thing. Stellan huffed and I heard him walk away. I realized then that I was setting myself up for something bad by hanging out over the glass if someone in the room decided to do harm me. I inched over to the wall so that I could see both the room and the fight, and was finally able to relax once I had everything in my sights.

Paxton's opponent was a beast. While Paxton's form was lean and perfectly cut, his opponent looked like he'd been on steroids his whole life. He was so huge it was almost cartoonish. He looked like he could lift a semi-truck without breaking a sweat. The butterflies only intensified, and I hated myself that I was actually worried about Paxton.

The crowd was chanting both fighters' names as Jack stepped to the side of the ring and raised his arm to signal the beginning of the fight. A bell clanged right as he lowered his hand, and Paxton's opponent immediately lunged toward him at full speed.

Paxton was faster and sharper, easily able to maneuver away from the guy's punch while leveling one of his own. He reared back and kicked the guy right in the gut, darting away before the fighter could retaliate.

Paxton looked...beautiful out there. It was almost as if he was performing an elaborate dance.

He was incredible. I obviously knew a lot about fighting and it was clear that Paxton Jones was a star. Although I could tell that Kaplan would be pretty good against most opponents, he looked like a lumbering troll out there compared to Paxton's movements. Paxton was cutting him down piece by piece, leveling hit after hit that continued to weaken and cripple Kaplan until he was a bleeding mess. Kaplan managed to get one hit in, striking Paxton right in the ribs, but Paxton didn't even flinch. In fact, the aftermath of the hit was the only time that Paxton didn't look bored during the whole fight. You could tell he'd savored that bite of pain, and I wondered if he hadn't let Kaplan hit him on purpose.

Cain was up against the glass, watching the fight closely, as was everyone else. The fight went on like that for what seemed like round after round. Paxton seemed to be toying with him, intentionally prolonging the fight. After the fifth round, it honestly seemed like a miracle that Kaplan was even standing. I wasn't sure how many brain cells he could still have after the last set of hits that Paxton had gotten in.

Cain leaned over the railing. "Finish him," he barked out in an authoritative voice that somehow cut through the noise of the crowd. Paxton clearly must've heard him, because all of a sudden he began leveling hits, faster and faster. Like a button had been pressed to push him into another level.

Kaplan began to sway in place, and I watched in lust-filled fascination as Paxton reared back and took him out with one last strike right to the nose. Blood splashed out all over the place, covering Paxton and setting my insides on fire. The announcer began to count down along with the crowd, and then it was done.

Paxton was the winner.

17

AURORA

Paxton held his hands up in the air, taking in the crowd's gleeful praise.

"Come on," said Remington, gesturing to where everyone was walking out towards the celebration that was starting. I followed the excited line of people, Remington keeping close behind me, so close that I could feel his breath tickling against my skin.

I was tempted to throw an elbow, but I refrained.

We made it down the stairs, led by Cain of course, and the crowd easily parted in front of our group as we made it over to the ring. Sweat was glistening all over Paxton's perfect body as he came over and did a fist bump with Cain and the others. Paxton and I locked eyes again, and I smiled at him, prepared to congratulate him on his amazing perfor-mance, but he looked quickly away, walking out of the ring and suddenly disappearing into the crowd before I could get a word out.

. . .

"WHERE'S HE GOING?" I asked Remington, thinking that it was odd he wasn't sticking around to celebrate longer. All around us the champagne was beginning to flow—the champagne and the drugs—like all the dealers had just been waiting in the wings for the aftermath of the fights.

Remington gave me a Cheshire cat grin. "He's just going to burn off some steam, I'm sure," he told me. "There's always a plethora of ladies waiting around the locker room for a chance with the victor."

My stomach felt like I'd swallowed a rock. I grinned weakly at Remington and he continued to smile at me all too knowingly, like he knew exactly the effect that his words had had on me.

Before I had a second to dwell on it for too much longer, an alarm sounded, echoing around the whole room and sending the crowd into panic.

"Fuck. Someone called the cops," said Remington, not sounding too upset about it.

Just as he said that, and I began to panic along with the crowd, loud footsteps pounded down the stairs from the main entrance where we'd come in, and police officers made their way into the room, yelling at everyone to freeze.

Fuck that. There was no way I was going to stick around to get picked up by the cops. Yes, I had perfect identification papers to go with my new face and name, but I was sure that one of the assholes around me would give me away in five seconds if given the chance. I'm sure the cops would like nothing more than to make my life even more miserable, even with all the help I'd given to pick up The Demon in the first place.

Nope, it wasn't happening.

"I'm getting out of here," I yelled at Remington. "Where are the other exits?"

Remington smirked and pointed to two doors across the way. I rolled my eyes and looked for Cain and Stellan, finally spotting them and seeing that they'd already started to head for completely different doors, confirming my gut feeling that Remington couldn't be trusted with helping me to get away from the police.

I punched Remington in the arm and headed after Cain and Stellan, elbowing a couple of people away just in case they got any bright ideas to get me in trouble. Cain and Stellan went to a door underneath the staircase that led to the glass viewing boxes and disappeared inside.

The police were making their way through the crowd, so I picked up my pace, making it to the door and getting inside as well. The staircase was dimly lit, and I took the steps quickly, wondering why Remington hadn't tried to follow.

I gasped in relief when I made it to the top of the stairs and the door led out to the chilly night air. This part of the warehouse was empty, with no one around. I could hear the din of the police sirens from somewhere on the other side of the building, so I took off in the opposite direction, trying to find Cain's car. I went down an alleyway and found myself by the road, only to see Cain's car driving towards me, Stellan in the passenger seat. Stellan saluted me as the car flew past, leaving me stuck in who knows where without any means of transportation.

I sighed, knowing I had a long night ahead of me trying to figure out how to get back to campus.

I should've been furious, but I couldn't find it in myself to be that mad. Images of the fight played in my head, and a shiver that had nothing to do with the coldness of the night passed down my spine as I thought about how Paxton had looked in the ring.

Yes, I should have been furious, but some part of me, a big part, thought that perhaps it had all been worth it. Just to see that.

❧

Remington

I'd been dropped off by the cops at the steps of my father's mansion over an hour ago, and here I sat, waiting outside his office like an errant schoolboy. It was all an enormous inconvenience, but I'd brought it upon myself. I could've easily slipped away with the others, but sometimes I couldn't help but rebel when I had the chance.

Obviously, there was no way that the cops were *actually* going to take me in once they realized who I was, but I knew that it would have annoyed my father to have his son dropped off in front of the mansion in a cop car for anyone to see. Not that there was really anyone around at 3 AM, but my father wouldn't care about that.

Our long-time butler, Paul, opened the door to the study and stared down at me disapprovingly. "Your father will see you now," he said disdainfully, as if I was the one who kept him at his beck and call twenty-four seven.

"Good to see you too, Paul," I said with a smirk as I ambled past him, in no hurry for the lecture I was about to endure. It was only recently that these visits had just been lectures; growing up they'd been much different. But no one who knew Senator Taylor, the finest politician that the state had ever seen, and current Majority Leader of the United States Senate, would ever suspect him of the things he did...on a daily basis.

"Stop," Paul ordered, and I gritted my teeth as Paul walked over to me and waved a metal detector down my front, back, and sides. Paul holstered the metal detector in his belt and then began to personally pat me down. I winced when he brushed against my dick a few too many times. I would have killed him, but Paul was one of the many things I had to put up with to keep my little brother and sister safe.

Finally, the sexual assault/strip search was done and Paul ushered me into the office.

I walked in, feeling the need to wash my skin in bleach, and immediately came to a screeching halt. My father was sitting behind his enormous desk that hailed from the time of the Mayflower, two Eastern European prostitutes kneeling in front of him and taking turns licking his leaking dick. Now I wanted to claw my eyes out after a bleach bath.

I knew my mom was probably comatose upstairs at the moment, safely encased within the haze of her favorite cocktail of Vodka and fentanyl. I was pretty sure that my dad administered the fentanyl himself, giving her just enough to make sure she didn't die on him and raise questions. She knew what happened in this house but had long since stopped caring as long as she got her "fun" juice, as she called it.

"Where's Andrew?" I snapped, averting my eyes as one of the girls took an especially long lick down my father's dick. I wish I could've said this was the first time I'd walked in on a scene like that, but growing up, my father had actually delighted in forcing me to sit on the couch behind him and watch.

Like I said, if the public could only see the man in front of me when he was in his element.

The senator smirked at me before leaning over his desk and rolling up a crisp hundred-dollar bill so that he could snort the pile of cocaine on his desk. One of the girls cried out as his fingers tangled and pulled on her hair, and he forced her farther down until she was choking and crying. He closed his eyes in ecstasy, and I wasn't sure what was doing it for him more, hurting the girl or the drugs coursing through his system.

A nerve near my eye twitched, a sure sign of how stressed I was, but I said nothing. I just stood there waiting for him to stop torturing me and speak.

At least twenty minutes passed before he realized he wasn't going to get the reaction he wanted from me, and he sent the girls away in tears—after finishing loudly, of course.

He leaned on his desk, his hands folded in front of him in his signature power position that the press always raved about. "Do you have an explanation for tonight?" he said sternly in a voice that would have starred in my nightmares if I had any. Sleeping pills every night made sure that wouldn't happen.

"A harmless side hustle," I told him, and he chuckled darkly.

"Is that what you called tonight's date with The Demon's daughter?" he purred, his eyes sparkling maliciously.

I snorted, although my insides felt anything but amused. "Your sources are wrong, old man, if they told you I was on a date."

"Really?" he asked, pressing a button on his phone. He picked it up to show it to me and started scrolling through picture after picture of me next to Aurora. In all the pictures I was staring at her like a man obsessed, the cameraman obviously catching the wrong moment and the wrong angle to create an image that hadn't actually happened.

"I think you of all people know how a situation can be skewed under the right lens," I commented, making sure to keep eye contact and my voice steady so he couldn't tell that my pulse was beating for reasons I wasn't really sure about.

I already had enough people I had to keep safe. The last thing I needed was a serial killer's daughter being added to that list.

Not that Aurora was even a thought for that.

It just made me sick to hear her name on his lips. Because everything about him made me sick.

That was all.

"The last thing I need is my wayward son being seen with a murderer. Don't let it happen again. You won't want to see what happens."

"When are you going to realize that you're not in charge anymore," I said darkly, immediately regretting the words as soon as they left my mouth.

My father leaned back in his chair, a wide smile breaking out across his face.

"Paul," he barked.

A moment later I heard the soft sniffling of my little brother as Paul dragged him into the room. My brother Andrew was clutching his teddy bear, dressed in a pair of dinosaur pajamas as tears ran down his face. "I'm tired," he cried out before he saw me. He tried to run towards me but was hauled back by the scruff of his shirt by Paul.

"Still think I'm not in charge, Remington?" my father asked triumphantly.

I gritted my teeth, trying to resist the urge to drag my brother away from Paul's nasty grip and get us both the hell out of here.

But then there was my little sister to think of.

My father held all the cards, and as always, I was just playing to survive...never to win.

"Is she going to be a problem anymore?" my father sneered.

"No," I muttered.

"No, what?"

"No, sir," I added reluctantly.

"That will be all, Remington," he said, already picking up his rolled-up bill to snort some more coke.

I quickly strode towards my little brother and practically ripped him from Paul's grip, hustling out of the room before he could see anything.

"I love you, Remy," Andrew sniffled into my shoulder.

"I love you too, buddy," I murmured, rubbing his back as I strode up the stairs to place him back into his room.

I put him into his bed and walked towards the door and locked it, sliding down to sit in front of it.

She wasn't going to be a problem. I'd make sure of that. Nothing was going to interfere with my goals.

Especially not The Demon's daughter.

18

AURORA

I sighed as I pulled the last textbook out of my backpack. I had so much studying to catch up on. Remington, Stellan, Cain, and Pax were definitely not good for my grades so far, although I wasn't sure how fairly any professors were going to grade my work anyway. That girl's threat that I would fail out kept bothering me.

As I slammed the book onto my desk, a piece of paper floated off the back and landed on the floor. I frowned as I picked it up and unfolded it.

Familiar handwriting was sprawled across the page, and my stomach clenched.

Dad.

How the hell had this gotten to me? Someone must have slipped it into my bag, but when?

Even from prison, he had gotten close to me. I rose from my seat, but there was nowhere to go. My legs felt shaky beneath me, and I sank back into the chair, trying to fight the adrenaline suddenly coursing through my body.

My hands shook as I opened the page, and I bit down on

the inside of my cheek to steady myself, so hard I tasted the iron tang of blood but barely felt the pain.

My girl,

I hear you've started a new life for yourself. How exciting.

Are you being good? Remember our rules.

You can't trust anyone but family.

I'm always with you in spirit, even when we're apart. But I know we'll be together again soon, having fun.

Dad

I folded the letter in half, then again, then again, then again, until I'd worried it into a tiny square. I stuffed it into the back of a book as if I could hide it away and protect myself from him.

He was trying to escape. He was trying to come find me.

He wrote as if he didn't know I was the reason he'd been caught, but that didn't mean it was the truth.

Everything was a game with my father.

If he knew, though, he'd want to torture me and kill me himself. He'd never delegate such an important kill. So his 'friends' might hurt me but they wouldn't kill me. My mind raced, trying to think of what he would do and how to get two steps ahead of him.

My skin crawled at the thought of him, my chest tightening, my muscles heavy as if he'd already injected the drugs to make me helpless. I shook my head, refusing to let him make me feel that way.

I had to get out of here. I had to ground myself. I moved in quick, jerky movements to pull out a sports bra and a pair of leggings, to lace up my running shoes.

I never wore earpods. I couldn't afford to let my guard down and lose myself in the music. I reached for my knife and clipped the sheath onto the high waistband of my leggings, before jerking a baggy t-shirt over my head to cover it.

Maybe Remington or Pax would go with me... I longed to have Remington jog with me, his easy smile and flirtation helping distract me from my racing thoughts. Or Pax. Pax would be quiet like always, but there was something steadying and comforting about his presence. Cain was terrifying and yet I felt safe when I was by his side.

I hesitated in the hall, debating trying to find one of them. I glanced down the hall at the row of bedroom doors. Cain was right next door, although I hadn't overheard any orgies lately. I'd noticed which room each of the guys was in as I happened to run into them in the hallway. I took a step forward, about to knock on Remington's door.

But I shouldn't feel safe with them.

They were just as dangerous to me as anyone else.

Maybe worse, because some rogue part of me wanted to trust them.

Before I could do something stupid, I broke into a light jog down the hall, headed down the stairs to the hidden door. Whenever I came back now, someone opened the door for me without fanfare or tormenting me—a reminder that I was always being watched, which was creepy, but it was convenient.

Once I let the doors slam behind me, I broke into a full-on sprint, eager to burn off my frantic energy. The wind slapped my face, ruffling my hair as I jogged through a parking lot behind a fraternity and broke onto the busy roads that led around the perimeter of campus.

I tried to stick to bright, well-lit areas that had plenty of people and traffic. I didn't trust anyone to help me if I needed it—no one should—but witnesses helped discourage most predators.

Part of me wished that I'd had the combination of strength and vulnerability to knock on one of the guys' doors and ask them to come with me. Although, knowing them, one of them was probably tailing me at a distance anyway.

I couldn't let my guard down around them and start thinking that they were going to protect me. They weren't my friends. Charged heat stretched between us all, but that didn't mean that I could start to look to them as protectors.

After all, they had tortured me by leaving me in that dark water; Stellan had known what it would do to me.

Even if Cain had dived into rescue me. The memory of Cain's hands on my body, the way he'd looked at me with desire written across his face, distracted me from the terror of my father's letter.

It was strange to imagine my father versus Cain. What Cain and I had done together would definitely not classify as being good in my dad's book.

But when I thought of the practiced way Cain interacted with other humans, as if he wasn't quite like them, the darkness in his eyes, the aura of danger that clung to his skin.... Well, my father loomed large in my memories, until I imagined him next to Cain. Then he seemed smaller, grayer, older. He looked more like the man who had shuffled into the courtroom looking weak and tired, his hands that once wielded a scalpel chained in front of him.

When I imagined him next to Cain, my father looked like someone I could beat.

I ran until my legs felt exhausted and my mind felt clear. I'd taken a hundred runs like this when I was growing up, and the long open road had been my only respite from The Demon. When everything was quiet except for the sound of my feet impacting the cement over and over again and my own labored breathing, I'd had the peace I needed after hearing people scream under The Demon's knife.

My legs were weak as I cut through the parking lot again. The towers of the secret society house rose above the trees in the distance as I threaded between cars.

Suddenly, a guy was walking fast toward me in between cars. I barely registered him before I was darting forward, and as soon as I reached the front of the car, I turned hard right and broke into a sprint.

But another man slammed into me. He seemed to come from nowhere in between the cars and then tackled me. There were two more guys behind him, their faces intent.

The Demon's men?

Or my internet friends?

Whoever they were, I was already reaching for my knife, but one of the guys grabbed my arm and slammed it into the car behind me. He drove his shoulder into my stomach, trying to pick me up, but I slammed my elbow into a nerve in his shoulder and his knees buckled, his teeth gritting. But I was still pinned against the car by him and his friend who had piled behind him.

I screamed, and a couple walking at the edge of the parking lot turned and looked. The girl made eye contact with me, then turned away.

The Demon had said, you can't trust anyone but family. The truth was you couldn't trust anyone.

The men were still trying to sweep me away. One of them grabbed my legs, wrenching them and knocking me off balance. He managed to get my feet off the ground, and I sagged between him and the other man gripping me. I needed my knife, but the first two guys each had control of one of my arms.

The fourth guy had disappeared. Then I glimpsed him

again behind the wheel of a black van; he'd pulled it up behind the car I was trapped against. He got out and opened the side door.

There was no way in hell I was going to a second location. I was very familiar with what happened once they got you where they wanted you to be.

I lashed out, kicking and fighting what seemed like an ineffectual struggle to them, because there were four of them and they were all far bigger and stronger than I was. All I cared about was getting to my knife.

I yanked an arm free, going for the knife that I'd concealed earlier. When I finally wrapped my fingers around the hilt, it resisted coming out of the sheath for a second. Then it was loose, a silver glint in my hand, and the man gripping my shoulders looked shocked. I didn't hesitate. These men didn't intend to show me any mercy, and I wasn't going to show them any.

The men pulled me away from the car, carrying me swaying between them toward the van, cursing. I shoved the knife into the kidneys of one of the men who was trying to carry me. He gasped, his eyes going wide as he fell to his knees.

My head and shoulders slammed into the ground, and a jolt of pain ran up my spine.

One of the men was still holding my feet, and I kicked out at him, trying to get free. The other two guys were trying to edge toward me, but I slashed with the knife, making myself too dangerous a target, and they stayed out of range. I threw myself forward, bending at the waist to slash the legs of the man gripping my ankles. The knife cut through his khakis, a shallow graze that still drew blood, but he let out a shocked cry.

The man dropped my feet. I barely hit the ground before

I was rolling onto my knees, getting my feet beneath me and throwing myself upward. The three men were still ringing me, trying to edge toward me, and I needed to make myself an escape route. I was going to have to take down at least one of them.

I drove toward one of them without hesitation, plunging the knife into his ribs as I grabbed his shoulder with one hand so I could push the knife in deep. His gaze met mine, his mouth twisting in an expression of sheer terror.

Well, welcome to the party, asshole. I imagined I looked pretty damn scared too.

As I pulled the knife loose, blood flowed over my fingers. Blood made the hilt slippery, but I clung to the knife, my survival.

He crumbled in front of me, and I didn't hesitate in throwing him aside and sprinting away.

But I didn't make it far. Something slammed into my head from behind and red stars burst across my vision.

I slammed to my knees as the world started to go black at the edges.

I'll never try to run again. I'll always fight.

That was the last thing I thought before the cement was rushing up toward me and the world was fading.

19

AURORA

I woke up with my throat burning as if I'd been screaming. My head ached sharply when I turned my face, and I blinked sleep from my eyes only to realize that I was in total darkness. But the space around me felt close, confined.

My arms slammed out to the sides, but not far. My fingers crashed into wood. More carefully, I felt for the confines around me. There was a ceiling three inches above my face.

Casket. I was in a casket.

Was I buried alive?

Frantically, I racked my brain, trying to figure out how much air I might have, but I didn't know how long I'd been here. I pinched my hand, desperately trying to channel some calm, because the rasp of my breathing in the dark was edging my panic higher.

"Are you still scared of the dark?" The Demon's voice rose out of my memories. "You're not going to go back to being weak little Gabriela with her little girl fears, are you? I thought you were my Delilah now."

He'd told me he would help me. I'd taken his hand when he smiled at me and let him lead me into the darkness he said would cure my nightmares.

And he'd left me there, in the dark root cellar with the quicklime that burned my knees, that left scars on my legs. It wasn't until I grew a little older, a little more familiar with The Demon's ways, that I understood the quicklime. That I understood I hadn't been alone down there like I'd thought.

The bodies had been keeping me company.

Why had those guys taken me and put me in a casket? My analytical brain finally kicked on. No one on the internet forum had ever brought up such an idea. The Demon would never have been so hands-off with his victims. Could The Demon have already escaped, could this be where his friends had stashed me until The Demon dug me out?

A distant sound, the faintest whine, reached my ear, and I froze, holding my breath. *An engine.*

Something fast and expensive, from the sounds of it.

I wasn't buried.

My lips parted in surprise. Was I near the garage beneath the secret society house?

Had Stellan done this to me? Was this torture round two?

I ran my fingertips over the faint seam along the edge of the coffin, then drew my legs up, trying to wiggle until I could brace my knees against the lid and try to kick it up. Pain exploded through my feet and ankles at the force of my kick, but it was my best chance. I gritted my teeth, preparing to try again and again until the coffin broke or I did.

Was there someone out there, watching me and laughing?

"Aurora? Aurora, are you in here?" The voice sounded

muffled through the coffin, but even so, she sounded terrified. And familiar.

I slammed my legs into the coffin again, doubting anyone was actually going to help me. Then reluctantly, afraid to be disappointed, I called, "I'm in here!"

There was a straining noise, then a *thud.* Something heavy must have been rolled off the coffin. Then it was being flung open.

Jenna's wide eyes stared down at me in the dim light of her flashlight. She looked terrified.

I pulled myself out of the coffin and jumped out before I could be trapped in there again. My running shoes hit the stone floor beneath us and I stared around. The further reaches of the room were lost to the darkness, but Jenna's flashlight illuminated a long stone table where my coffin rested, the stone wall, and more cobwebs than I wanted to examine too closely. We were in some kind of crypt.

"What are you doing here?"

She hugged her chest, her eyes wide. "I've been hanging out with some of those frat guys ever since the... the party... and I overheard them talking about what they were going to do to you. Supposedly being buried in the crypt is part of the initiation for secret society members, and someone said that you were always with them, that it seems like..." she licked her lips nervously. Maybe some of her terror wasn't for the dark confines we were in. "Like you'd found a way to take over the secret society."

I let out a short, sharp laugh. "Maybe next week."

She jumped as if she'd heard a noise, shining her flashlight erratically around the room. It seemed like she had a nice life, a nice family, the things that left a girl unprepared to deal with the not-so-nice things.

I wanted to know why she'd come, but first things first. "How'd you get in? Let's get out of here."

"Let's." Her voice came out fervent. She held out the flashlight, and I was confused, staring at her until she thrust it toward me. "I've got my cell phone for light. It's dead down here but at least we can both have light."

"Thanks," I said, taking the flashlight from her. What the hell was going on? I was more confused and unsettled by Jenna's apparent rescue attempt than by being kidnapped and locked in the crypt. This had to be some kind of trap.

She held her cell phone high, shining the way as she headed toward the door. Her hands were shaking so the light kept bobbing. "They came in this way. There's a long tunnel. I came from the frat house, but I don't know where else it leads."

"You followed them?" Or came with them, as part of their plan to torture me?

She nodded as she reached the door, then let out a scared gasp as her light illuminated the seam. "I thought I left it propped open... oh, it's okay. It opens."

She swung the door open and nudged a rock out of the way with her foot. It was too small to hold the heavy door. Then the two of us were out in a long narrow tunnel. It felt claustrophobic... and intriguing. Where else did the tunnel lead?

Rough masculine voices echoed down the hall, and she turned toward me, her fingers rising to cover her mouth in horror.

"Turn off the light," I whispered, clicking my own flashlight off. She fumbled, then we were both submerged in darkness.

In the distance, I heard the faint drone of an engine again. Toward our left, while the voices came from our right.

If she'd truly come from the frat, then I had an idea how we could escape... through the secret society. I reached out in the dark and my hand bumped her back. She was tense as I found her arm and grabbed her hand. I tugged her with me, fully expecting that she might prefer to risk her chances with the men in the dark, but she followed.

I trailed my fingertips over the wall with my other hand, moving quickly and purposefully even through the dark. I didn't have supernatural night vision—that would have been nice—but I'd spent enough time in the dark, honing my other instincts, that I moved as if I did.

Far behind us, flashlights flickered, then thankfully we turned a bend. A man's voice said, "What the fuck? The door is open."

Her quick intake of breath seemed loud to me, but they couldn't possibly have heard it. I moved faster and faster down the hall, toward where I thought I'd heard the engine.

Then my racing fingertips found a seam in the wall. I stopped abruptly, and she almost crashed into me.

"Spread out and search for her."

"That bitch. I can't believe Jonny might not make it—"

Oh, Jonny must've gotten stabbed when he was kidnapping me. Poor guy.

I didn't have my knife anymore, and I wasn't carrying my lock picking kit today. I dared to whisper, "I don't suppose you're carrying your wallet and have a credit card on you."

"What are you going to buy—oh, I've got my student ID."

I could've hugged her. She passed it to me in the dark, her fingers trembling when they brushed mine, or maybe she was already shaking even before she touched me. I hurriedly inserted it into the crack between the door and the jamb, leaning my shoulder into the door and moving the credit card with quick, practiced movements as I pushed down on the door handle.

It gave with a *click* that seemed far too loud. We had to get out of here, and fast, so I threw my shoulder into the door and it opened into brighter light. She slipped in behind me just as I heard voices in the hall, loud and angry. They'd seen some glimpse of us.

I closed the door behind us, locked it quickly, and turned to find we were indeed in the guys' garage. A familiar McLaren was parked nearby, the spaces to either side empty. No one dared get close enough to ding Cain's precious car.

I had a lot of questions for Cain and the other boys.

"We've got to get you out of here," I said impulsively, deciding to believe she'd really come to rescue me, even though I couldn't understand why. What did she want from me? Maybe there was someone cruel and awful in her life that she needed offed, or maybe one of the frat guys had hurt her and she needed protection. "No one's allowed in the secret society."

She looked around, her lips parting as if she were awestruck. "Is that really where we are? Under the secret society?"

"It loses its charm and excitement quickly," I warned her. I eyed the cameras nearby; someone would know we were here soon. The unblinking eye watching me might not see her, given the way it was angled and how she still stood right by the door.

I handed her back her student ID. "Don't lose it down here. You don't want anything tying you to me or to this building."

Then I waved at the camera, climbed onto the hood of the McLaren, then the roof. Balanced on the shiny metal, I yanked off my t-shirt, then rose onto my tiptoes to cover the camera.

I turned back. "Okay, there's another one by the ramp to the exit. You stay here while I take care of that one."

There were muffled angry voices on the other side of the door, and the sound of guys slamming into it before one of them said, "I don't think you want to go in there without permission."

I had to get Jenna out of here fast. I kicked off my sneaker and yanked off one slightly blood-stained sock—well, shit—before running to cover up the other camera. Then I reached the garage door's controls, which was a screen prompting me for a code. The guys obviously had some kind of special sensor in their cars that opened the doors automatically for them. I didn't have time to fuck around with code-breaking. I paced to the nearest car, tried the door, and when it didn't open, I backed up and kicked in the window. Pain arched through my foot but the window shattered inward.

"Wow," she said, her eyes wide.

Was she impressed? There was an unfamiliar warm glow of pride in my chest. I reached in, unlocked the door, and searched frantically for the sensor. I found it mounted on the dashboard, a small black circle, and I wrenched it loose and carried it toward the door.

The doors rumbled open.

"You've got to run," I said. "I'll stay here and lead off any welcome party. By now, someone in the house knows something is off."

She shook her head. "Come with me. You aren't safe here."

"I'm not safe anywhere," I promised her. "But this is sort of my home now. And thanks. I... I needed help back there."

It was hard to admit.

"Any time," she said, then frowned as she must have realized what she'd just said, and I burst out laughing. She stared at me for a second, then started to laugh too. It sounded shaky, but it was still a good sign.

"Why'd you come?" I asked, and my heart froze when I asked, even more than when I was in some life-or-death situation.

"I was a bitch the other day," she said freely, surprising me. "I'm sorry, Aurora. You were nothing but nice to me, and I thought about it and... you should be treated like your own person. You *are* your own person. Not just The Demon's daughter."

"Maybe I need to learn to be both."

A noise from above drew both our attention. The door stood open, the night dark and stark outside. I gave her an encouraging look. "Be careful. I'll check in with you later to make sure you made it safely."

"You be careful!" she shot back, a bossy edge overcoming some of her fear.

Then she raced off into the night.

I turned back, knowing that someone would be coming for me.

But I wanted to go have a conversation with Cain and the others. Had they set me up to be locked in the crypt, sending frat boys to do their dirty work? Because I could bring the stabbing party to them.

I slipped back through the garage and made my way up the stairs. This time, they were illuminated. I stopped at the first landing to let myself into the floor to my right, and found myself in a room where artificial lights glowed overhead, illuminating the blue-green waters of an enormous, Olympic-sized pool. I shuddered at the sight, pressing my back against the wall so no one would see me as footsteps rang down the stairs.

Two men raced past me. Once they were gone, I made my way calmly up the stairs and through the door back into the main hallway.

I went up the stairs and listened outside Cain's room first. It was quiet. No obvious evidence of an orgy. Was he asleep? Out?

Funny that I felt more nervous outside his door than I had all night. Being here reminded me so strongly of walking into that hot, dark scene by accident, of the way girls writhed at Cain's feet.

I tried the knob, and it turned. I walked into Cain's room as if I belonged here.

The room was only faintly lit by a lamp on his desk. The dungeon equipment was cast in shadows. It took me a second to even see him, lost in the shadows himself. He was sitting up in bed with one elbow draped on his knee, his gaze amused as he watched me.

Cain drawled, "Hey, little devil. Why are you covered in blood?"

20

AURORA

I glanced down and realized my arms and legs were splattered with blood from the knife fight. I'd wiped off my hands at some point, but that was as far as I'd gotten. I looked up and met Cain's eyes, which seemed to glow with interest as if he'd just come alive.

"It's not mine." I shrugged. "Surprised to see me?"

"Should I be?" His tone gave nothing away.

"Someone kidnapped me today. I thought they might be operating under your orders."

His brows rose slightly. "No."

He was always hard to read. "How do I know you're not lying to me?"

"You don't." He dropped his book beside him, pushed aside the blankets and rose. He was wearing only boxers, his big cock tenting them as he stalked toward me. He crossed his arms over his chest, studying me. "Are you hurt?"

"No." The headache had already faded, healed by my adrenaline rush escaping the frat boys.

"Did you hurt them?"

"Yes."

"Yes, of course you did." His thumb swept along my jawline, turning my face up to his as he studied me. "Are you going to hurt them more?"

"Undecided. Right now, I'm not so sure about you, either."

"Oh, little devil. I'm disappointed in you. I'd never send anyone else to hurt you when I'm so happy to do it myself." His gaze flickered toward the cross in the corner. "Did you want to play tonight?"

"No," I said, and as soon as I said the word, I realized maybe it was a lie.

Remington had gotten me started thinking about taking my life back from The Demon. My father's letter had made me imagine how hard it would be for The Demon to hurt Cain. One psychopath in my life might well be the match for the other.

I wasn't going to play by The Demon's rules anymore.

He was watching my face, and his fingertips slid up my cheekbone to rest on my temple before he tapped my forehead twice. "What's going on in there?"

He sounded genuinely curious.

"Always trying to figure out how real humans work, Cain?"

He tilted his head to one side, his gaze intent. "You've got me figured out, don't you, little devil?"

"I think I've got some of the pieces."

"The question is, do you know if *you're* a real human or not?" He was studying me, then smiled faintly at whatever he saw on my face. "No, you're sure about me; you see something you recognize, but you don't know about yourself yet, do you?"

"I don't know," I admitted. I didn't feel a damn thing about stabbing two men tonight, but there was a flicker of warmth, of vulnerability, I felt with Jenna and even these men that made me wonder if some spark of humanity was alive in me still, despite everything I'd seen and done.

True psychopathy requires both a genetic predisposition and a trigger, but humans can be broken enough to mimic psychopathy pretty damn well.

"Tell me what happened tonight," he said, then moved away, falling into his desk chair. "Amuse me, Aurora."

"Why would I do that?"

"Because you want to. You want to tell someone."

I let out a laugh. He reached for a bottle of whiskey on his desk, poured two glasses, handed me one. He added, "You want to tell *me.*"

"I don't like whiskey," I said as I took it.

"Drink it anyway." He always sounded so commanding. Why did that turn me on?

"Tell me," he said again.

And I did tell him about the night, skipping over parts that would endanger Jenna, making it sound as if I'd escaped alone, although I was careful not to lie directly. He'd find out the truth when he watched the videotape. There was something comforting about talking to Cain, who laughed out loud when I told him about my stabby escapades.

I was starting to believe that he didn't plan what happened tonight. I perched on the edge of his desk, so close that my leg brushed his, and his brows arched again. My daring surprised me too.

"Oh, Aurora. Are you the sweet, innocent virgin or the cunning monster all the other monsters should fear?"

"Why not both?" I kicked my legs back and forth, the strange reckless comfort I felt around Cain taking me over, making me slightly giddy. "Although I don't know how much longer I'd like to keep that *virgin* title."

His gaze sharpened. "Oh?"

"Help a girl out, Cain." My voice came out in a whisper, and I wasn't sure if it was seductive or vulnerable.

But from the way heat flared in Cain's gaze, maybe it was both. "One problem with that, little girl."

"And that is?"

"You told me you didn't want me to touch you, remember?"

"Maybe I changed my mind."

"Maybe you need to show me, then." He half-stood, sweeping the items on his desk to one side. They fell to the floor in a cascade of *thuds* and the tinkle of breaking glass, and I stared up at him in shock as he settled back into his seat.

He leaned back, propping his feet on the desk beside me as he leaned back, making himself comfortable although his dick straining at his boxers seemed so hard it had to hurt. "Undress for me, Aurora."

There was nothing sexy about my shorts and sports bra, soaked in sweat and blood, or my running shoes with one sock. But somehow, when Cain's intense gaze raked over me, I felt like the most beautiful woman to ever seduce a man.

I pulled my sports bra over my head, and his gaze flared on my breasts as my arms were above my head. "Slower," he ordered.

I stopped, the bra half off, realizing how I'd arched to slip it over my head. More slowly, I worked it up my body, watching the way he watched me, the way his eyes dilated as if he were intoxicated.

I dropped the bra next to his desk, then leaned back and hooked my thumbs into my shorts to wiggle slowly out of them. He watched me with obvious desire, then said drily, "The lone sock can go too. I do wonder what you've been up to tonight."

I peeled it off and dropped it in his lap with a saucy smile. He shook his head as he threw it over his shoulder. "Brat. Give me your panties."

I arched back, pushing my breasts out, resting a foot on either arm of his chair. I could feel his gaze like a throb between my thighs as I rolled my panties slowly down my thighs, slipped them down my calves.

He held out his hand, and I deposited them into his palm. He looked down at the pink cotton and lace and said, "I bought these for you," with a tone of evident satisfaction.

"You remember them, weirdo?" My voice came out light.

"I pay attention when it comes to you, Aurora. It's the only way to make sure you don't knife me in the back." Unlike the disdainful way he'd treated my sock, he folded my panties into one of his big fists as he leaned back, his arms across his powerful chest.

"What are you going to do with that?"

"Whatever I like."

I shook my head at him, amused by his need to dominate. I started to move off the desk, but he grabbed my ankle, forcing my bare feet to stay planted on the wooden arms of his chair. "Stay like that. I like the view."

I followed his gaze, which fell from my face to between my thighs. I squeezed my knees shut, feeling suddenly embarrassed. The Demon's face rose in my mind, the way he would've punished me for this wanton display.

"Stay with me, Aurora," Cain said, and my gaze snapped to his face, wondering what he'd just seen. "No one's ever going to hurt you again except for me."

"I don't think you can promise that."

"I'm not going to promise. I'm going to prove it." He sounded so sure of himself that some of my anxiety fled, as if The Demon didn't matter anymore, as if he and I were at the center of the universe and everyone else had faded away. "Touch yourself."

I'd always been scared of what would happen if The Demon caught me touching myself. He was always watching, always lurking. So it felt forbidden and awkward at first to slip my hands across my thighs, to delve tentatively between my folds and stroke myself. If it weren't for Cain's orders, for the way his breath froze in his chest as if watching me was pushing him over the edge too, I probably would've stopped, would've given way to my old fears and shame.

But with Cain's gaze and his low, commanding voice urging me on, I toyed with my clit, pulsing my fingers against it until a low moan came to my lips. Putting on a show for him made me feel powerful. I sank down, my shoulders pressed against the cool, hard wall behind me so I could roll my hips up and spread my knees, giving him a show.

"That's my girl," Cain said, his voice tinged with pride as I opened myself up to him. "Touch yourself for me. Find your g-spot."

As I worked my clit with one hand, I pushed a finger inside, searching uncertainly until my finger found a sensitive nub deep inside me. I pressed hard, feeling liquid warmth spread through my belly. Cain leaned forward, one hand braced on either side of my thighs, so close he was almost touching me as he watched. His gaze seemed to intensify every sensation.

Then he stood, pushing the chair back. I wrapped my

calves around his lean, hard waist, trying to pull him toward me.

He shook his head. "Greedy girl. You have to be punished for telling me you didn't want me to touch you. That means you don't get this. Not tonight."

He pulled himself free of his boxers, revealing his enormous dick, hard and ridged in his hand. He wrapped my panties around his cock and began to work himself back and forth.

The sight of him masturbating with my panties sent an unexpected extra spike of lust through my body. I moaned, feeling myself coming closer and closer, until I finally shattered. And when I did, my channel convulsing around my fingers, my hair flying as I moaned and shook and came on his desk, he did too. His cock seemed to jerk in his hand as his hot cum soaked my panties, and I wished he was coming inside me.

He stopped, dropping my panties to the ground. When the magic of the moment had passed, the spell between us breaking, I felt suddenly exposed.

I couldn't believe what I'd just done, and I jumped off the desk with my clit aching and throbbing, grabbing my shorts and my t-shirt to dress again. I bent for my panties, and he stopped me, grabbing my throat with one hand to pull me back to my feet again, his touch gentle but firm.

"Leave the panties. I'm not done with them."

Fuck me, why was the thought that he might want to masturbate with them again strangely hot? That Cain was thinking about me even when I wasn't in the room?

Cain probably saw other people as nothing. Psychopaths don't think about other people after they're done hurting them any more than we think about a discarded tissue in the trash.

So why was there a part of me that dared to think that Cain didn't see *me* that way? There was something alive in his gaze when he looked at me, something that wasn't there when he looked at other women, even as they sucked his cock or stroked his ego.

Cain stepped closer to me, dominating me with his size, with the heat that came off his skin, with the dark, sexy scent that was his aftershave or maybe just him. "Are you sorry for saying you didn't want me to touch you?"

"Yes." The word seemed jerked from my lips before I even realized I was going to admit it. But I was sorry at the moment, god damn it; I wanted more.

"I forgive you, then. Next time, I'll touch you." A small smile touched his lips. "Best prepare yourself, little devil."

He moved to the door, opening it for me. I stared at him, disappointed to be dismissed, aroused and annoyed and excited all at the same time. All the usual emotions I felt around Cain.

I reached the door, but before I could leave, he grabbed my hips and spun me toward him. His lips descended on mine, and my hips ground forward against his as he gripped me tightly. Cain's lips were soft, no matter how domineering his touch was, and my lips parted against his hungrily.

He kissed me breathless, then suddenly pushed me into the hall. I stared at him, my lips bee-stung, as he gave me one of those rare angelic smiles.

"Good night, little devil. Try to stay out of trouble."

Then he shut me out.

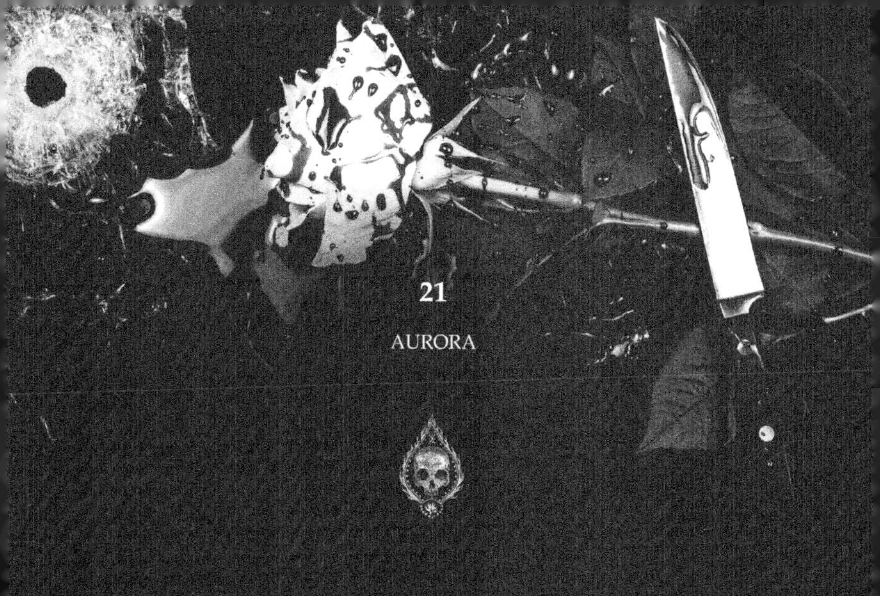

21

AURORA

I was still hot and bothered as I made my way back to the hallway, making a mental list to purchase a vibrator or something to help with the never-ending ache that I had nowadays.

Wonder how that Hitachi Magic Wand thing was that I'd always heard about.

I was so lost in my vibrator musings that I almost stumbled right into Stellan who, for some reason, was standing in the middle of the hallway.

"Whoops," I said, rather breathlessly. Because thinking about vibrators and Stellan was a little too much for my fluttering insides.

I tried to go around him, because I didn't feel like fighting with Stellan after everything that had happened today, but he grabbed my arm before I could get past him.

"Not tonight, Stellan," I murmured, trying to yank my arm away from him...unsuccessfully.

"Cain will destroy you, little girl," he said through gritted teeth, and I scoffed as I glared at him.

The anger quickly disappeared when I looked into his gaze and realized he was...jealous.

“You almost sound like you care,” I told him in a taunting voice.

His face crumpled then, and his grip on my arm loosened. "I'm so tired of fighting you," he whispered. "I can't take picturing them touching you. You were mine."

My heart clenched. I felt like I'd been waiting for him to show me anything, but I certainly hadn't been expecting it to happen right now.

"That was a long time ago, Stellan. You've made it clear that you're done with me."

He sighed and his eyes closed, like my words had caused him actual pain. Maybe they had. I'd survived the edge of a knife many times, but sometimes it didn't feel like I'd survive Stellan's ugly words.

"It's her birthday," Stellan told me, a hitch in his voice, and my eyes widened.

Sophia's birthday. How had I forgotten? For years I'd made sure to remember it, making sure it was a day that I remembered how good she'd been, and wondered what she was doing. But lately there'd been so much going on...I'd forgotten. A rush of guilt hit me.

Stellan's fingers were suddenly tangled with mine, and he was leading me down the hall to where his room was. I followed him inside without an argument, savoring the momentary truce we seemed to have called.

Stellan's room was tidy. There were pictures of his family scattered here and there, and some of him and the guys. I stopped looking around when I noticed the box from Sophia's favorite bakery sitting on his bed, a candle and lighter laying beside it.

I didn't have to open the box to know what was inside. It

was German chocolate cupcakes with coconut pecan frosting. Sophia's favorite. The bakery had been owned by one of their family friends, and he'd actually named the cupcake after Sophia since she'd been so obsessed.

I hadn't eaten one since I'd left.

Every year we'd lived in town, Sophia's family would invite me over and she'd have one pink candle on her perfect chocolate cupcake. And then that night, after the rest of the family had gone to bed, we'd sneak out of our beds to eat another.

And Stellan was always there too.

"You remember," Stellan commented. My breath came out in a sorrow-filled gasp as I realized that he was watching me.

"How could I ever forget?" I choked out.

Stellan went over to the box and opened it, pulling out a single cupcake. I watched as if in a trance as he placed the pink candle inside of it and then lit it, before walking towards me.

The candle light flickered across his face as he walked towards me. He was so sad, and so freaking beautiful all at the same time.

Stellan held the cupcake in between us, and we watched as the wax from the candle began to drip down.

"I miss the way that she was my best friend, the best person I knew," he murmured.

"I miss the sound of her laugh and the way that she'd loved everyone around her," I added softly.

We both just stared at the candle for another long moment, lost in thoughts of childhood and a different life.

Stellan finally blew out the candle and then pulled it out of the frosting before putting the cupcake up to my mouth. I didn't hesitate to take a bite, the sweet chocolate and coconut frosting lighting up my tastebuds like fireworks.

"Mmmh," I moaned, closing my eyes in pleasure as I savored the bite. I'd forgotten how freaking good it tasted. Maybe the best taste ever.

When I opened my eyes, I almost choked because Stellan was staring at me, so much hunger and longing in his gaze that it felt hard to breathe. He lifted his hand and wiped some frosting off the side of my mouth with his finger before placing it in his own mouth and licking all the frosting off.

My chest was heaving, my breasts felt heavy and tight. Stellan abruptly dropped the cupcake he'd still been holding, and I was only faintly aware of it splattering to the ground.

STELLAN

The energy between us was palpable and wreaked havoc on my ability to concentrate on anything other than what I wanted to do to her. To Delilah. To Aurora. The blonde. The brunette.

I wanted all of her. I didn't want anyone else to have her. I wanted to be the one to make her breathless, make her moan, make her feel pleasure...and pain.

A blush crept up her chest, and somehow it was one of the sexiest things I'd ever seen. Only she could seduce me in an instant. I'd never tell her this, but I'd been caught by her spell the moment our eyes met, even all those years ago. The fall had been hard and fast. She blinked her eyes slowly, the same hunger that I was sure was featured in mine reflected in those violet eyes of hers.

It only hit me now that I'd been searching for her all this time, looking for those violet eyes in every face I passed.

She tilted her head, and the slow sinking of her lids to half-mast was enough to make me feel desperate. I took a step until I was right up against her, my nose pressed into her ear. I bit down softly and then whispered, “I need you."

She shivered, and that was it. I couldn't stop myself anymore. It had been torture to have something that I wanted more than anything at the tip of my fingers these past few weeks, and to not let myself have it. I'd always lived my life taking whatever I'd wanted. It was time to take what was mine.

I swept up her legs and she gasped. I half expected her to push me away, but instead she wrapped her arms around my neck, her fingers tugging at my shirt.

Good girl.

“Stellan.”

The whisper of my name from her lips hit me in the chest hard enough to take my breath away. The way she said it...I wanted to hear her say it that way forever. I moved towards the bed.

“Deli-Aurora, ” I said, choking on the sound of her old name. It was how I knew her. It was the name I'd been calling her in my head this whole time because it kept me angry. Her old name was thick and heavy in my throat, torturing me as it threatened to ruin everything.

Which was why she would be Aurora tonight. Somehow I was going to take all the good from the old her and tangle it with this beautiful, fierce creature currently in my arms.

But was she really that different now that I'd had hours to stare at her, even when she wasn't looking?

I sure couldn’t look away from her now. The light dusting of freckles on her nose was the same, even with this new face of hers. Her tilted head and narrowed eyes hinted at the trouble I was beginning to learn always followed closely behind her, the same as when we were young. Her obliviousness was still the same. Even with her father and the cloud of suspicion that followed her everywhere, every man wanted her. Even my brothers.

They all hadn't realized yet that she was mine.

My hope for a second chance. A way to escape the pain of the past.

"Baby." A hum resounded through her chest, sounding more like a purr. Her cheeks flushed in embarrassment.

"Is this real?" she blurted out as I set her down on the bed and leaned over her, brushing my nose down the smooth skin of her cheek, smiling when I felt her shiver from my touch. I wanted her to be affected. I wanted her to feel me imprinted beneath her skin.

"It's fucking real," I answered her, and she tentatively pulled her arms from around my neck, trailing them down my chest to the bottom of my shirt before pulling my shirt up.

Finishing what she started, I slipped the shirt up and off of me.

"This is your last chance to get away," I warned her as I slipped my hands into her hair, gently massaging her head as she moaned softly."

She didn't answer me. Her eyes were closed and her breath was coming out in halted gasps.

"Sweet girl," I murmured, pulling her hair gently to get her attention. Her eyes opened and she stared at me as if in a daze. Her pupils were blown out and a smirk tugged on my lips, seeing how turned on she was already. I didn't know what I wanted to do first. I'd been jacking off since the day I'd seen her, imagining everything I wanted to do. The orgasms had been intense, laced with guilt for wanting someone that I was trying to hate so much.

It wouldn't be like that tonight. Tonight, I'd actually let myself get lost in her. I'd think about everything else in the morning.

For a second I got lost in the daydream, thinking about what it would have been like to have her with me all this time, to have her by my side with how fucking hard my life had gotten. Would she have been able to keep all my demons at bay? Would I have become a better man?

This new version of her was strong. When I'd first met her, all those years ago, she'd been like a shy, quiet colt, skittish with any sudden movement. She was laced with iron now. Yet even with that strength, there was a fragility woven throughout her that seemed to draw me like a moth to a flame.

When I'd seen her in the cafeteria that first day, I think my heart had started beating again. I just hadn't realized it. Parts of me had become alive, infused with purpose, even if the purpose had been to destroy her.

Since she'd come back, I was no longer just moving from one day to the next. I'd become starving...for her.

“Mine,” I blurted out, and her breath hitched again as she studied me.

"Please," was all she said in response, but it was enough. It was everything.

I squeezed my eyes shut against a sudden wave of emotion. I didn't want her to be able to look into my eyes and see...me.

I pushed myself away from her for a brief moment to take off the rest of my clothes and watch her reaction as she took me in. Everything about her intensified; her widened eyes, the dilated pupils, the spiked breathing and parted lips when I stroked up and down my dick. My name fell from her lips in a whisper, her gaze desperate as it flicked from my hand to my face and back again. It was a heady feeling to have a perfect creature like her look at you like you were a god.

I didn't know what I wanted to do first. I was desperate to experience what it felt like to be inside of her. At the same time though, I wanted to take my time. I wanted to kiss and bite my way over her entire body, worship every inch of the girl I'd been obsessing over.

My gaze flicked all over her face. "What have you done to me? I can't decide whether you're an angel or a devil. All I know is that I want you with every piece of my soul."

Her lips trembled. "Stellan, please...," she whispered.

I began to kiss a path from her ankle up to her hip, taking a small break to pull down her shorts as I went. I growled as I made it to the apex of her thighs and realized that she wasn't wearing underwear. I wasn't going to think about why.

Nudging at her clit with my nose, I groaned and hardened to the point of pain from her scent and the gasp that filled the silence.

I teased her with my tongue, drawing out a soft cry before sliding up her body. We kissed then.

Finally.

Hard and deep, long strokes of my tongue against hers, and I demanded more.

I was frantic as I pulled off the rest of her clothes, taking small sips of her lips between every piece of clothing like I'd die without her taste. Her skin glowed under the light of the one lamp I had shining in the room. She was the most fucking gorgeous creation that I'd ever seen...even covered in blood. I made a mental note to ask her about that later.

"Beautiful."

I wasn't sure how someone could be strong and perfectly soft all at the same time, but she was. Her body was every wet dream embodied. Curves. Breasts with tight pink tips and legs I wanted wrapped around my waist. Immediately.

Her thighs parted for me and I pressed down on her. I hovered over her mouth, our eyes locked together, and I just breathed her in.

I was a junkie, fresh out of rehab, who had just gotten my first hit. I rocked against the soft heat of her sex, pushing my dick against her clit until she was a squirming, writhing mess beneath me.

Aurora's gasp was loud when I dipped to take her nipple in my mouth, and I smiled, hoping her screams would fill the hallway and torture every fucker in this building who'd been dying for her.

I licked at her nipple before sucking on it. She pulled my hair, and gasped my name again. Each time she called my name it spurred my need to drown in her softness and bring about the insistent pleas that followed. I bit down, resisting the urge to make it hurt.

That could come...later.

Leaving her breast wet from my tongue and red and swollen from my teeth, I went back to her lips, desperate to have another hit.

"Say I can have you," I murmured, not sure why I was so insistent to get her permission now when I'd almost taken her just a few days ago without it.

"Yes. Take me. I'm yours," she responded, and I swore my heart skipped a fucking beat. I didn't know if I actually could have stopped at this point, not when I finally had her like this.

Everything sped up then, my pulse as my hand skimmed

down her stomach, to her thighs, finally dipping into her perfect heat. She was dripping for me. I muffled her cry with my lips. Stroking deep lashes with her tongue, she clawed my back and I moaned at the bite of the pain. It felt like it was holding me here, taking the edge off the sorrow I held onto every day.

I pulled away so I could watch her tremble around my fingers.

"Come on, baby," I hissed into the crook of her shoulder, looking at where we were joined. I'd fucked too many girls to count, but this was without a doubt the sexiest thing I'd ever seen, watching her come undone for me.

She was in her most raw, primal state, all the walls she kept up decimated in her search for pleasure.

Her skin was flushed with sweat now, her head thrown back as she arched into me. Then suddenly she was calling my name as her orgasm hit, and I fell, wondering if I'd ever find a way to come back from this.

I pulled my fingers out, and then my cock was pressing against her entrance. I should have gone slow. I believed her when she said she was a virgin. I should have savored the gift she was giving me.

But all I could think about was making her mine.

I pushed in hard and fast, and a soft scream pulled from her throat.

Fuck. Fuck. Fuck. She was soft and tight, choking my dick. She moaned again, a lick of pain in the sound.

"Aurora," I whispered, and she squeezed her eyes closed for a second longer before finally opening up, a tear falling down her face that should have made me feel guilt, but only made me feel pride. Only I would ever have this moment. Only I would ever be her first.

She rippled around me, and I was a panting, writhing

mess. I felt like the virgin. I took some deep breaths, trying to stop myself from coming. She just felt so fucking perfect.

Her legs wrapped around me and I groaned as she clawed up my back again.

"I have to move, baby," I murmured.

"Yes," was all she said, but somehow it was enough to send my lust spiraling even more.

I pulled out and then buried myself again until our hips met. "Fucking. Perfect," I growled.

I feasted on her flesh as I moved in and out of her frantically, licking, biting and kissing a path to her mouth to claim that too. We moaned and fed on each other for long moments. Our rhythm was ravenous, anguished, like we both feared this was our last moment.

I hiked her leg over my shoulder so I could go deeper and deeper again. I wanted her to feel me...forever. If there was a way to make our bodies one in this moment, I would have done it. But if I couldn't have that, I wanted her sore, aching, reminded of me with every step she took when I wasn't around.

She bit her bottom lip, biting so hard a drop of blood beaded down from it. I couldn't stop myself from licking it, wanting every part of her to be a part of me. She gasped at the sting and grabbed my ass to push me to go faster.

"Please," she begged again, and unbidden images of her on her knees, a blindfold over her eyes as I fed her my cock flashed through my brain.

I groaned, the fantasy, combined with the very real feel of her surrounding me right now, overwhelming me with lust.

It was so intense, as I continued to move I feared I wouldn't last long. Not like this, with her wrapped around me in every possible way.

I kissed her long and hard, our breaths mingling together in gasps.

I pushed and pulled into her again and again. And it felt like she was working some kind of witchcraft while we moved together. It was like she was dragging everything from inside of me. All the feelings and emotions I've done my best to keep locked away in a little box.

I didn't realize until she came back into my life how exhausting it was to keep myself numb, to never let me feel everything thrashing around inside of me. I hadn't let myself care about anyone.

What the fuck was she doing to me?

"Come with me," I ordered when I could feel her start to tighten around my cock. I sunk down against her, chest to chest, and rested my elbows on either side of her head. I was so far gone, so desperate to feel every inch of her that I pressed her legs farther apart with my hips so I could fully seat myself inside, so far apart I'm sure it hurt. Taking in her cry, I started moving, long, deep thrusts that pushed her up the mattress each time. Her arms grabbed onto the headboard. It bounced against the wall and I hoped everyone in this fucking building heard it.

The sound of the headboard, the creak of the bed, the slapping rhythm as our bodies met...our groans. It was an erotic soundtrack that I just wanted to hear over and over again.

My name fell from her lips, repeatedly, just adding to everything.

And it was suddenly too much. Aurora, her voice, the breath rushing along my neck and the reality that she was really here, in my bed. Panic thrummed through me. I wanted to keep her here, tie her up so that this moment could never end. Because once it did...

Holding tight, I tried to focus on the feel of her, the soft panting cries she was giving me.

"Good girl, baby. I'm so fucking close."

Evidently, she liked that because she was suddenly so fucking wet I felt like I'd just entered nirvana. Trembling beneath me, she started crying out.

"Stellan. So good. Fuck yes. Please..."

I gritted my teeth at her first spasm, and a burning sensation built in my lower spine. I clamped my teeth down on the soft skin that connected her neck to shoulder, wanting to break the skin and leave a lasting mark.

And then I spiraled into oblivion. The best kind. The only one I wanted from then on.

"Aurora." Groaning out her name, I got to the edge of the cliff, pressing deeper, harder, faster into her. Wanting more, more, more.

I fell over the edge, and in that moment, the only thing I cared about was her coming apart around me and the feeling that she was suddenly the center of my life.

We laid there for a long moment, intertwined, and I never wanted to be apart.

"Mmmh. I think I need another cupcake," she said with a giggle as she opened her eyes and stared at me like she used to.

Like I was the sun and the stars and her...hero.

I pulled out of her, the emotion of the moment suddenly too much for me. That panic that I'd momentarily pushed away came flooding back. My skin felt hot. I felt suffocated. My breath began to come out in gasps that had nothing to do with sex.

Fuck.

I squeezed my eyes closed, knowing that I was on the verge of a panic attack. It hadn't happened for a while, but fuck. Aurora. She was breaking parts of me that I needed to be able to function.

"Get out," the words came out harsh, much harsher than intended. But I didn't want her to see me like this. I didn't want her to see what a fuck up I was. How weak I was.

"Stellan—" She reached out to touch me and I jerked away.

"Get the fuck out," I practically screamed, and she flinched like she'd been burned.

She jumped off the bed, and I could hear her grabbing her clothes, but I couldn't even look at her, because I was a coward. And I was falling apart. I couldn't do this.

I wasn't strong enough to feel like this.

The door slammed behind her as she left, and it felt like she'd taken a vital piece of me with her.

I threw myself face down on my bed, trying to get myself under control.

But I didn't. I couldn't.

Because I'd just ruined everything.

22

PAXTON

I knew who was outside my door just from the heavy-handed knock. I yanked my sweatshirt over my head as I moved to pull open the door.

Cain waited outside, his eyes blank and cold. "Ready to go to work?"

"What's up?" I moved into my room, opening the drawer in the desk and pulling out my 9MM pistol. I checked that it was loaded, safety on, then clipped it to my waistband. I laced up my boots, then clipped my knives to the inside of my boots, though it was a bad day if we needed those.

Cain was staring at my knife as I straightened, letting the hem of my jeans cover it. I knew he wore them too, so it seemed strange until he said, "Did you know Aurora carries a knife all the time too?"

"I knew I liked her," I said lightly.

Cain's gaze swept toward mine, hardening. "She stabbed two men tonight."

Interesting. "Did we like *them?*"

"We did not. They were unruly—I didn't give members

of the frat permission to kidnap her and stuff her into the crypt."

I whistled. "Someone ran their mouth about society rituals at some point, I guess."

He grunted. "Shit's all over the internet. Everything's all over the internet at this point, although at least half of it is lies."

He headed to the garage, and I followed him.

"You going to tell me where we're going?" I slid into the passenger side of his McLaren. I half expected he was going to say we were visiting the frat; he didn't exactly give a fuck about girls most of the time, but he'd seemed...fixated... on Aurora. I'd never seen him like that before.

"The casino. Remy found irregularities in the books. Looks like the blackjack manager is skimming."

"And Remy didn't want to go?"

"I didn't invite him."

That meant Cain had dark plans for the evening. Remington was more sensitive than the rest of us, and even Cain sheltered him sometimes. It had to be because of Remy's past. It struck me as strange Remy didn't ask us to help him bury his father, but maybe he was attached to the old monster.

We pulled into the parking lot of the casino, and by the time we reached the doors, they were opening for us. The casino manager hurried to talk to us. Cain looked at him, dead-eyed, and told him to call the blackjack manager into his office.

The blackjack manager looked terrified when he saw Cain, but most people who knew him reacted that way, so it wasn't exactly an admission of guilt.

"We have a discrepancy in blackjack money making it off the floor." Cain turned toward the man, who was balding in front, which revealed a wide expanse of skin beginning to sweat. "You've got a newfound appreciation for coke, hm?"

"No," the man started.

Cain reached back for his holster at the back of his waist, pulled his gun, and shot the man in the head. He crumpled to the floor, blood splattered across the wall behind where he'd been standing.

The manager and I stared at Cain in shock.

"I hate liars," Cain said, holstering his gun again.

Normally, Cain would've taken the man for a drive with us to a second location. He would've given the man plenty of time to lie—and plenty of time to pay for those lies.

Cain cast a dispassionate eye over the mess. "Make sure that gets cleaned up. I'll send someone over."

"Of—of course, sir," the man stammered.

I texted for a clean-up. By the time I looked up, Cain was already stepping over the body.

In the casino, there was a low throb of constant chatter, of people streaming by toward the gaming tables. A cocktail waitress who looked vaguely familiar tried to catch Cain's gaze, but she failed. She looked downcast when she saw me, then her face brightened.

I flashed a smile at her as I walked past, but I wasn't interested.

Truth was, I hadn't felt too interested in any girl since Aurora walked into my life, with her signature brand of wide-eyed innocence and hidden badassery. She seemed like something special.

And I didn't like the sensation.

Cain jogged down the steps of the casino, his shoulders relaxed in his leather jacket. Then he pulled out his cell phone as if he'd gotten a text, and his posture stiffened. Remy? More business?

Once we'd slammed the doors shut and were sequestered in the peace of the McLaren, I said, "We usually go to a second location."

"I'm bored with all that shit."

Interesting, because torturing people used to be the one time Cain looked cheerful. I'd been gearing up for his kind of crazy, and it was unexpected that Cain had taken care of the situation so succinctly.

"Remington was sure?" I asked.

"Is he ever wrong?"

"No." Remy was an expert in discovering what people were up to. He'd been the brains behind our own hunt, when we'd found the man who murdered my mom.

But it was Cain's special skills that came in handy when it was time to take that man apart.

I leaned back in my seat, relaxed no matter what Cain did. I'd follow him into hell, and I knew he'd do the same for me. There was something wrong with Cain—but we had a bond anyway.

There's no love like brotherhood, especially a brotherhood bathed in blood.

We pulled up outside the frat house. I gazed through the window at the house, a three-story brick building with all the personality of an Amazon box. So we'd come for revenge for Aurora after all. "I see."

"Remy said Aurora put two of them in the hospital, but they got out." His voice was bleak.

They were better off in the ICU.

"Fine." I got out of the car.

He looked at me over the roof. "You don't want to know the plan?"

"I can guess the gist of it. I've been around with you before."

Cain paced ahead of me into the frat house. We walked into the living room, and two guys were sitting on the couch, obviously bandaged. Six of their other friends were in here, and they started to scatter before Cain turned and closed the doors behind him. The lock snapped shut.

I stepped in front of the doors. The guys were backing away, their eyes wide.

"Those two," Cain said, pointing at one of them, then at the other. They both looked like they were about to piss themselves. "They helped take her."

Remy must have gotten his hands on video.

"What—what happened?" One of them started to say. "We didn't do anything—"

"I hate liars. Don't tell me none of you knew," Cain said quietly for a second time today, and the room went even more still than it had before. He glanced around the room. "We're going to have a conversation about playing with my toys."

Fuck. "Four to one, Cain?"

He didn't bother to turn around. "Never said I needed you, Pax."

He raised his hand and gestured for them to come at him.

None of them wanted to, I could tell. They traded frantic glances, but they knew there was no other way past him and out those doors.

Suddenly, three of them flew at Cain, their movements almost synchronized.

Not that it mattered. Cain whirled to attack each of them in turn, blocking their hits, not appearing to give a damn when they landed one on his rock-hard body.

I leaned against the doors, beginning to grow bored. The first three had fallen, but four others had moved in to take their place. One rushed at me, finally, trying to stop me from blocking the doors.

I hit him over and over again, pulling my punches just enough to keep him from going down, until he slammed into the wall, his eyes rolling back in his head.

He fell to the ground on his knees, then slumped over onto his face.

Cain's eyes were bright for once when they met mine, as he was surrounded by all those bodies.

But by the time we were driving back to the house, he seemed quiet and preoccupied. The high he usually had after a fight like that had already faded.

There was something wrong.

Sometimes, a rare event shook Cain's sense of himself as a psychopath. Once we'd gone to visit a rival gang leader to find the man had an eleven-year-old girl drugged up, hollow-eyed and bruised, sitting on his lap.

Cain had destroyed him and the top hierarchy of his gang—and even though he'd said it was for territory, he'd also carried that girl to our private doc to make sure she got help. Remy found out what happened to her and made sure she reached a safe, loving family.

The whole thing fucking haunted Cain—not what he'd seen, not the blood bath he'd created, but the fact he'd given a shit about something.

Cain slowed the car. Aurora was sitting on the imposing front porch of the house, which was usually unused. She looked over her shoulder, as if she sensed us. She was gorgeous, her long hair swept over one shoulder, her gaze magnetic even from this distance. Her face looked sad. Had she been crying? The thought made me feel a sudden burst of protectiveness that tightened my hands into fists.

Cain was staring at her too, then he abruptly hit the gas and we sped past her.

Judging from the way Cain looked at her, we were in trouble.

Every single one of us... especially Aurora.

23

AURORA

The next morning I reluctantly got out of bed. Time to face another day. I couldn't believe that I'd finally been brave enough to rebel against The Demon and claim what I wanted, and it had been so heartbreaking.

I'd always heard that the first time a girl had sex was disappointing, but the sex itself hadn't been disappointing. It had been the aftermath that was going to haunt me all day. I hated the fact that I was going to have to go out there and see Stellan after he hurt me...again. After I'd been stupid enough to give him the chance...again.

But such was life. I took a shower, then pulled on a pair of black leggings and a slouchy gray cashmere sweater. The expensive cashmere sweater had definitely come from the guys' attempt to make sure I wouldn't embarrass them.

The leggings were my own. I deserved to wear leggings today. Something about my life should be comfortable.

When I headed out into the hallway, Paxton was just coming out of his room. His joggers hung low on his hips and he wore a sleeveless t-shirt that highlighted all the tattoos across his powerful arms.

For a second, our gazes met. Something hung, charged, between us. He was just standing there with his hand on the doorknob of his room, but he looked at me as if he wanted to devour me. His face was always handsome and magnetic, but at the moment his eyes smoldered as if he'd come to life when he saw me. Some crazy part of me wanted to forget Stellan, kiss Pax, walk him backward into my room and see if I could have a happier post-orgasm glow this time around.

"Good morning, pretty girl." His voice was pure sex.

Well, I liked that a whole lot better than little *devil.*

"I was just heading to the basement for my morning workout before breakfast. Want to come? You look like you could really use the chance to try to beat someone's face in."

Ha, he wasn't wrong. After a night with Stellan, it was hard not to wake up and choose violence. "I'm not looking to get hurt, Pax."

A wounded look came over his handsome features. "I'd never hurt you."

Lies. Those were absolute lies.

"Come on," Pax said. "Give me half an hour before breakfast. If I bore you, you can go find Remy."

It would be smart to walk away from Pax. It would also be boring.

Then he held his hand out to me.

And even knowing better, I reached out and took it. His strong, warm fingers clasped mine, and the two of us walked down the hall to a wooden panel that slid aside, revealing an elevator.

"Are you kidding me?" I demanded. "There's always been an elevator and Cain dragged me down all those dark stairs?"

"Cain is an ass," he said, "and the elevator is for people we trust."

I stared at him, but the elevator doors dinged open and he stepped into it as if he hadn't just dropped an emotional bomb in my lap.

Pax and I rode down the elevator. I shivered when the doors dinged open on the balmy warmth of the pool room, but he headed to the side, to another hall off the pool room where there was a weights room and a small dojo space.

The moment I stepped into the room with the ring, I knew I'd made a mistake. I didn't want to be on the receiving end of his brutal fists.

"Don't be scared of me," he said.

"Shouldn't I be?"

"Should I be scared of you?" The little smile playing around the corners of Pax's mouth was sexy as hell. "You've got some moves, don't you? Where'd you learn them?"

"My father made me learn quite a bit."

"So did you find learning to fight empowering?"

"No," I said honestly. "For a while, I'd wanted to make him happy, and I guess maybe when I was really little and trying to convince myself I was safe, it made me feel good. But as time went on, it felt like he always wanted me to be more aggressive, more mean. I never wanted to hurt anyone. But sometimes when I don't have a choice, I'm glad I have the skills."

He frowned, and I wasn't sure which part of what I'd said he disagreed with. "Did you have a choice the other day? When you came into the house all blood-splattered?"

My stomach dropped. I knew the guys would find out; they always seemed to know everything, but I still hated it. "Nope."

"Then I'm glad you had the skills." He climbed over the rope that led around the ring, looking sexy as he did so, then gestured to me. "Come on. Let's just play."

Reluctantly, I took my place across from him. The two of us circled each other. He lashed out first, incredibly fast, and I dropped low, ducking his blow and kicking out a leg. He jumped over my leg adeptly.

The two of us circled each other, trading blows but evading more strikes than landing. He crashed into me, bringing us both against the ropes. His arms wrapped around my waist, the hard planes of his chest against my breasts, and suddenly everything between us felt different—not a fight but a dance. His gaze was on my lips, and I couldn't help staring at his lips, which looked soft above that hard jaw.

For a second, I was sure he was going to kiss me, and I was sure I was going to kiss him back.

Then he straightened, his hands on my waist, making sure I was on my feet. He tweaked the end of my ponytail. "I had to stop you from kicking my ass somehow."

"You're full of shit, Pax."

He grinned at me, and that grin was so warm that it made me want to kiss him all over again.

"You didn't come to my room last night," I said softly, certain now that it wasn't a dream anymore.

"I thought you were sleeping in Stellan's bed." He said the words levelly, no hint of jealousy.

I shook my head, catching my lip with my teeth. He looked as if he might touch me, then said, "Well, Stellan's a fool."

I didn't know what to say to that, but I didn't have to say anything, because he said, "Come on. I need caffeine to deal with the day ahead."

"Me too," I said fervently.

Pax and I walked through the formal dining room where

some of the society members were eating and into the cozy blue breakfast room.

Cain and Remington were already there. They were having a heated conversation, but they immediately smothered it when I walked in. Remington turned his magnetic smile on me, but Cain just leaned back in his chair, a commanding presence, as always, that seemed to fill the room.

"What were you talking about?" I expected one of them to tell me that it was none of my business.

Remington's eyes filled with mischievous light. "Nothing nearly as interesting as what you were up to last night."

"Do you mean the part where I stabbed someone or..."

Remington waved it off as if it were nothing. "No, no, that's not very interesting. We expect a bit of a murderous impulse from you. What I'm interested in discussing is how desperate you've been to lose your virginity, and why you didn't come to see me about it."

Cain smirked. "She wanted her first time to be good, Remington."

Remington threw a piece of toast at him, and Cain just seemed amused. I wasn't used to seeing Cain's lighter side, and even when his smile was just a faint smirk, it was still sexy.

Just then, Stellan walked in, skirting Pax and me to reach a chair.

"Well, how about it?" Remington asked. "*Was* your first time good?"

Stellan froze, halfway into his chair, then sank all the way in and reached for the cup of coffee waiting for him as if he didn't give a damn. For some reason, watching him take a sip as if nothing impacted him made my last fuck pop like a bubble in the breeze.

"I had been told that my first time would probably be disappointing," I said crisply.

A collective heckling of Stellan went up from around the room, but I cut it off by adding, "Oh, the actual sex was great. Afterward, afterward was incredibly disappointing."

"Well, at least Stellan's dick didn't let you down, just his personality," Remington said. "I could have told you that would happen."

Stellan was the only person in the room who didn't seem to be having any fun. He kind of looked like a kicked puppy. Was I supposed to feel sorry for him? He'd been the one who'd hurt me last night.

As I headed for my chair, Cain grabbed me around the waist and pulled me into his lap. I wasn't sure what to do, but then, Cain was so dominating I didn't have to make any decisions. He had already decided for me. He wrapped his big arm around my waist and I found myself straddling his powerful thigh.

"I'm sorry I turned you away, little devil. It should have been me," Cain said.

Stellan's eyes flickered up to Cain, something hot and furious in them, but all he did was sip his coffee.

"I'm sure it was for the best."

His breath was hot against the back of my neck. It made me want to grind down on his lap.

One of his hands rested casually on the inside of my thigh. His fingertips weren't touching anything important and yet they still sent tingles of electricity through my body.

"Wrong," he growled into my ear. "And I'll teach you better one day."

"Stellan, Stellan, Stellan." Remington shook his head mournfully. "You know Pax is gonna move in on you and teach your girl how to fight so she can knock your head off."

"She's not my girl," Stellan said.

At almost the same time, Pax winked at me and said, "She doesn't need me to teach her anything."

I was beginning to really like Pax. Lord help me.

"Yeah, of course she's not your girl," Remington said. "Not when you act the fool. Or maybe it's not an act."

"All right, leave Stellan alone," I interrupted. Something in me did feel sorry for him, even though he didn't deserve it. He was so messed up from losing Sophia...and so was I. How did I hate him for that? "His brain probably short circuited when he realized that he treated me like I was an actual human being for fifteen seconds."

"Are we really having this conversation?" Stellan demanded. "We're just bringing all of our shit out into the open now."

Cain scoffed. "Stellan, all your shit has been on clear display all this time."

Stellan's jaw set. "You guys are taking her side. You don't realize how fucked up that is?"

Cain laughed as if it were ridiculous. I felt that laugh like a rumble through his chest and my back, like a lion's purr. But even if the guys played Stellan's protest off as if it were ridiculous, it had kind of felt that way for a moment.

When I saw the four of them teasing each other, when I saw them acting *human,* it made me want to be around them more. It was the thing that made me feel some of the same desire for them that every other woman on this campus seemed to feel constantly.

"Are we going to talk to the frat boys about staying out of the tunnel?" Stellan asked, as if he were trying to change the subject. "That's our territory. Doesn't matter if there's a door into their house."

Pax, Remington, and Cain shared a quick glance.

"What did you do?" I demanded.

Remington leaned over the table, propping his chin on his hand. "Why? Did you have big vengeance plans?"

"I don't need any. I already showed them the error of fucking with me." I offered Remington a bright smile, hoping they'd all taken notes.

When we'd eaten and Cain released me from his lap, Stellan lingered as I headed toward the door.

"Can we talk?" he asked.

"I don't want to," I answered. He'd hurt me, and as much as it was in my nature to forgive Stellan—because of all the history we shared, because of how strong my feelings were for him. I was not doing it this time. Not this morning at least. Let him suffer. Let him grovel. I was pretty sure Stellan had never groveled in his life, and the man needed to get some experience.

Just then, Remington got a text on his phone. The look on his face was relaxed as he pulled it up, then shifted. He whistled, a short, sharp sound that got everyone's attention. "Nobody leaves. Something interesting just came in. I think you all might want to see this."

He rose and picked up a remote from the sideboard, then keyed something in which made a picture on the wall recede, replaced by a television screen. He cast something from his phone to the wall.

I drew in a breath as a familiar setting came up. The Demon's torture chambers had looked much the same as often as we'd moved. He'd always found a way to recreate his happy place everywhere we went. Now the place that had haunted my dreams was frozen in a still frame on the screen.

"Where did this come from?" My voice came out in a whisper.

He'd recorded everything.

And I'd destroyed it all.

But he must have made backups.

"It's all over the internet, all over the news. Apparently, someone released some footage to the police and to the news simultaneously—just ten minutes of video from your father's collection."

Bile crawled up my throat and I pressed my fingertips to my mouth. I didn't want to see this again. Seeing it once had been enough. One of The Demon's friends must have the footage. Why had he sent out ten minutes, when there had to be days and days worth of video? Would they want me to buy the footage from them?

Remington hit *play*. I shook my head no, but there was no stopping them.

I could feel Cain watching me, his gaze like fingers up my spine as my knees went weak.

There was a man on the screen, bound and tied. I'd been there that day.

He was the man I'd broken apart to protect Stellan and Sophia.

I'd helped my father more than I ever wanted to.

The Demon moved into the scene, smiling and handsome, his hair gray at the temples by now. The man thrashed and begged.

"Come here, darling. Don't be shy," The Demon said.

The music started up then. I remembered putting the record on the record player, stalling, taking my time setting the needle. Then I'd come to my father's side.

I stepped into view, and I squeezed my eyes shut. I didn't need to watch it to know what happened. But how much of the scene was there? How bad was it?

I had to see how they were taking it. I opened up my eyes and met Cain's, which were quiet and judging. A look of horror wrote itself across Stellan's face. I couldn't bear to watch the video. Besides, it was everywhere; I'd look up the transcript later, find out just how visible I was.

Instead, I watched their eyes as every spark of care they'd felt for me faded.

I fled back to my room and slammed the door. I sank down in front of it, burying my face in my hands.

I'd lost my second chance when Aurora became connected to Delilah. But then I'd started to feel as if I did have another chance, in a way, with these men by my side.

It was all over now.

24

AURORA

I came back to my room defeated. There hadn't been anyone to let me into the Sphinx, the guys obviously having decided I no longer should be helped. I'd had to wait by the door for someone to come back from class and then I'd booked it into my room, unable to deal with the whispers and taunts for one more fucking second.

"Out of the darkness and into the light, to all that is good and all that is bright," I whispered to myself, the meditation mantra, one that I hadn't had to use for a long time.

But it was necessary now. Because just when I'd thought things were beginning to get better, everything had crashed down around me.

I couldn't tell you what I'd been taught today. The only thing I'd heard were all the voices calling me murderer, over and over again until I couldn't remember if I was or not.

And the scary thing was, that had only been ten minutes of video. What would happen if more of those recordings were revealed?

I didn't think the protection I'd been given for turning

my father in would stand. When they saw those tapes...they'd know I was a monster.

Liquid dripped on my arm and I realized that I was crying. I was always so surprised to see my tears. It felt like it had happened a lot here, but before...I'd never cried.

I'd never been allowed to.

To find out that I was capable of crying was still shocking to me every time it happened.

"Out of the darkness and into the light, to all that is good and all that is bright," I whispered again, desperately.

A knock sounded on the door and I flinched like I'd been hit. What was it now?

"Aurora," Remington's voice purred through the door. "Sweetheart, open the door."

A sob hitched from my throat, and I don't know why I did it—I must have lost my mind, because I opened the door and let him in.

"Come here," he said, opening his arms wide. I threw myself into his arms, desperate for at least a small smattering of comfort from the day

I sniffled into his chest, and he stroked my hair, holding me tightly in his arms.

It took me a second to realize that he was wearing some kind of suit. I pulled away to look at him closer, confused.

He was wearing a fucking tuxedo.

"Got a fancy fundraising event tonight?" I asked, figuring he must be going somewhere for his father.

Something glittered in his eyes, and then it was gone. And I thought I must have imagined it.

"Actually, we have a surprise for you," he told me, giving me every ounce of his charm in a smile.

I stepped out of his embrace warily. "What kind of surprise?"

"We're having a party tonight. An official welcome into the Sphinx to show everyone that you're ours."

The frown I'd been sporting only deepened as suspicion flashed through me.

"I hadn't gotten the impression that you were my biggest fans at the moment," I told him, searching his face for any tells.

But I couldn't see anything but his smile.

"We all have our dirty secrets, Aurora. We're not going to hold that against you. You were a child. It's not like you could say no to The Demon. We understand that."

Relief flushed through my veins. Relief...and hope.

"So, you understand. You know that I didn't want to do any of that. I would never—"

"Of course," he said soothingly, not letting me finish my sentence. He smoothed a lock of hair out of my face. "Just come party with us for a couple of hours. Get drunk with me. This day will seem like nothing but a bad nightmare. It's going to be okay."

My brain was screaming at me not to trust him, but my heart, and the lost lonely girl that resided permanently inside of me, was desperate for this to be real. For everything not to have been ruined. I'd just go and have a couple of drinks, and then it would be over and everything would be fine. I'd seen the guys in action. They could fix this.

At least that's what I was telling myself.

Remington stepped out into the hallway and came back in with a sleek black bag. "I got you a dress to wear tonight. Go put it on."

I took the bag and pushed aside the matte black tissue paper, a flash of white peeking out. Reaching down, I stroked the silky fabric, anticipation rushing through me.

"I'll go get dressed."

"Hurry, little devil. The party's about to start."

We were back to "little devil" apparently. But maybe we'd never left.

His words sounded like a warning.

A warning I should have listened to.

We stepped into the ballroom, yes, a fucking ballroom, that existed somewhere in the Sphinx. I didn't think I was ever going to find all the rooms in this place. It was completely ridiculous. And I still hadn't figured out why they had the largest water bill in the state.

My dress was a skintight, floor length white silk gown with spaghetti straps. I felt like a princess when I'd slipped it on, definitely never wearing something so nice before. There'd been a sparkly white mask to go with it because evidently this was a themed party...a masquerade. I'd slipped the dress on and then put on some red lipstick. The mask covered my eyes and nose and I kind of felt like I'd become a different person as I put it on.

Remington had been waiting for me in my room, wearing a black mask that covered his whole face. It cast a sinister feeling to his look, and I shivered involuntarily as I stared at him.

"Shall we go?" he asked, holding out his arm like the gentleman I knew he wasn't.

"Yes," I responded, trying to sound confident as I took his arm and we walked out of the room and down several hallways.

We entered the room filled with people clothed in fancy dresses and suits and masks, and I gazed around suspiciously, waiting for the other shoe to drop. Remington was being charming, more charming than I'd ever seen him, quite frankly.

It was only adding to my unease.

I'd seen behind the mask Remington wore, the real one, and we were past the need for him to be like this.

What was going through his head right now?

It felt like every eye was upon us as we walked towards the center of the room. Remington led me over to the bar where a tuxedoed bartender was pouring a line of people drinks. There were other waiters around the room with trays of food. The bartender immediately gave Remington his full attention, abandoning the other drinks he'd been preparing to get him whatever he needed.

"Drink of the night," Remington ordered, and the bartender nodded and immediately went to work.

"What's the drink of the night?" I asked, watching the bartender's hands closely...just in case he decided to slip something in mine.

"It's called Delilah's Smile," Remington responded with an amused grin.

I shifted uncomfortably, unsure at first that I'd heard right. “What?”

He brushed some of my hair out of my face and leaned in close. “Because you don't have to hide anymore,” he whispered.

"Pomegranate, bourbon, raspberry liquor, and lemon. It's been a big hit tonight," the bartender inserted, and I broke away from Remington.

"Hmmm," I said in response as Remington grabbed the cocktails from the bartender and handed me one of them.

I looked down at the drink. It was a dark red color, the same exact shade of blood actually. My stomach swirled uncomfortably.

"What's the matter, Aurora? Don't like your drink of honor?" Stellan murmured as he came up behind me. I jumped at his sudden appearance, almost spilling my drink.

Cain and Paxton were with Stellan, looking like fallen angels in their perfectly fitted tuxedos. They were all wearing identical masks, the same as Remington, so their faces were completely covered. I didn't like not being able to see them. It felt like they had too much of an advantage this way. I wasn't able to see any of their facial expressions; their eyes were totally blank staring out at me.

I fiddled with my dress, wondering how soon I could slip away. I could practically taste the danger in the air. No matter what Remington had said, this wasn't safe for me.

"Glad you decided to join us, Aurora," Cain said, but there was a flatness to his voice that was all wrong. He held out his hand, and I stared at it like it was a viper about to strike. "Dance with me," he asked, but the tone of voice made it seem much more like an order.

I took a sip of my drink, and then another. It was delicious. Maybe the first alcoholic drink that I'd actually really, really liked. Even if it did make me feel like a vampire when I was drinking it. I drained the glass and then handed it to a still amused looking Remington as I took Cain's hand.

Cain led me out to the center of the room. "Waiting Game" by BANKS began to play as he smoothly pulled me towards him until I was pressed completely against him.

The music pulsed around us. No one else was dancing. It was just me and Cain.

And they were all watching us.

The lyrics of the song were dark and sensual, spinning into my head as Cain expertly swirled me around the dance floor. It felt familiar, this dance of ours—he led...and I followed. I wasn't sure if I'd even be able to dance with someone else without looking like a fool, something about Cain just made it so that my body did what he said.

"What's going through that head of yours, Cain?" I murmured as he spun me around. His eyes were dark and unreadable, the dark jade color sparkling under the lights of the room.

One of his hands came up to hold my face. He pressed his thumb on my lips and smeared my lipstick. I frowned and slapped his hand away.

"It's quite the dichotomy isn't it? The fact that you look like an angel tonight. So pure and lovely, you seem incapable of sin," Cain remarked as he spun me by where Paxton, Stellan, and Remington were all avidly watching us.

I wiped at my face, trying to get the red lipstick off that he'd smeared so I didn't look like a demented clown.

"It's not really fair for you to look so perfect on the outside, when we all know how messy you are on the inside. Is it, little devil?" he whispered, his fingers stroking my back lightly.

My insides froze at his words. He said them casually, but only a fool would miss the threat in his words.

The song ended and Cain brought us to a slow, elegant stop. Cain stared at me for what must have only been a second, but it seemed like forever. He took my hand and brought it to his lips, placing a long, slow kiss on my skin that sent shockwaves swirling through my insides.

"Where are our manners? We haven't introduced you to anyone here tonight."

"Oh, that's not necess—" I began, but Cain had already pulled me towards a couple nearby.

"This is Aurora," he announced to them.

"Dale and Shirly Layton," the couple answered blankly.

I frowned, wondering why those names sounded

familiar and thinking they were a bit old-fashioned for two college aged people.

Cain didn't wait for small talk. He pulled me away immediately before I could say anything.

"David Penniweather," was how the next guy introduced himself. Something was trying to knock at my brain, another hint of familiarity, but I just couldn't place it.

"Clarissa Adams," a woman said, and goosebumps sprang up on my skin. An image of a beautiful brunette who'd abused her children filled my head. The Demon cut that one's head off when he was finished, a departure from his M.O. that had him spiraling for weeks.

But that was just a coincidence...right?

"Jasmine Able," the next woman said, and I visibly flinched, thinking of the particularly messy death that The Demon's Jasmine Able had endured.

The game they were playing became very clear.

I tried to yank my arm away from Cain, but he held it fast. "We aren't done with the introductions yet," he purred.

"We're done," I snapped, not wanting to make a scene but seconds away from trying to break his face.

Their voices all came at once then, the whole room of masked strangers circling me as they called out the names of all The Demon's victims, many that I'd seen meet their demise. The voices swirled around, and it felt like I was going mad. I'd tried so fucking hard to forget. The faces I saw in my dreams were enough, but I couldn't forget the names either. He'd shown me their licenses, told me of their crimes. And the terrible part was I never could be sure if it was the truth or if he'd created an alternate storyline to push me along the path he wanted for me.

Either way, their names felt like they'd been carved into my mind with a knife, and this...this I never would have expected. I half expected for Cain to somehow have arranged for all their corpses to be rolled into the room too.

The room felt like it was spinning, my breath was coming out in gasps, like I was losing my grip on reality. I looked at the four of them, looking more like the four horsemen of the apocalypse than boys I'd ever thought I'd known.

I tried to push through the crowd, but they pushed me back towards the center of the room...and there were so many of them. Cruel gazes that I knew would join the other specters that haunted my dreams.

A waiter appeared beside Cain then. He handed him one of the glasses filled with the vibrant, crimson cocktail.

"A toast," Cain called out to the room, and everyone turned, almost in unison, to give him their full attention. "To our guest of honor tonight."

My hand fluttered to my throat. Paxton, Stellan, and Remington were all flanking Cain, a united unit. They all had drinks, and they were all staring at me.

I forced myself to hold my ground. I could read their gazes clearly now. There was a malevolence there that they'd clearly been hiding.

"To the murderer," Cain said, his voice seeming to echo around the room.

"To the murderer," the crowd repeated.

Cain reared back, and he tossed his entire glass all over me, the red staining my skin and dress. Before I could even react, Stellan, Pax, and Remington were doing the same. The red liquid splashed all over my face, some of it going down my throat, and I coughed, trying to get it out of my eyes.

I turned and began to run through the crowd, punching and kicking my way through as I fought desperately to get to the exit. As I ran, the crowd threw their drinks all over me. All I could see was a red haze as it splashed in my eyes...and everywhere else. In my desperation, I slipped on some of the spilled drink, falling to the floor.

My body shook as I struggled to get up. And then suddenly Stellan was there. "Where is Sophia?" he asked, shaking me so hard my neck snapped back.

"I don't know," I gasped as another cup was poured over my head.

"Where is she!" he roared.

I finally got to my feet and yanked myself away from him. I slapped him across the face before picking up the bottom of my sodden, crimson stained dress and again running towards the door. More drinks splashed against me, and I shrieked when an actual glass hit me on the side of the head.

The journey to the door was probably only fifty yards, but it might as well have been fifty miles for how long it took.

By the time I'd reached that door, I'd been changed, bathed in blood and fire until I wasn't sure who I was at the end.

I don't know why I did it, but I took one last look behind me as I ran through the doorway.

The four of them were all there, staring after me, identical grins on their faces. They'd taken off their masks and I could see them now for who they really were.

And wasn't it a shame that I'd once thought maybe I could love them.

Because all that was left was hate.

25

AURORA

I sank to the floor in the hallway. The marble felt cold against my palms, cold as the hearts of the men I'd dared to trust for a moment.

I'd been crying when Remington came to my room. But now as I ran my hands up the stained bodice of my gown, I didn't feel like crying anymore.

I felt like burning down the world that would never accept me.

Slowly, all my sadness, all my *longing* crystallized into something cold and dangerous.

I think I have to find a way to be both my own person and The Demon's daughter, I'd told Jenna.

But had I truly, fully accepted that?

Because The Demon had taught me a lot of useful things.

I rose to my feet, feeling ice run through my veins. I'd be as cold as those men from now on.

I caught a glimpse of myself in the mirror that hung above a rose-adorned table across the hall. I looked ruined

—my stained dress, my smudged makeup, my sinner's empty eyes.

And then I smiled at myself in the mirror, a slow, cold smile.

I'd given up Gabriela to please The Demon.

I'd abandoned Delilah to escape him.

I'd lost Aurora when Pax, Remington, Cain and Stellan stripped my new self from me.

I'd let men name me or take my names away my whole life, and I'd lost myself.

The desire for revenge hummed through my blood, just as cold as the ice. I knew one thing that one of those men loved, and it was here below this house, while they were still laughing in the ballroom. Why not start there?

But it would only be a start.

I picked the lock to Cain's room. I would've expected them to be watching me through one of those video cameras, but maybe they didn't have them in the halls, or maybe they were so very certain that I was weeping helplessly in my room.

The keys to the McLaren were thrown carelessly on his desk. I tossed them in my hand as I walked across the room to the bar Cain kept in the corner. I pushed a flogger abandoned on the floor out of the way with my toes and crouched, pulling open his cabinet doors.

Thoughtfully, I pulled out bottles of vodkas and rums with the highest proofs. I had special plans for this cocktail. The higher the proof, the higher the flammability.

He'd even left a lighter on the bar top alongside a humidor of expensive cigars. How very thoughtful of the bastard.

Carrying a line of bottles cinched to the damp bodice of my dress by one arm, the keys and lighter in the other, and humming "Just Like Fire" by Pink, I made my way to the dark stairs. I stood there for a moment, wanting to turn on the light and illuminate the flights that led down to the garage.

I was still scared of the dark, no matter how much I wanted to be new and different today.

But I walked down in the damn darkness anyway.

I stepped into the cool of the garage. The McLaren glinted even in the dim light down here. I hit the key fob to unlock it as I walked toward it, then set the bottles down on the hood of the car. Cain would lose his shit if he saw me scratching up the hood, but it was hardly the worst thing I was doing to his car tonight.

I opened the driver's side. The memory of having to scoot over the stick shift, the way he'd watched me with a glint of hunger in his eyes, surfaced.

"Here's to your true love, Cain," I said, raising my bottle of vodka in a toast and then taking a swig. I almost gagged—nope, new and improved me still thought straight booze tasted like straight ass—then upended the bottle, splashing it over the front seats. I did the same thing with the rest of the bottles. Then I grabbed the garage door sensor from his dash and slipped it into the bodice of my dress.

I lit the lighter, jammed the safety to keep it from turning off, then watched the glow of the flame for a second. Was I really going to do this? Was I really going to pit myself against Cain?

Hell yeah I was.

I tossed the lighter into the car and took a step back.

The lighter hit the driver's seat, and for a fraction of a second, nothing happened. The garage was still and quiet.

Then flames rushed over the seats, leaping and glowing and chasing each other playfully. I took another step back as the flames suddenly heated my face, making my cheeks burn, but not as hot as I'd burned with embarrassment in front of those men.

As I headed up the ramp toward the garage door, there was a *whoosh* behind me as the flames ate up the rest of the car, swirling over the engine block.

I was walking into the cold night air when it exploded behind me. Even though I was far enough away not to be hurt, the power of the blast still knocked me to my knees.

I got up and brushed myself off. How many times had the world knocked me to my knees now, anyway?

Without a backward glance, I made my way into the dark night.

Continue the Rich Demons of Darkwood series in Make Me Beg

AUTHOR'S NOTE

Pretty fiery ending...hehe. Pun intended of course. Would it really be one of our books without an explosive ending? (I can't help myself at this point).

We absolutely love this book and hope that you did to! We have so much in store for you guys. We wanted to write a book that combined our love for everything alpha-hole bully romance with our obsession with true crime.

Just you wait.

A huge thanks to our betas: Summer, Caitlin, Rebecca, Lisa, Kelly, Denise, Brandy, Becca, and Angie. Your feedback was amazing and helped make this book.

Thank you to Jasmine for proofing our baby and making her shine.

Thank you to Victoria for creating two beautiful covers.

And last but not least...thank you to you, our readers. We couldn't do what we loved without you.

XOXO,

C.R. & May

BOOKS BY C.R. JANE

www.crjanebooks.com

The Fated Wings Series

First Impressions

Forgotten Specters

The Fallen One (a Fated Wings Novella)

Forbidden Queens

Frightful Beginnings (a Fated Wings Short Story)

Faded Realms

Faithless Dreams

Fabled Kingdoms

Fated Wings 8

The Rock God (a Fated Wings Novella)

The Darkest Curse Series

Forget Me

Lost Passions

The Sounds of Us Contemporary Series (complete series)

Remember Us This Way

Remember You This Way

Remember Me This Way

Broken Hearts Academy Series (complete duet)

Heartbreak Prince

Heartbreak Lover

Ugly Hearts Series Contemporary Series

Ugly Hearts

Hades Redemption Series

The Darkest Lover

The Darkest Kingdom

Academy of Souls Co-write with Mila Young (complete series)

School of Broken Souls

School of Broken Hearts

School of Broken Dreams

School of Broken Wings

Fallen World Series Co-write with Mila Young (complete series)

Bound

Broken

Betrayed

Belong

Thief of Hearts Co-write with Mila Young (complete series)

Siren Condemned

Siren Sacrificed

Siren Awakened

Siren Redeemed

Kingdom of Wolves Co-write with Mila Young

Wild Moon

Wild Heart

Wild Girl

Wild Love

Stupid Boys Series Co-write with Rebecca Royce

Stupid Boys

Dumb Girl

Crazy Love

Breathe Me Duet Co-write with Ivy Fox (complete)

Breathe Me

Breathe You

Rich Demons of Darkwood Series Co-write with May Dawson

Make Me Lie

Make Me Beg

BOOKS BY MAY DAWSON

May Dawson's Website

The Lost Fae Series

Wandering Queen

Fallen Queen

Rebel Queen

Lost Queen

Their Shifter Princess Series

Their Shifter Princess

Their Shifter Princess 2: Pack War

Their Shifter Princess 3: Coven's Revenge

Their Shifter Academy Series

A Prequel Novella

Unwanted

Unclaimed

Undone

Unforgivable

Unstoppable

The Wild Angels & Hunters Series:

Wild Angels

Fierce Angels

Dirty Angels

Chosen Angels

Academy of the Supernatural

Her Kind of Magic

His Dangerous Ways

Their Dark Imaginings

Ashley Landon, Bad Medium

Dead Girls Club

The True and the Crown Series

One Kind of Wicked

Two Kinds of Damned

Three Kinds of Lost

Four Kinds of Cursed

Five Kinds of Love

Rich Demons of Darkwood Series Co-write with C.R. Jane

Make Me Lie

Make Me Beg

Subscribe to May Dawson's Newsletter to receive exclusive content, latest updates, and giveaways.

Join Here

ABOUT C.R. JANE

A Texas girl living in Utah now, I'm a wife, mother, lawyer, and now author. My stories have been floating around in my head for years, and it has been a relief to finally get them down on paper. I'm a huge Dallas Cowboys fan and I primarily listen to Beyonce and Taylor Swift...don't lie and say you don't too.

My love of reading started probably when I was three and with a faster than normal ability to read, I've devoured hundreds of thousands of books in my life. It only made sense that I would start to create my own worlds since I was always getting lost in others'.

I like heroines who have to grow in order to become badasses, happy endings, and swoon-worthy, devoted, (and hot) male characters. If this sounds like you, I'm pretty sure we'll be friends.

I'm so glad to have you on my team...check out the links below for ways to hang out with me and more of my books you can read!

Visit my **Facebook** page to get updates.

Visit my **Amazon Author** page.

Visit my **Website.**

Sign up for my **newsletter** to stay updated on new releases, find out random facts about me, and get access to different points of view from my characters.

ABOUT MAY DAWSON

May Dawson lives in Virginia with her husband and two red-headed wild babies. Before her second career as an author, she spent eight years in the Marine Corps and visited forty-two countries and all seven continents (including a research station in the Antarctic). You can always find her on Facebook in May Dawson's Wild Angels or on the internet at MayDawson.com

Printed in Great Britain
by Amazon